"You seem to be a most unusual nobleman."

"As you seem to be a most unusual lady."

Even *he* could not have said whether he meant that for a compliment or not, but it was true. "I'm impressed with your concern for your sister," he added as he strolled toward her, and that, at least, was the truth.

Lady Mathilde backed away as if she were afraid. Of him? That was ridiculous—he had given her every reason to believe he would be the opposite of dangerous to her.

The woman before him flushed, but didn't look away. Her mouth was half parted, her breasts rising and falling with her rapid breathing. She swayed forward a bit—enough to encourage him to think she was feeling the same pull of desire and curiosity.

Responding to that urge, he put his hands on her shoulders and started to draw her closer....

MARGARET MOORE

HERS To COMMAND

HQN™

ISBN 0-373-77095-2

HERS TO COMMAND

www.HQNBooks.com

Printed in U.S.A.

With thanks to everyone who has offered support
and encouragement during my writing career,
and the readers who buy my books.
I couldn't do it without you!

PROLOGUE

London, Michaelmas, 1243

SIR ROALD DE SAYRES'S nostrils flared with disgust as he stepped over the refuse in the alley in Cloth Fair between the slaughtering yards of Smithfields and the bulk of St. Bartholemew's Church. Aware of the sword he wore on his left, he firmly clasped the hilt of the dagger stuck in his belt on his right and scanned the alley for the man he was to meet.

"Sir Roald!" a coarse Yorkshire-accented voice called out in a harsh whisper. The bulky shape of a big, brawny man stepped into the alley from a shadowed doorway. He wore breeches, tunic and cloak, patched and none too clean.

Roald peered at the figure in the dim light, trying to get a good look at his face. "Martin?"

"Aye, sir," the man replied with a nod of his shaggy head.

Roald relaxed a little, but he didn't take his hand

from his dagger. "You told no one you were planning to meet me here?"

"No, sir," the former garrison commander of his uncle's castle answered.

"And you told no one in Ecclesford you were going to London?"

"Not daft, am I?" Martin replied with a hoarse laugh.

Not daft, but not clever, either, Roald thought as he regarded the traitorous fool. "It's as you promised? The garrison—?"

"Will be like lambs to the slaughter. Taught 'em next to nowt, and their weapons are older'n my mother. Paid for the worst, told Lord Gaston—who wouldn't know a decent sword from a pike—they was the best."

And pocketed the difference in price, no doubt.

"Them that are left won't know how to mount a proper defense, neither," Martin bragged, the big brute clearly not caring a ha'penny about the fate of his former comrades-in-arms. "They'll be running 'round like chickens if you march on 'em."

"And his daughters? Prostrate with grief, I assume?"

Chuckling like the fool he was, Martin nodded. "They was weepin' and wailin' when I left. They think that father of theirs was a saint or summat." Martin grinned again, the corner of his wide, ugly mouth lifting. "Told 'em I wouldn't take orders from no women—and I wouldn't, neither, especially that Lady Mathilde."

Roald didn't care what excuse the man gave for leaving his cousins' employ as long as it didn't involve him. "You told no one you were meeting me tonight?"

"No, my lord."

Pleased his alliance with this traitorous oaf was still a secret, Roald reached into his finely woven woolen tunic and produced a leather pouch. He had no immediate financial needs, thanks to the money-lenders who were only too happy to help him when they learned he was the heir of Lord Gaston of Ecclesford and soon to be in possession of one of the most prosperous estates in Kent.

As always, it wasn't just the thought of his new wealth and power that warmed him. How he'd make that shrew Mathilde grovel before he sent her off to a convent for the rest of her life. As for Giselle…his loins tightened at the memory of her ethereal beauty. He'd marry her off to the highest bidder, but not right away. Oh, no, not right away.

Martin cleared his throat, clearly anxious for his reward.

Roald held out the pouch, mentally assessing the man's strengths and weaknesses. A trained fighter Martin might be, but all men had their vulnerabilities. Big men were slow, and stupid men were the most easily defeated of all.

Grabbing the leather bag, the soldier eagerly emptied it into his calloused palm, the coins gleaming in the moonlight. With a slow deliberation that set Roald's teeth on edge, the lummox began to count them as he returned them, one by one, to the pouch.

"Do you think I'd try to cheat you, Martin?"

Martin glanced up, frowning. His gaze faltered, and he swept the coins, half of which were below their proper weight and value, back into the pouch. "No, my lord."

Roald fingered the jeweled hilt of the dagger in his belt. "What will you do now that you're quite rich?"

Martin grinned. "Enjoy some sport, then get meself a wife. Maybe buy an inn."

"I could always use a trained fighter," Roald proposed.

Martin shook his head. "Beggin' your pardon, my lord, but I'm done with that. Not gettin' any younger, nor any faster. Time to take what I've earned and settle down."

"Like a horse put out to pasture, eh?"

Martin frowned as if the comparison displeased him, but he nodded nonetheless. "Aye, you could say that."

"Well, it's a pity, but of course, if that's what you'd prefer," Roald said amiably. "I give you good night, then, Martin. And if there's ever anything I can do for you, you mustn't hesitate to come to me and ask."

With a bow and another grin, the soldier tugged his forelock and started to pass the French nobleman, heading for the end of the alley.

He never made it. With the speed of an adder, Roald grabbed him by the neck from behind and shoved his pretty silver dagger up under the man's ribs.

His eyes wide and wild, gasping for breath, Martin flailed like a landed fish as he tried to free himself. Unfortunately for him, while Roald was not as big or muscular, he was strong. And determined. Still holding the bigger man around the neck with his arm, he pulled out the dagger and shoved it in again.

Weak, the blood pouring from his side, Martin sank to the fetid ground, falling with a thud when Roald finally released his hold.

Out of breath and with a look of disgust, Roald pulled his dagger free and wiped it on the man's no doubt flea-infested tunic. "Should have worn mail, you stupid ox," he muttered as he grabbed the pouch. Twenty marks—or even a portion of that—was still worth holding on to. His greedy little whore of a mistress had been demanding a present from the new lord of Ecclesford. He would give her a ring or some such bauble, and he trusted she'd be suitably grateful. After all, there was no need to go rushing off to his estate. Mathilde and Giselle would be too upset by their father's death to do anything but mourn for days yet.

As for Martin, when his body was found, people would assume he was just another fool who came to London and got himself murdered.

They'd be right.

CHAPTER ONE

THE FOX AND HOUND in the county of Kent lay ten miles from the castle of Ecclesford along the road to London. It was a small but comfortable inn, with a walled yard, a taproom frequented by the local farmers and food slightly better than one usually found in such places. Inside the building was the aforementioned taproom, redolent of damp rushes, ale and cheap English wine, smoke from the large hearth and roasted beef. A little natural light shone in through the wooden shutters, now closed to keep out the cool, moist morning air of late September.

Five days after Roald de Sayres killed the former garrison commander of Ecclesford Castle, two women went up the rickety steps leading to the chambers where guests could lodge for the night. One of the women, beautiful and blond, trembled with every step that brought them closer to the rooms where the guests slept. The other who led the way appeared full of confident conviction as she marched briskly upward, oblivious to the creaking of the stairs and motes of dust swirling around them. Nothing was going to dissuade Lady Mathilde from her quest, not even her own rapidly beating heart.

"Mathilde, this is madness!" the lovely Lady Giselle hissed as she grabbed hold of her sister's light gray woolen cloak and nearly pulled the white linen veil from her head.

Grabbing at her veil to hold it in place, Mathilde turned toward her anxious sister. In truth, she knew what they were doing was outrageous, but she was not about to lose this opportunity. The innkeeper's son, who knew of their troubles and their need, had come to them the day before and told them of the young nobleman who'd arrived alone at the Fox and Hound—a merry, handsome Norman knight with a very thin purse.

His looks mattered not to Mathilde, and indeed, she would have been happier had he been homely. But the knight's nearly empty purse caused her to hope that he would be glad of the chance to earn some money, even if he had no personal interest in their just cause. The lordly brother and equally lordly friend the knight had mentioned also made her hope he might be the answer to her prayers.

"What else are we to do?" she asked her sister, likewise whispering. "Sit and wait for Roald to take Ecclesford from us? If this fellow is who he says he is, he could be exactly the sort of man we need."

"Perhaps Roald will not dispute our father's will," Giselle protested, as she had every time Mathilde mentioned her plan to discourage Roald from trying to take what was not his. "He has not yet come and—"

"You know as well as I how greedy he is," Mathilde replied. "Do you really believe he will accept losing Ecclesford? I do not. He may come today or tomorrow, demanding that we turn the estate over to him. We must do everything we can to prepare for that."

Giselle still didn't budge from her place on the step. "This knight may not want to help us."

"Rafe said he was poor. We will offer to pay him. And after all, we aren't going to be asking him to risk his life."

"But why must we go into the bedchamber?" Giselle asked piteously, wringing her hands with dismay. "We should stay in the taproom. He will surely awaken and come downstairs soon."

"We have been waiting for too long as it is," Mathilde replied. "We cannot sit all day in the taproom, especially when there is much to be done at home, and did you not see the clouds gathering over the hills to the south? If we do not start for home soon, we may get caught in a storm."

"We know nothing of this man beyond what Rafe has said," Giselle persisted, "and he was only repeating what the Norman told him last night. Maybe the Norman was merely bragging. A man may say anything when he's in his cups."

Perhaps the young man *had* been drunk, or exaggerating or lying, and if that was so, obviously he wasn't the man to help them. But if he wasn't lying, Mathilde wasn't about to let a knight related to a powerful Norman nobleman in Scotland and who was a friend to an equally powerful lord in Cornwall slip through her fingers without at least asking for his help. "If this fellow seems a liar and a rogue, we will leave him here."

"How will we be able to tell if he's honest or not?"

"I will know."

"You?" Giselle exclaimed, and then she colored and looked away.

Shame flooded Mathilde's face, because Giselle had good cause to doubt Mathilde's wisdom when it came to young men.

"I'm sorry," Giselle said softly, pity in her eyes even as Mathilde fought the memories that flashed through her mind.

"I once made a terrible mistake, but I have learned my lesson," Mathilde assured her sister. Then she smiled, to show she wasn't upset, although she was. "But since I may misjudge this man, I'm glad that you are here to help me."

Without waiting for Giselle to say anything more

lest her sister's doubts weaken her resolve, Mathilde ducked under a thick oak beam and rapped on the door to one of the two upper chambers. Each would contain beds made of rope stretched between the frame, bearing a mattress stuffed with straw, as well as a coarse linen sheet and a blanket. Each bed would be large enough to hold at least two grown men, possibly three. There was little privacy at an inn; however, Rafe's father had assured them the Norman was the only guest still abed.

"Maybe he's already gone," Giselle whispered hopefully when there was no answer to Mathilde's knock.

"The innkeeper would have said so, or we would have seen him leave," Mathilde replied as she knocked again, a little louder this time. She pressed her ear against the door.

"Perhaps he left in the night," Giselle suggested.

"Maybe he's dead," Mathilde muttered under her breath.

"Dead!" Giselle exclaimed.

Mathilde instantly regretted her impulsive remark. "I do not believe that," she said, lifting the latch of the rough wooden door. "More likely the man is dead drunk and if so, he will be of no use to us."

"Oh, Mathilde!" her sister moaned as Mathilde sidled through the door, the leather hinges creaking. "Wait!"

It was too late. Mathilde had already entered the small, dusty room beneath the eaves sporting three beds, a table and a stool. Articles of clothing had been tossed on the stool beside the bed closest to the door, and an empty wine jug lay on its side on the table, near a puddle of wax that had once been a candle. The large, disheveled bed was still occupied—by a man sprawled on top of the coverings.

He was completely naked.

With a gasp, Mathilde turned to flee—until she saw Giselle's worried face.

What would Giselle say if she ran away? That she had been right, and Mathilde wrong. That Mathilde's plan was foolish and impossible. That they should wait and see what Roald would do, rather than take any kind of action.

That she didn't want to do, so she mentally girded her loins and reminded herself that this man was merely lying on the bed, apparently fast asleep, or passed out from drink. If he was in a drunken stupor and since he had no weapons near him while she carried a knife she wouldn't hesitate to use, surely she had nothing to fear.

He certainly looked harmless enough in his sleep, although his back bore several small scars and welts that were surely from tournaments or battles. She also couldn't help noticing that there wasn't an ounce of superfluous fat on him, anywhere. But then, the

Normans were notorious warriors, descendants of piratical Norsemen, without culture or grace, so what else should she expect?

"Is he alive?" Giselle whispered behind her.

"He's breathing," Mathilde replied, moving cautiously closer. She sniffed, and the scent of wine was strong. "I think he's passed out from drink."

Closer now, she studied the slumbering man's remarkably handsome face, slack in his sleep. He looked like an angel—albeit a very virile one, with finely cut cheekbones, full and shapely lips, a straight nose and a strong jaw. His surprisingly long hair fell tousled in dark brown waves to his broad shoulders. His body was more well formed than most, too, from his wide shoulders and muscular back to his lean legs.

She glanced at the clothes lying on the stool. He might be alone now, but he likely hadn't been last night. She wondered where the wench had gone, and if he'd even noticed.

Her lip curled in a sneer. Probably not. Like most men, he had likely thought only of his own desires.

She turned away. "This is *not* the sort of man we require," she said to her sister. "Come, Gis—"

A hand grabbed hers and tugged her down onto the bed. Mathilde grabbed the hilt of the knife she had tucked into her girdle with one hand and struck him hard with the other.

"God's teeth, wench," the young man cried, releasing her as he sat up, still unabashedly naked. "No need to rouse the household."

His eyes narrowed as she jumped to her feet, weapon drawn, panting and fierce, before he tugged the sheet over his thighs and belly. "Tell your husband or father or whatever relation the innkeeper is to you that I have paid for a night's rest, and I will get up when *I* decide, and not before."

"Our apologies, Sir Knight," Giselle said from the foot of his bed as Mathilde breathed deeply and tried to regain her self-control. "We should not have intruded upon you."

The knight glanced at Giselle and then, as often happened when men first beheld Mathilde's beautiful sister, his eyes widened and his mouth fell open. Giselle, meanwhile, lowered her eyes and blushed, as she always did when forced to endure a man's staring scrutiny.

Totally ignoring Mathilde, the Norman got to his feet and wrapped the sheet around his slender torso. He should have looked ridiculous, but he carried himself as if he were a prince greeting a courtier.

"May I ask what brings you to my chamber, my lady," he asked as genially as if they were in their hall at home, "for I can tell you are a lady by your sweet and lovely voice."

Giselle looked at Mathilde with mute appeal.

"We require a knight's service," Mathilde decisively announced, her dagger still in her hand, "but—"

"Indeed?" the Norman interrupted, his brown eyes fairly sparkling with delight, as if they were offering him a present.

"How charming," he continued, addressing Giselle, "although I must confess, I usually prefer to choose my bedmates. In your case, however, my lady, I'm prepared to make an exception."

Of all the vain, arrogant presumptions! "That is *not* what I meant," Mathilde snapped, her grip on her weapon tightening.

The knight turned to look at her. "Why are *you* so angry? I'm the one who ought to be offended. You invaded my bedchamber when I was asleep and unarmed."

"But not for…for that!"

"No need to dissemble if it was," he replied with an amiable smile and a shrug of his broad shoulders, and completely ignoring her drawn dagger. "This wouldn't be the first time a woman has sought my company in bed, although they don't usually come in pairs."

"You…you scoundrel!" Mathilde cried, appalled at his disgusting comment, as she started for the door.

The Norman moved to block her way.

"Let us go!" she demanded, tense and ready to fight, while Giselle shrank into the nearest corner.

"Gladly, after you explain what you're doing

here," the knight replied, no longer amiable or merry as he grabbed her wrist and forced her to drop her dagger. He let go of her as he kicked the dagger away, but continued to regard her sternly.

Looking at him now, she could well believe he was a knight from a powerful family, and of some repute.

"Is this some sort of trick?" he asked, raising a majestic brow and crossing his powerful arms. "Should I be expecting a visit from an irate father or brother insisting that I marry this lady? If so, he's going to be sorely disappointed. I might have welcomed her into my bed, but I will *never* be forced to take a wife."

Giselle let out a little squeak of dismay. "Mathilde, tell him why we are here," she pleaded, her face as red as a cardinal's robe.

"If we explain, will you let us go?" Mathilde asked warily.

He inclined his head in agreement.

"Then I will explain," she replied.

Determined to get this over with as quickly as possible, she planted her feet, looked him straight in the eye and said, "We require a knight, and we thought, since we heard you did not have much money, that you would—"

"Do I look like a mercenary to you?" he interrupted, lowering his arms, his face flushing and his brown eyes glowering.

"At the moment, you don't look anything except

half naked," Mathilde replied, managing to sound much calmer than she felt. "Perhaps if you had some clothes on, I would better be able to judge."

He snorted a laugh. "Aren't you the coolheaded one," he remarked, leaning back against the door and once again crossing his arms. "So, you need a knight. For what, if not for pleasure?"

Mathilde cringed at his reply, but gamely continued, still determined to get away from him as swiftly as she could. "To be at our side should our cousin come to the estate our father left us and try to take it from us."

"You seek a knight to fight this cousin over an estate?"

"Not fight," Giselle anxiously interposed from the corner.

The knight regarded her with confusion. "Why do you need a man trained for battle, then, if not to fight?"

"To impress him," Mathilde said. "To show him that we are willing to defend our rights and that we are not without some means to do so."

"I am to be for *show?*" the Norman asked with a hint of indignation.

"We hope to make Roald think twice about trying to steal our inheritance."

The knight tilted his head as he studied her. "Roald is an unusual name. Might I have met him at court?"

Perhaps he had, Mathilde reflected, and if so, she would have to be careful. It could be this man was

Roald's friend, or as much as any man could be the friend of anyone so selfish as Roald. "Our cousin is Sir Roald de Sayres."

The Norman's lip lifted with derision. "I thought that might be who you meant. You're related to that blackguard?"

"You know him?"

"God help me, I do, and I hate the knave."

Sweeping the sheet behind him as a lady would the skirt of her gown, the knight strode to the table. He picked up the wineskin lying there and lifted it over his mouth, shaking out the last few drops.

Mathilde glanced at Giselle. If this man truly hated Roald… "Why do you dislike him?"

"As there is a lady present, I would rather not say," the Norman replied as he tossed the empty wineskin back onto the table.

A lady? What did he think *she* was? "I am Lady Mathilde of Ecclesford," she declared, "and this is my sister, Lady Giselle."

The knight ran an incredulous gaze over her and her plain clothing. "*You're* a lady? I took you for a servant."

"Well, I am not."

"Forgive me my mistake," he replied, not very contritely, as his hand moved to his waist and the sheet wrapped around it.

"What are you doing?" she exclaimed, turning away.

"I want to hear more about your dilemma, so I think I should dress. Don't you agree?"

It would be much easier to talk to him if he were dressed, so she didn't disagree. However, since there was no reason for them to be here while he put on his clothes and indeed, every reason they should not—she retrieved her dagger and started sidling toward the door. Unfortunately, Giselle was apparently fascinated by the corner at which she stared and before Mathilde could catch her eye, the knight declared, "There. Now I am presentable."

And so he was. He wore plain woolen breeches, a sleeveless leather tunic bound by a wide sword belt holding his scabbard and broadsword over a white shirt loosely tied at the neck. He'd put on a pair of boots that were certainly not new, although they were polished and well cared for.

Without the distraction of his near nudity, Mathilde focused on his handsome face and intelligent brown eyes—when she should be thinking only of how, and if, this man could help them.

Determined to do just that, she said, "We may be related to Roald, but I assure you, he is no dearer to us than he is to you, and not just because we dread what he may do. He has done great harm in the past, and we fear he will do more in the future. He has no honor, or kindness, or mercy."

"That sounds like the Roald I know," the Norman agreed.

"Our father died a short time ago," she continued, a slight catch in her voice, for her grief was still raw. "In his will, he left Ecclesford to Giselle and me, the land to be divided equally between us, with a small sum of money for Roald.

"However, there are still many who believe inheritance should follow the male line above all other concerns. Then Roald should be lord of Ecclesford, and I am certain he will argue so, and try to steal our inheritance away."

"And likely marry you off to form alliances to his advantage," the knight added, proving that he knew about Roald's greed and ambition. "So you want a knight to scare him off and stop him from making any such claim, is that it?"

"Yes. We were told you are the brother of the lord of Dunkeathe in Scotland, and the boon companion of the lord of Tregellas of Cornwall. Is that true?"

"I have that honor, yes," the knight replied with a courteous bow, smiling in a way that made him look more handsome still. "As it happens, my lady, I have no particular calls upon my time at present and indeed, it would be my pleasure to thwart any plans of Roald de Sayres. Therefore, since it's also my duty as a knight of the realm to help ladies in distress, I will gladly assist you. And of course, as I am an honorable knight, I would not expect to be paid."

"Then, Sir Knight—"

"Mathilde," Giselle interrupted. "May I have a word with you? Alone?"

Mathilde was not pleased by the amusement in the knight's brown eyes that appeared when he heard Giselle's request, but she wasn't willing to ignore her sister's plea. "Of course," she said, moving to the door.

Giselle eagerly followed. Once on the stairs, Giselle stopped when they were halfway to the taproom, as if she couldn't wait to speak any longer. "Mathilde, surely we need not decide about this knight right now, or even today. Let us think on it some more."

"He might not be here tomorrow—and what more is there to think about?" Mathilde replied, once again struggling to control her impatience. "How many other knights with such associations are likely to ride through this county in the next few days? How many others will hate Roald as he does?"

"We still know very little about him," Giselle protested. "We don't even know his name."

Good God, Giselle was right. Still, that was not so important as his connections. "Whatever this Norman's name may be, we should accept the aid he offers."

Giselle's gaze went from wary to searching. "He's a very handsome fellow."

Mathilde couldn't blame Giselle for her unease. She had good cause to doubt Mathilde's judgment when it came to men, and this one was very handsome and charming and probably persuasive. Even so, Giselle should also believe she had learned from her mistake.

"Have no fear, Giselle," Mathilde assured her. "I will be on my guard, as I'm sure you will be, and if it seems he is not behaving as a noble guest should, we can ask him to leave. Now will you accept his help?"

Although she looked far from certain, Giselle sighed and said, "Since I can think of no better plan myself, I will agree—with the understanding that if I think he should leave, you will not argue with me until I cannot think straight."

Mathilde embraced her sister. "I promise."

When they returned to the chamber, they found the knight sitting on the bed, one ankle on his knee, whistling a merry and rather complicated little tune. He rose when they entered and gave them another smile. "So, what is it to be? Do I go to Ecclesford or not?"

"Yes, if you will, Sir…?"

He laughed and made a sweeping bow. "Egad, forgive my lack of manners! I can only plead the unusual nature of our meeting. I am Sir Henry D'Alton, knight of the realm, sworn protector of women and children, guardian of the faith, brother of Nicholas of Dunkeathe, brother-in-law of the chieftain of Clan Taran and sworn comrade-in-arms of Lord Merrick of Tregellas."

His connections were even more significant than

Mathilde had been told and she was duly awed. Nevertheless, he looked so pleased with himself as he rattled them off, she was tempted to take him down a peg. But, since he'd agreed to help them, she didn't. "Most impressive, Sir Henry. If you will gather your things, our escort is in the yard awaiting us."

"Please ask the innkeeper to have Apollo saddled," he said, opening the door for them, "and for a crust of bread for me to eat along the way, if you intend to leave immediately."

"We do." Indeed, the sooner they were back home, the better she would feel. Although they had no such word, it was possible Roald had come while they were away.

Sir Henry's lips curved up into a smile. "I can hardly wait to see the look on Roald's face if he comes to your castle and finds me there."

Mathilde made no response as they hurried past him, but in truth, she would far rather never see Roald again, and fervently hoped all her precautions would prove pointless.

WEAVING THEIR WAY through scratching chickens, waddling geese and puddles left from last night's rain, with a gray sky threatening more rain overhead, Mathilde and her sister headed toward their escort. Some of the soldiers leaned against the wattle and daub walls of the stable; others sat on the end of a hayrick. A few had hunkered down in a dry spot under the eaves, and all held cups of ale the innkeeper must have provided them.

Cerdic spotted them first. Barking an order to the rest of the men, their muscular friend set his ale down on a nearby barrel while the other soldiers scrambled to their feet or jumped from the hayrick and prepared to depart.

Like the knight, the tall, blond Cerdic was also a fine example of a warrior: broad shouldered, narrow hipped, with powerful arms and legs. Like many of his Saxon ancestors, he was an expert with the battle ax and if he wasn't as handsome as Sir Henry, he was hardly homely. His strong features were framed by thick hair that hung past his shoulders. He wore a leather tunic loosely laced and his breeches were of leather, too. His dark cloak was held closed by a large, round bronze brooch that had been his father's, and his father's before him. He had the fur of a wolf wrapped around his booted shins, tied on with thin leather strips. All in all, he was an imposing figure.

"It is just as Rafe told us," Mathilde said with a smile when they reached him. "The Norman knight is the brother of a powerful man in Scotland, the brother-in-law of another, and the friend of the lord of Tregellas in Cornwall. Even better, Sir Henry has agreed to help us."

Cerdic frowned, for like Giselle, he had never been enthused about Mathilde's plan. "What wilt thou do if this Sir Henry does not send Roald running off like a hound with its tail between its legs?" he asked, his French tinged with the accent of his people.

Although she had not expected otherwise, his disapproval stung nonetheless. "I don't question your skill as a warrior, Cerdic," she replied with a hint of pique. "I wish you would not be so quick to question my plan, especially when I hope it will spare the lives of many of the garrison. But rest assured, if my plan fails and we must fight, I know our men will not fail us."

That brought a smile to Cerdic's face, until he caught sight of Sir Henry sauntering toward them, his shoulders rolling with his easy, athletic strides. He wore a thick black cloak and carried a large leather pouch thrown over his shoulder. From inside it came the clink of metal—his chain mail and other armor, she supposed.

"Thou thinkst that little man is going to frighten Roald?" Cerdic asked with amazement.

Only Cerdic would think Sir Henry "little." To be sure, the Norman was lean, but there was plenty of muscle on his slender frame, as she well knew, and while Sir Henry was not as tall as Cerdic, he was taller than most of their soldiers, especially the dark-haired Celts.

"If not the man himself," she replied as she looked back to Cerdic, "then his family and friends."

Sir Henry had to notice Cerdic's furrowed brow and glaring gray eyes, yet when he reached them, a merry little smile played about his well-cut lips, as if he thought they were going to celebrate his arrival.

Or was he amused by her men? Did he think himself superior? That Normans were naturally better soldiers?

To be sure, her men looked a little slovenly after waiting in the yard, and Cerdic's hair could use a trim—but Sir Henry's hair was astonishingly long for a Norman's, and he was hardly dressed as befit a nobleman. He looked more like a well-to-do merchant, except for his sword.

Or maybe, she thought as she remembered his behavior in the upper chamber, this was simply the man's normal expression when he was with noble-women, especially one as beautiful as Giselle.

"Sir Henry, this is Cerdic, the leader of our escort and the garrison of Ecclesford," she said by way of introduction.

"Your forefathers must have been Saxons," Sir Henry said amiably, "judging by your hair and that battle ax."

"I knew thou wert a Norman by thy pretty face."

Sir Henry continued to smile, yet she could see a growing determination in his brown eyes, and his knuckles started turning white. So did Cerdic's, and for a moment, it was like watching two powerful stags about to butt heads.

She didn't want them to come to blows. Cerdic was her friend, and they needed Sir Henry.

"Cerdic," she interposed, her voice taking on a slightly warning note, "Sir Henry is going to be our guest at Ecclesford."

Mercifully, Cerdic let go of Sir Henry's arm and stepped back.

Sir Henry laughed with apparent good humor. "Well, my brawny friend, what say we get on our way? Unless I'm very much mistaken, there's a storm brewing and I would rather not get wet."

CHAPTER TWO

AS A COOL AUTUMN BREEZE carrying the scent of rain blew across the hedgerows, Henry studied his companions and contemplated this rather odd turn of events. It wasn't every day he awakened to find himself being scrutinized by unknown ladies, but as he'd told them, it wasn't the first time he'd discovered women in his bedchamber, either. Women had been chasing after him since he was fourteen years old, which meant that the flattery and pleasure of such encounters was far from fresh, or even entertaining anymore. He had been far more annoyed than happy to discover two ladies examining him, especially after another nearly sleepless night.

However, he'd also meant it when he'd said he would have considered bedding the beautiful Lady Giselle. Indeed, he had never seen a woman more lovely. She had perfect features, pale skin with a hint of a blush on her cheeks, and lustrous blond hair. She wore a fine mantle of wode-dyed, dark blue wool, held together by a broach of silver. Her gown was fine, too, of deep blue damask and belted with a supple leather girdle. Her veil was made of soft white silk that floated about her round cheeks, and she had stood with her blond head bowed, her eyes demurely downcast, as modest as a nun in a cloistered convent.

Her sister, on the other hand…she was something completely different. She wasn't pretty, especially when her face was pinched with anger and disapproval, and she had been much more plainly attired. She had been as strong as a young man, too, at least judging by the blow she'd struck when he mistakenly—very mistakenly—grabbed her hand. Was it any wonder he'd thought her a serving wench?

Then she'd acted as if he'd burst in on *them*. Her nut-brown eyes had fairly snapped with displeasure, and her full lips thinned to near invisibility.

In spite of his annoyance, which he took chivalrous pains to hide after he'd seen Lady Giselle, there'd been a moment when Lady Mathilde glared at him that he recalled bold women made the best lovers, for they were never shy to tell him what they liked, or to ask for his preferences.

Once he learned Lady Mathilde was of noble birth and the beauty's sister, however, he quickly turned his attention back to Lady Giselle. He became mindful of the sorry state of his purse, his lack of an estate and his age. He was not so young that he hadn't started to think of marrying and starting a family, especially with the example of his brother and sister, as well as his friend Merrick, to illustrate the joys of domesticity. Years of traveling from place to place, of being always a guest, had lost their luster, too.

His brother would surely counsel him to woo and wed Lady Giselle if he could. She was rich, she was young, she was beautiful—what was lacking? Well, one thing, but at the moment, it didn't seem like much of a hurdle. Henry had vowed he would be in love with his bride when he wed.

His smile grew as he watched Lady Giselle's slender body swaying in the saddle. It would surely be an easy thing to fall in love with such a beauty, and he was not without some confidence that he could arouse a similar feeling within her. He had his looks and years of experience with women on his side, and to win the love of such a woman, who would bring lands and wealth as her dowry, was surely worth whatever effort it might take.

And if he won the fair Giselle, Nicholas would finally have to say something good about his younger brother. Nor would he be able to accuse Henry of leading a wastrel existence anymore.

So why not begin the wooing? Henry thought, spurring Apollo to a slightly quicker pace until he was between the ladies.

"Have we much farther to go?" he asked Lady

Giselle, giving her his most charming smile. "I'm not sure how long the rain will hold off."

"Not far now," Lady Mathilde answered, while her sister nudged her horse forward to ride beside Cerdic.

Whether that was due to her modesty or not, Henry was slightly disgruntled at being so obviously left behind to ride beside Lady Mathilde.

That lady immediately fastened her inquisitive brown eyes onto him and asked, "Why do you hate Roald?"

God save him, she was as bold and blunt as her sister was shy and maidenly.

"You need have no fear of offending my delicate sensibilities, Sir Henry," she said when he didn't answer right away. "I can believe anything of Roald."

Despite her curiosity and her confidence that his reason wouldn't upset her, the explanation was not a tale he cared to share with a woman. "Surely any man of honor would dislike him."

She didn't bat an eye or look away. "He can be charming and sly, and he has more influence at court than we will ever have. Perhaps, if you don't hate him as much as I think, you may decide it is not worth the risk to offend him. You may even decide you should help him."

It was an insult to even imply that he was capable of such duplicitous behavior. "I've said that I'll help you, so I will—and even if I hadn't, Roald will make no overtures to me, nor would I accept them if he did. He hates me as much as I hate him."

"I must assume, then, you quarreled. Over a wager? Over a woman?"

God's wounds, she made him sound like a confederate who'd gotten in a bit of a tiff. "I would certainly never wager with Roald and his cronies. For one thing, they probably cheat."

She slid him a glance that was both shrewd and appraising, but in a complimentary way. "A woman, then?"

That was close to the truth, and yet their animosity sprang from a far different cause than she surely imagined.

Rather than endure her interrogation and who knew what other implications she might come up with, he decided to tell her the truth, if not in complete detail. "When we were both at court, I came upon him trying to force himself on a serving girl."

As always, the bile rose in his throat as he remembered the poor girl's terrified face, and a girl she was. She couldn't have been more than ten years old, but he would spare even this bold, prying lady that unsettling information. "I made him let her go at the point of my sword, so Roald has no love for me."

At first he thought he saw grim satisfaction on the lady's features, but it was quickly replaced by a piercing, searching gaze that was as uncomfortable as his brother's. "When did this happen?"

"Two years ago."

"He was not charged with trying to rape her?"

Henry winced inwardly at the harsh, if accurate, word. It was disconcerting to hear a lady speak so directly of such an act. "No."

"So although you caught him in the process of committing a crime, you let him go?"

Henry flushed, feeling a twinge of guilt at her accusation, although he'd told himself that night, and ever after, that he had done nothing to feel guilty about when he had allowed Roald to leave. "You didn't see the girl, my lady, or hear her sobs and pleas not to call the guard. She was sure no one would take her word over Roald's, and that Roald would say she led him on, and then her reputation would be ruined. I could not disagree, so yes, I let him go."

The lady tilted her inquisitive head with its pointed little chin. "Many noblemen would not interfere at all, believing a servant's body theirs by right, whether she was willing or not."

"*I* don't," he answered with firm honestly. "I would never take a woman against her will, whether high born or low, and I have never made a woman cry out in pain and anguish, or left her bruised and bleeding."

Lady Mathilde looked ahead at Cerdic and her sister, and he regretted speaking with such force. He should have remembered that, no matter her appearance or her manner, she was still a lady.

"That girl was fortunate you were there to help her," Lady Mathilde said quietly, and with sincerity and compassion—a hint of gentleness and sympathy that was rather unexpected, and not unpleasant.

Inspired to be pleasant in return, Henry nodded at Cerdic at the head of the cortege. The fellow had a sword at his side and a rather fearsome battle ax strapped to his back. The shaft of his ax had to be four feet long and the head looked sharp enough to split hairs. "It's rather unusual to see an Englishman in a position of such responsibility and trust."

In truth, he couldn't think of any Norman nobleman he knew who would give an Englishman that much responsibility, or consider one a friend. It had been nearly two hundred years since the Conquest, but old enmities died hard.

"Cerdic's family was royal before the Normans came," she replied.

She obviously admired the fellow. Henry wondered just how much, and if that extended to being on intimate terms. Not that it mattered. He had no interest in the bold and brazen Lady Mathilde. "You're from Provence, aren't you?" he asked, commenting on her accent.

"Yes, we were born there and lived there for most of our childhood."

Just like the queen Henry detested, the woman he believed was spurring his countrymen to rebellion with her selfish advancement of her own family.

"The same as Queen Eleanor," he remarked, wondering how she'd react to that.

Lady Mathilde looked as if she disliked the queen as much as he did. "If what Papa said about her family is true, it is a pity for England she is married to the king."

That was interesting. "What did your father say about her family?"

"That the only thing they produced was beautiful women, and the only intelligence they showed was in arranging marriages."

That was so close to the mark, Henry had to laugh. Then, because he was Henry, he smoothly said, "The queen's family isn't the only one capable of producing beautiful women."

Lady Mathilde frowned.

Clearly, he had erred. Obviously, this lady would never be impressed with flattery or, perhaps, reminders that her sister was beautiful while she was not.

"My father didn't like Normans, either," she declared. "He said they always wanted to make war and didn't appreciate music or art."

He *had* upset her with his comment, and since he was well aware of what it was like to be compared to a sibling and found lacking, he didn't take offense at her umbrage.

Her observation was also unfortunately true, at least in his case. He had little appreciation for art or music, except a clever, ribald ditty. Yet never before had he been made to feel that was a failing. "Someone has to defend the kingdom," he noted.

"William was defending England when he invaded it? I must have been seriously misinformed."

He would have found her remarks more amusing if she didn't look so smugly superior. "Well, sometimes we get carried away—and sometimes, such men are necessary to defend estates."

A blush colored her smooth cheeks, nearly overwhelming the few freckles on her nose.

"I meant no offense, Sir Knight," she said after a moment, and looking not nearly so well pleased, "and I do not necessarily share my father's views about the Normans. He did admire some things about your countrymen—*Magna Carta,* for instance, and how it set a limit on the king's power. That is why Papa gave up all claim to his French estates to his elder brother, Roald's father, in exchange for Ecclesford. Then Papa discovered that the English court is not very different from that of France. He was sorely disappointed."

Henry couldn't disagree. Noblemen were men first, and noble second, so they brought their ambition, greed, desires and needs to court with them.

"So Papa retired to Ecclesford and never went near the royal court again."

That would explain why he'd never seen either of the ladies there, or even heard of them.

"And that is why we have no noble friends to call upon, you see, or I would not have to ask a stranger for his help."

He suddenly felt like a lout for being annoyed with her, or anything she said. She and her sister were ladies in need of his aid, and that should be all that concerned him.

Maybe this would be a good time to do as Nicholas was always telling him, and keep his mouth shut.

Doing just that, he rode in silence beside Lady Mathilde, listening to the soldiers behind them laughing and talking. God's wounds, they sounded more like men on a hunt than soldiers.

The man who'd trained him and his friends in the arts of war would never have tolerated such a lack of discipline. Henry could just imagine the things Sir Leonard de Brissy would say if he were here, and the curses that would accompany his comments.

"Ecclesford is on the other side of this wood," Lady Mathilde remarked after they'd gone another mile or so, and the wind had started to rise. It tugged at the edges of the ladies' cloaks, and sent brown and yellow leaves swirling down the rutted, muddy road.

Henry noticed that the clouds were darker, too. He

hoped the rain wouldn't start before they arrived at Ecclesford. Chivalrous knight or not, he didn't want to get soaked to the skin.

THE RAIN didn't hold off and Henry was soaked to the skin before they reached Ecclesford Castle. He could barely see where he was going though the downpour, although he did note that the fortress had a dry moat that encircled it, except for the road leading to the large wooden gate, and only one outer wall. It was certainly not the most well-fortified castle he had ever encountered.

Once in the cobblestone courtyard, everyone hastened to dismount. Covering their heads with their arms, stableboys ran out to help with the horses. The animals snorted and refooted, their iron-shod hooves clattering on the cobblestones and adding to the din. The soldiers, grumbling about the weather, splashed heedlessly through puddles.

In the midst of the clamor, Lady Mathilde's voice came clear and strong. "Follow me to the hall, Sir Henry," she commanded as she headed toward a building directly across the yard.

He required no urging. Indeed, it was all he could do not to grab her arm to hurry her along.

It wasn't just that his clothes and hair were getting wet; it was the smell of wet stone—a potent and vivid reminder of those long hours in that cold, damp dungeon when he feared he would be dragged out and executed at any moment. That scent made him relive the beatings and, worse than any physical blow, the sickening realization that the man to whom he had sworn an oath of loyalty and brotherhood did not trust him.

Once out of the driving rain, Henry handed his soaking cloak to a servant who appeared beside him, then shook himself like a dog, as if that could rid him of not just the damp, but the unhappy memories, too.

In a way, it worked, and as the fear and dismay dwindled, he straightened and took in his surroundings while Lady Mathilde bustled off, saying something about a chamber and some food.

The hall itself was small, although comfortably furnished with benches, stools and even chairs upon a raised dais at one end. The well-scrubbed tops of large trestle tables that would be set up for meals leaned against the walls, along with their bases. Bright tapestries depicting scenes of hunting and ladies in a garden lined the wall behind the dais to keep out the chill of the stone walls. There were metal sconces for torches along the walls, and great smoke and age-darkened oaken beams held up the slate roof.

Best of all, though, was the large fire burning in the central hearth. Henry went there at once and, sighing, held out his hands to the welcome warmth. They had put in wood from an apple tree, and the scent mingled with that of wet wool, damp linen and the moist rushes below his feet.

Meanwhile, Lady Mathilde flitted about giving orders like a general in the midst of battle. Lady Giselle disappeared up some curved stairs that led, he assumed, to bedchambers and dry clothes. Cerdic and the rest of the sodden escort came in and arranged themselves on the opposite side of the fire. Each and every one of them cast hostile glances at Henry as they shuffled their feet and jockeyed for a place closest to the heat.

Henry ignored them. He was used to scrutiny, whether speculative or hostile.

Once or twice a pretty and particularly buxom serving woman wearing a gown that seemed molded to her full-figured body passed by. She made no secret of her interest in Henry, surreptitiously and coyly smiling at him.

Henry was used to this, too, and he supposed she would come to his bed if he so desired. He didn't so desire. First, it had never been his way, despite what many assumed, to fall into bed with any young woman who happened to catch his eye. Secondly, he had already discovered the few times he'd bedded a woman since his days in the dungeon that not only did making love *not* inspire sleep, it actually made him more wakeful. And last, but not least, he doubted the lovely and modest Lady Giselle would be inclined to accept him as a worthy suitor if he was bedding one of her servants right under her very nose.

As for any wayward fancies concerning Lady Mathilde and such activity, they were surely borne of fatigue and the unusual events of this strange day. To be sure, she was a bold and spirited woman, but not at all the sort he preferred. She was too audacious for his taste. While he was here, he would stay as far away from her as possible.

Lady Giselle appeared at the bottom of the stairs. Now she wore a gown of soft blue velvet that matched the color of her eyes. Her white, virginal veil was shot through with matching blue threads and held in place by a thin coronet made of intricately twisted gold. The long cuffs of her gown were embroidered with gold and emerald-green threads, the green matching the silken lining of the garment. A slender gilded girdle sat upon her hips.

She was the epitome of beauty, and as she paused on the bottom step, as uncertain as a fawn, he thought that he would surely be a fool not to woo and hope to wed her.

"Would you care to change your clothes?" Lady Mathilde asked, startling him out of his reverie.

He looked down to find her at his elbow, and with a disturbingly astute expression on her face. If someone were to tell him she possessed the ability to read his mind, he'd be inclined to believe it.

"There is a chamber ready for you now," she added.

He was aware of Lady Giselle gliding toward the hearth and decided he wasn't that wet anymore. "No, thank you, my lady. I'm quite comfortable."

Lady Mathilde's pursed lips revealed her reaction to that little lie—and then her eyes lit up like a bonfire on Midsummer's Eve.

"Father Thomas!" she cried, brushing past Henry and rushing toward a middle-aged priest who'd just entered the hall.

Maybe Lady Mathilde hoped to be a nun.

If that was so, he doubted any convent, or any Mother Superior who expected docile novices, was quite ready for *her.*

Instead of continuing toward the hearth, and to Henry's chagrin, Lady Giselle seated herself on one of the chairs on the dais. He contemplated leaving the fire to join her, but Lady Mathilde was coming toward him, leading the priest like a proud mother hen with a single chick. The priest followed serenely in her wake, a gentle smile on his pleasant face topped with a graying fringe of hair and a bald pate.

"Sir Henry, this is Father Thomas, the chaplain of Ecclesford, although he refuses to live here," she said, relaxed and happy, her eyes dancing with delight.

He wouldn't have been surprised if she'd started to giggle. She looked so different, it was hard to believe this was the same woman who'd confronted him not so long ago.

It suddenly seemed rather a pity she wasn't a serving wench, and one who would welcome the chance to spend a night in his bed.

God save him, he must be more exhausted than he knew.

Father Thomas smiled at Henry with beatific apology. "I fear Lady Mathilde will never forgive me for preferring to live among the villagers," he said, his accent marking him as a well-educated man who'd probably been the younger son of a noble household in the south of France. He shrugged his shoulders with elegant grace. "They need me more."

"More than soldiers?" Henry asked genially. He instinctively admired men of cloth—at least, most of them. "I would think soldiers are more prone to sin."

The priest's patient eyes seemed to reveal a knowledge of the world few worldly men possessed. "All men are tempted, my son. At least a soldier knows he will be housed and fed. The poor in the village have no such security, although the ladies of Ecclesford are more generous than most." He sighed. "But it is as our Lord tells us, the poor will always be with us, and their lives are difficult."

Although Henry wasn't ignorant of the lives of the poor, rarely did the fate of such people intrude upon his life. Standing before the kindly, soft-spoken priest, he suddenly felt rather ashamed that it should be so.

"Father Thomas says there has been no word or sign from Roald," Lady Mathilde said. "The more days that pass and we do not see him, the more I hope he has accepted my father's desire."

Her words and her smile made Henry think of a very different kind of desire, one that had nothing to do with her late parent. His mind instantly conjured the image of the bold, lively Lady Mathilde in his bed beneath him, smiling that smile, laughing, then sighing with pleasure as he loved her.

"Now it is time to eat," Lady Mathilde announced, forcibly returning him to the here and now where he was hungry and still slightly damp. "Sir Henry, you may take my father's chair. Giselle, you will sit to his right, Father Thomas to his left."

Like soldiers under her command, they all dutifully took their places, Lady Giselle keeping her eyes demurely lowered and never once looking his way.

As the meal progressed, Henry ignored the lively Lady Mathilde on the other side of Father Thomas and instead tried to amuse, entertain and impress the beautiful Lady Giselle. During the first course of fresh bread, butter and a dish composed of turbot cooked in a sauce of leeks and saffron, he told his best, most amusing stories of some of the people he'd met at court.

She never smiled. Not once.

When a fine frumenty of beef cooked with onions, parsley and sage followed, he spoke of the tournaments he'd been in, and the knights he'd defeated. He told her some tales of his friends, Merrick, the lord of Tregellas and Sir Ranulf, now the garrison commander there. She made appropriate gasps and exclamations of dismay as he described the combat, but with a detachment that spoke of mere polite attention. As a pudding of eggs, cream, bread crumbs and ground meat, spiced with pepper and something more exotic that he couldn't quite name, was set before them, he tried telling her about his sister and her exciting elopement with a Scot.

That finally got a reaction from Lady Giselle. Her eyes widened and her cheeks flushed. "To put her family through such fear and near disgrace," she murmured. "It must have been so difficult for you."

"Well, I wasn't there at the time," he admitted, delighted he'd finally gotten some kind of rejoinder from her.

But then Lady Giselle lapsed back into silence, causing Henry to subdue a disgruntled sigh. Never had he been met with less interest.

This did not bode well.

Maybe he should see if that buxom serving wench was as friendly as she seemed, even though he knew a tumble wouldn't guarantee him a good night's sleep. On the other hand, it might clear his mind of these ridiculous fancies featuring Lady Mathilde that persisted in dancing about the edge of his mind even as he spoke to Lady Giselle.

As the last of the baked fruit was cleared away, Lady Giselle pushed back her chair and got to her feet. "If you will excuse me," she said quietly, her gaze on her sister and Father Thomas, and without so much as a glance in his direction, "I shall retire early tonight."

"It's been a tiring day," Lady Mathilde agreed, although she herself didn't seem the least fatigued.

"Thank you for this fine meal, my lady," the priest said as he, too, rose. "If you will excuse me, I will take the leavings to distribute to those who wait at the gate."

"Certainly, Father," Lady Mathilde said. "It has been a pleasure, as always, and if there is more I can do, you have but to ask."

"Thank you, my lady, and God's blessing upon you and all who dwell herein."

Father Thomas turned to Henry, who had likewise gotten to his feet. "Thank you, my son, for coming to the aid of these ladies in their hour of need," he said, his warm expression like a benediction. "God will surely bless you for your generosity."

Considering that his reasons were not entirely selfless, Henry couldn't quite meet the priest's friendly gaze. "It is my honor, Father."

After the priest left the dais, Henry decided he

might as well retire. "I should sleep, too, my lady."
Or try to. "It's been a long and rather unusual day."

A rush light in her hand, that pretty maidservant
appeared at once, as if she'd been waiting for just this
moment. "I'll light his way, my lady."

Lady Mathilde reached for the rush light. "You
should help in the kitchen, Faiga. *I* shall show Sir Henry
to his chamber. If you will follow me, Sir Henry."

She briskly set off for the curved staircase, leaving
Henry to trail after her as the priest had. While Henry
obediently complied, he was more amused than
annoyed by her proprietary attitude. Perhaps she
thought Faiga required protection from the handsome
young guest, although he doubted Faiga would agree.
Or maybe she thought Faiga had been too forward.

Whatever Lady Mathilde thought about the
servant or her behavior, Faiga slid from Henry's mind
as they went up the steps. Instead, he found himself
hard pressed not to stare at Lady Mathilde's rather
attractive backside, her slim hips and rounded
buttocks swaying with every step. He smiled as he
thought of her happiness when she introduced him
to the priest, and the way she accepted the clergyman's preference to live among those most in need.

When they reached the second floor, Lady
Mathilde stopped at the first door. "This will be your
chamber while you are here. It was my father's, so it
is the largest. I hope it's to your liking."

Her tone made it clear she was sure he would.

"Considering some of the places I've had to lay my head," he honestly replied, "I'm sure it will be."

She made no answer as she opened the door and preceded him inside. The flickering light of the rush illuminated the large chamber, although the corners were still in shadow. A bed dominated the room, its curtains dark and thick, probably made of heavy velvet. A table with a silver ewer and basin and clean linen stood beside the door, and a chair and trestle table were near the window, where the sunlight would fall upon the surface during the day. He could smell the scent of lavender, either from the bedding or the lump of soap by the basin. Wherever it came from, it was welcome, reminding him of more pleasant times before he had been accused of treason and betrayal.

Outside, rain lashed against the walls and the wind moaned about the battlements. He didn't envy the men on watch tonight, provided there *were* men on watch. Given what he'd already observed, he wouldn't be surprised to discover that they deserted their posts in bad weather.

Lady Mathilde lit the thick yellow beeswax candle in the holder there. Another larger stand with several thinner candles stood in the corner.

For a moment, he thought her hands trembled, but she tucked them in the cuffs of her simple gown before he could be sure.

Why should her hands shake? Surely she wasn't afraid of him.

"Your baggage," she said, nodding at a familiar bundle in the corner near the bed.

"Thank you," he replied with a reassuring smile. "This room is most comfortable."

He thought she might go then, but she didn't move.

Why not? What was she waiting for, especially if she was uncomfortable in his presence? And surely it was unseemly for her to linger here, alone with him.

Unless what she was feeling was not fear, but something else that could make a woman quiver. Perhaps he wasn't the only one having lustful thoughts. "Is there something more you wish of me, my lady?" he asked, keeping his tone carefully neutral in case he was wrong.

Her gaze met his, steady and determined. "I should warn you, Sir Henry, that if you think to seduce my sister, you should think again."

He was so shocked, he actually took a step back. Seduction was not his aim, but *perhaps* marriage, if he and the lady suited, yet Lady Mathilde made him sound like some kind of disgusting scoundrel. "My lady, I play the game of seduction only with those willing to be seduced," he replied. "If a woman isn't interested, I don't pursue her, no matter how beautiful she may be."

"I am not blind, Sir Henry," Lady Mathilde replied, crossing her arms over her breasts. "I watched you trying to charm her. And I do not say mere seduction is your plan. After all, Giselle is an heiress, and the man who marries her will be rich."

His pride urged him to refute that mercenary motive, but since he honestly couldn't, he didn't. "Do you forbid me to speak to her?"

Lady Mathilde gave him a pitying look, as if she thought him stupid but was too polite to say so. "Not at all. You have offered to help us against Roald, and you are our guest."

"Yet you accuse me of plotting to seduce your younger sister."

"Not plotting, precisely. Hoping to marry her for her dowry, perhaps, and so I seek to save you a useless effort. Giselle may be beautiful, but she is not a fool. I assure you, she will not succumb to any honeyed words or meaningless promises. And Giselle is not the younger sister. *I* am."

Given Lady Mathilde's command of the household, he had assumed she must be the eldest. She certainly behaved as if she were.

Recovering as quickly as he could, he said, "If I were to make an offer for your sister, it would be because I love her. I have promised myself I will be in love with my bride when I wed."

Lady Mathilde's expression betrayed her skepticism.

"Believe it or not as you will," he said with a shrug, "but I would have a marriage such as that of my brother and my sister, who care deeply for their spouses. They are very happy together. Why should I settle for less?"

Lady Mathilde's shrewd eyes narrowed as she studied him. "You seem to be a most unusual nobleman."

"As you seem to be a most unusual lady."

Even *he* could not have said whether he meant that for a compliment or not, but it was the truth. "I'm impressed with your concern for your sister," he added as he strolled toward her, and that, at least, was true.

Lady Mathilde backed away as if she were afraid. Of him? That was ridiculous—he had given her no reason to believe he would be dangerous to her.

"Giselle's husband will be the lord of Ecclesford. I must protect her from handsome, charming men who seek only to enrich themselves."

He regarded her quizzically. "If she is the elder, can she not look after herself?"

The woman before him flushed, but didn't look away. Her mouth was half-parted, her breasts rising and falling with her rapid breathing. She swayed forward a bit—enough to encourage him to think she was feeling the same pull of desire and curiosity.

Responding to that urge, he put his hands on her

shoulders and started to draw her closer. With her came the scent of lavender.

She gasped and in that same instance, her eyes were suddenly alive with what could only be fear as she twisted from his light grasp. "Don't touch me!"

Shocked by the force of her reaction, he spread his arms wide. "I didn't mean to frighten you."

"You were going to kiss me!" she accused, as if his kiss would kill her.

Not every woman he met was attracted to him, and he was not so vain as to expect that they would be. On the other hand, never before had he been to feel as if he were somehow unsavory, and his pride was pricked. She *had* been tempted to kiss him, and he would prove it.

"I thought you *wanted* me to kiss you," he said, his voice low and sultry, his tone one that had encouraged many a woman to express her passionate desires.

The look she gave him! It was a wonder it didn't strike him dead. "I did not, you base, vile, lustful rogue!"

The heat of a blush—something he hadn't felt in years—flooded his face. Embarrassed, his pride stung, he drew himself up like the knight he was. "If you would rather I leave Ecclesford, you have only to say so."

For a moment, he thought she was going to agree, but in the next, she shook her head, her cheeks as red as his scarlet hauberk. "Forgive me, Sir Henry," she said, twisting the cuff of her gown in her slender fingers. "I am sometimes too quick to anger."

Suddenly he realized exactly what her reaction reminded him of. She was like a horse that had been beaten and shied away from any person who came near it. No doubt some stupid lout had been too forward and too rough with her—a selfish youth or overeager suitor. The fool had surely gotten no further than a kiss, for a woman like Lady Mathilde wouldn't hesitate to fight off any unwelcome advances. It was unfortunate, but the damage had been done.

His annoyance fled, replaced with regret. "No, my lady, it is I who should be forgiven for presuming too much," he replied with a courteous bow. "I assure you, it will not happen again."

"Good," she murmured.

Then, keeping as much distance as possible between them, as if the very thought of touching him was repugnant to her, she sidled toward the door. "I give you good night, Sir Henry."

"Good night, my lady," he muttered as she closed the door behind her.

He moved the large, lit candle to the table beside the bed. He might have been a fool to come here, despite their need. Nicholas would probably say so, even taking the presence of the lovely Lady Giselle into account.

Ah well, this wouldn't be the first time his brother would think him less than wise, he thought as he started to disrobe, and Lady Giselle wasn't completely out of his grasp.

Yet.

AFTER SHE LEFT Sir Henry, Mathilde paused on the steps and leaned back against the curved wall, her hands clasped to her breast, her heart racing, her blood throbbing, her breathing ragged. Why had she lingered? Why hadn't she simply told him not to pursue Giselle and left the chamber at once?

Because he was handsome and friendly and charming. Because she had both feared and hoped that he would kiss her. Because she was weak and lustful, and he aroused a desire in her so overwhelming, she felt almost helpless to resist, in spite of the chiding of her conscience.

At least now one thing was very clear: she must never be alone with the handsome Sir Henry again.

CHAPTER THREE

THE NEXT MORNING, after another restless night disturbed by dreams of the dungeon and the beating and the pain his friend had inflicted, Henry leaned over the basin in the lord's chamber of Ecclesford and splashed cold water over his face. God's wounds, would he never sleep well again? It had been weeks since those terrible days. His injuries had healed. So why could he not sleep soundly? Why did the memories still come so vividly, as if he were again chained to that wall and despairing that Merrick, a man to whom he had sworn to be loyal even to death, had been so quick to believe that he was a traitor?

A soft knock sounded on the door.

When he bade the person enter, he more than half-expected Lady Mathilde to march over the threshold. Instead, it was that full-figured serving wench, carrying a tray, and with a coy smile on her face.

"Good morning, my lord," she said brightly. "Lady Mathilde said although ye're not an early riser, it's well past mass, so you should be getting up and I was to bring you something to eat and wake you."

Lady Mathilde had seemed to believe he was lust incarnate last night, so he was rather surprised by her choice of servant...unless this was some sort of test. Or perhaps it was a trap intended to "prove" his lascivious nature to her sister, and so prevent any hope of a marriage.

Clever, but doomed to fail. "What o'clock is it?" he inquired, drying off his face with a square of linen.

"Nearly noon, my lord," the wench replied, setting the tray on the table beside the bed and running a blatantly lascivious gaze over him.

"Thank you."

"My name's Faiga, my lord."

He bowed as if she were a lady. "Thank you, Faiga."

Grinning with delight, the maidservant whipped the cloth napkin from the covered tray. "Here's fresh bread, my lord, and honey, and ale. Good ale, too, not like some you get. The alewife here's a good one."

"Excellent. Now you may go."

The maidservant's expression could only be called a pout and her progress to the door was desultory at best, but he ignored her in favor of the delicious bread and welcome honey. The ale *was* excellent, too, some of the best Henry had ever tasted.

His repast complete, Henry contemplated what he should do. He had no duties here, beyond waiting for that lout Roald. A glance toward the window showed that the storm had blown itself out overnight. The sky was clear, and the sun shone as if it were still summer, so he decided to take a stroll about the castle.

As he passed through the hall, he noted that neither lady was there. Lady Mathilde was probably running around issuing orders somewhere. As for Lady Giselle, maybe she was trying on gowns or brushing her hair or whatever it was beautiful ladies did while their sisters ran the household.

He halted on the steps leading down to the court-yard and surveyed the fortress of Ecclesford. A keep—square, squat, ugly and old—stood at the southern end of the yard, while various other build-ings had been built against the inside of the protec-tive wall. The stables were to his right, with barracks above, judging by the men's garments hanging out of the open windows to dry. At least one was a gambeson, the quilted padded jacket soldiers wore beneath their mail.

The small building in the corner opposite the stables with the carved door was probably the chapel. Good Father Thomas could have spent his days lei-surely there, saying mass once a day and otherwise doing whatever he wanted. Truly, he seemed a kind and honest churchman, and Henry hoped he saw more of him.

The kitchen had to be the building attached to the hall by a covered corridor, so that should fire break out, it wouldn't spread to the hall. He sniffed the air and recognized the wonderful smell of baking bread and gravy.

When he had been released from his imprisonment, the first thing he had asked for was wine, but what he had enjoyed most was his first bite of a loaf of freshly baked bread. It still seemed to him the very taste of freedom.

Turning his thoughts from those days, he noted the well near the kitchen, which meant that if the castle were ever besieged, water wouldn't be a problem, unless some bloated carcass of a beast was thrown over the wall and landed in it by a stroke of luck for the attacking force. As was usually the case, several women were clustered around it, drawing water and gossiping, no doubt. He wondered what they made of his presence here.

He looked up at the wall walk, trying to determine how many men patrolled the battlements. Not enough, that seemed certain, and several of them stood together, clearly much more interested in what was going on in the courtyard than keeping watch over the village and the approach to the castle.

Sir Leonard de Brissy would have had them all in the stocks and so would he…but this was not his castle or his garrison to command. He was a guest, so he would keep his opinions to himself. Besides, he could easily imagine how Lady Mathilde would take any suggestion he attempted to make.

When Henry started across the yard, the bustle came to a momentary halt while those at their work stopped to look at the Norman in their midst. The women gathered at the well eyed him with approval, while laborers repairing the base of the wall near the gate were considerably less impressed.

As before, Henry ignored their scrutiny, paying more attention to the guards, if they could be called that, at the gate. They leaned on their spears, chatting as if they were passing the time in a tavern. As Henry strolled out the open gates, they barely glanced his way.

God's blood, if he were in charge here, they'd be having bread and water for a week. No wonder Roald had not yet come to make his claim. He probably assumed he could simply saunter through the gates whenever it pleased him, demand the castle, and no one would be able to stop him.

How Lady Mathilde thought such a garrison could defeat Roald…

He came to an abrupt halt. In the open area between the dry moat and the village, Cerdic and another man, stripped to the waist, were fighting with clubs. Other men had formed a half circle around them, apparently offering advice or encouragement. Both combatants were intent on each other and clearly determined to win, yet he didn't detect animosity—just determination.

Not a fight between enemies or a settling of accounts, then. A practice? God save him, could it be? Was it possible there was some kind of attempt to train these men after all? But why clubs?

One of the men in the semicircle spotted Henry and made a comment to the man next to him. Soon others were staring at him, and in the next moment, Cerdic and his opponent had turned to look at him, too.

Having nothing better to do, Henry sauntered toward them.

"What dost thou seek, Norman?" Cerdic demanded.

"I was wondering what you're doing with those clubs."

Cerdic and his companion exchanged amused and smug smiles. "We use clubs instead of axes when we practice lest we slice off fingers," Cerdic replied. "We leave the swords for more dainty men."

So, that was the way it was going to be. "Then perhaps you'll let me watch and learn a trick or two."

Cerdic sniffed. "Why? Thou and thy countrymen do not use axes."

"I was taught to use any weapon that might be on a battlefield. Sir Leonard used to say a lance could be broken, a sword knocked away and a mace ripped from your grip, so the wise knight learns to fight with anything that might come to hand."

A challenging gleam appeared in Cerdic's storm-gray eyes. "I would see how a Norman fights with an ax."

The blood quickened in Henry's veins, as it always did when he was challenged. "It would be my pleasure. Shall we test each other here and now?"

The men muttered excitedly and Cerdic darted them a satisfied grin before addressing Henry again. "With these toys, or real axes?"

"Since I would rather not lose a limb, I'd prefer a club." Henry was determined to beat Cerdic, but he wasn't a fool. Accidents happened in practices, too, and it was obvious Cerdic didn't like him.

Cerdic's grin grew. "Very well, Norman. The toys."

Cerdic nodded to the man he'd been about to fight. With a sneer and a few words Henry was sure were not compliments, the fellow handed his club to Henry.

Cerdic could call them toys if he liked, Henry thought as he tested the feel and weight of the club, but this thing could break bones.

As he swung his weapon back and forth, then up and around his head, he studied Cerdic out of the corner of his eye. He wouldn't be easy to defeat. He was full of the confidence that came from skill, and he was one of the more well-muscled men Henry had ever seen. Although Henry didn't believe Cerdic would kill or seriously wound a guest of the ladies of Ecclesford, he didn't want to have to hobble about on a broken leg, or nurse a broken arm, either.

"Until the first man cries mercy?" Henry proposed.

His opponent nodded.

"Care to make a wager on who it will be?"

That brought another grin to Cerdic's face. "Ten silver pennies 'twill be thee."

"Done," Henry said. He glanced at the other men. "Wonder who they'll bet on?"

"Me to win, thee to lose," Cerdic said in a low voice.

And then, with a blood-curdling cry, the man ran at Henry, swinging his club back and up and around, to bring it crashing down on Henry's head—had Henry still been standing there. With lightning-fast reflexes honed by hours of practice, Henry deftly sidestepped the blow and shoved his shoulder against Cerdic, knocking him sideways.

Growling an oath, Cerdic righted himself and turned to see Henry holding his weapon with both hands, his body half-turned. Henry swung low, aiming for his calves.

Hissing like a snake, Cerdic leaped back, his arms wide with surprise. "Dog! Thou wouldst break my ankles?"

"You could have broken my head if your blow had landed. If this were an ax and I'd hit, you could have lost your feet."

Scowling, Cerdic raised his weapon again and

shuffled, by wary inches, closer to his opponent. Henry hesitated, not sure if he should try to strike low again, or knock the weapon from Cerdic's hand.

That hesitation cost him, for Cerdic suddenly jumped forward, bringing his weapon straight down. Henry lunged to the left, nearly sprawling on the ground. He righted almost at once and managed to hit Cerdic's club.

Cerdic struck back instantly, his club coming down on Henry's. Shoving it off, Henry backed up a step or two, but the men watching had surrounded them, ringing them in, and he had less room to maneuver than he thought.

Whatever happened, he wasn't going to give up. He was going to win and show these soldiers that he really did know how to fight with something other than a sword or mace or lance.

He would prove his skill and do Sir Leonard proud.

As fierce resolve coursed through his veins, he watched Cerdic like a hawk would a field mouse it wanted for its dinner and shouted at the men to give him room. They did, backing up a little, although they muttered in complaint as they did.

"I need no more room to defeat thee," Cerdic said through clenched teeth, also keeping his gaze on Henry, no doubt seeking an opening, too. "Canst thou not fight in close quarters, Norman?"

"Aye, indeed, I can," Henry replied, circling him in a crouch. "Very close."

With that, and although he was right-handed, he swung his club from the left. As he'd expected, that caught Cerdic off guard and he was unprepared to defend a blow from that side. The club flew from his hand, striking an unfortunate fellow in the front row.

That would teach him to stand too close, Henry thought, even as he seized his chance, and with a deft turn of his body, shoved Cerdic backward with his left shoulder. The man landed on the ground, spread-eagled, flat on his back and weaponless.

In the next moment, Henry's foot was on Cerdic's throat. "I believe I have the advantage, my friend," he said, still holding his club in case Cerdic was able to break free or grabbed his left ankle and tipped him back, as Henry would have done.

Apparently, however, that move didn't occur to Cerdic, who gave him a disgruntled frown. "I yield."

Henry removed his foot and reached out his hand to help Cerdic to his feet. The fellow would have none of it, however. He rolled onto his side and got up unaided. "Thou didst not say thou could use either hand."

"I wasn't born able to do that," Henry replied, prepared to be friendly, especially since he had won. "I was trained to do so. It isn't easy, but any man may learn how, with enough practice."

Cerdic merely grunted as he went to his clothes

on the ground nearby and fetched a small purse. The other men continued to regard Henry with wary caution, and perhaps—or so he hoped—a little respect.

He'd probably made more of an enemy of Cerdic, though. However, if a man hated you on sight for something that was not your fault—your birth, or your rank, or your looks—there was little to be done to change it, and Henry did have his pride. Even so, had he been staying at Ecclesford for the winter, he would have willingly lost the contest, if only to ensure himself a little less animosity from the men of the garrison.

"Here," Cerdic said, handing him ten silver pennies.

"Thank you," Henry replied, sincerely happy to have them. As Lady Mathilde had been informed, he had nearly nothing in his purse, and while he wouldn't take payment for helping ladies, he would certainly pocket the winnings of a wager fairly won, and with some effort. "Now if you'll excuse me, I believe I'll see what sights the town has to offer."

From the smirks on the faces of the men, he could guess how they thought he'd be spending his money. In that, they were quite wrong. He enjoyed wine, to be sure, and women, but not today, and not here. Not when there was a lady to woo.

So instead, the pleased, triumphant and slightly richer Henry sauntered through the village of Ecclesford, surveying the buildings and the wares in the marketplace, and trying not to notice that everybody stopped and stared at him as he passed by. He could also easily imagine what they'd be saying about him in the tavern and around the well when they heard of his defeat of Cerdic, and that it wouldn't be flattering. That was only to be expected, and since his visit here was not likely to be long, he wouldn't let their hostility disturb him.

All in all, Ecclesford seemed a fairly prosperous place. The main road skirted a green, and several two-story structures—stalls on the bottom, living quarters above—surrounded it. Women were both selling and purchasing goods ranging from bread, to chickens in small wooden cages, to bolts of woven cloth. He spotted the sign for an inn called, to his amusement, the Cock and Bull, and the ringing of a hammer on an anvil proclaimed the smithy. Another group, this time of men, were gathered outside the entrance, some standing, the older men on a bench that faced the west and setting sun. A massive oak grew near the smithy, and its spreading branches, now yellowing in the autumn, still provided some cooling shade on this warm day.

On the other side of the village beside the millpond, he paused to take a deep breath and realized that he stank of sweat. He needed to wash, and well.

He could always ask the servants at the castle to

prepare a bath, he mused, until he thought of the very friendly Faiga. He was tired after his contest with Cerdic and didn't particularly feel like fending off any unwelcome advances.

He glanced at the pond. It looked deep and inviting. A dip in those cool waters would be just the thing—except that he would be in plain view of half the village if he did that here.

Seeking a more secluded spot, he kept walking until he rounded a curve in the road and came upon a grove of willow trees along the riverbank, their graceful branches hanging to the ground, some grazing the river itself as it made its leisurely way toward the sea. Yes, this was much more to the purpose, he thought, ducking under the branches and removing his clothes.

Naked, he waded gingerly out into the water, wincing as he walked barefoot over the rocks and pebbles. When the water was up to midthigh, he dove.

The shock of cold water hit him like a blow, but he didn't come up for air immediately. He struck out with strong, clean strokes.

Sir Leonard had insisted his charges learn to swim, too. All had succeeded, more or less, and this was one skill in which he'd excelled. Merrick, who was otherwise the best warrior, had proven to be surprisingly awkward in the water, while Ranulf always seemed to be rowing Sir Leonard's boat.

Smiling at the memory of the time he and Merrick had overturned the boat and dumped Ranulf into the shallow water before Sir Leonard had embarked, Henry broke the surface and rolled over onto his back. Ranulf had been furious—but he'd deserved it.

How merry they'd been in those long-ago days, even the usually silent Merrick. Now Merrick was a great lord, married and with a child on the way. As for Ranulf, Henry wondered, and not for the first time, what exactly had happened that time Ranulf had been at court without them. Something certainly had, for he'd returned a colder, more cynical man.

No doubt it had to do with a woman. Who could understand the fairer sex? They were mysterious, unfathomable creatures, bold and haughty one moment, fearful and uncertain the next….

What the devil? When had Lady Mathilde become the model for her sex? If anything, she was the opposite of what a noblewoman ought to be—quiet, demure, gentle…dull, boring, lifeless.

He was being ridiculous. If there was any woman here worth pursuing, it was the beautiful Lady Giselle who, fortunately, wasn't already betrothed.

He wondered why. If Lady Mathilde had been the eldest, he would have assumed that their father believed that the younger daughter shouldn't marry before the eldest. Certainly finding a man willing to marry the brazen, outspoken Lady Mathilde would prove a difficult task. Since Lady Giselle was the eldest, perhaps no suitable candidate for either lady had been forthcoming.

Cooler now, and cleaner, and still determined to ignore any wayward thoughts involving the younger lady of Ecclesford, Henry walked out of the river. He swiped the water from his body as best he could, then tugged on his breeches. He threw on his shirt, but decided against putting his tunic and sword belt back on. He sat to draw on his hose and boots, then rose, grabbed his sword belt and, with his tunic hanging over his arm, started back to the poorly defended Ecclesford.

"Sir Henry?"

He halted and slowly turned around when he heard Lady Mathilde call his name. What in God's name was she doing here and had she seen him naked—again? He wasn't normally the most modest of men, but he didn't enjoy feeling as if his entire body was available for her perusal.

Fortunately, Lady Mathilde was far enough away that she probably hadn't seen him in the river or on the bank. Thank God.

Her head was uncovered and she carried a basket in her hand. Her chestnut hair hung in a single braid down her back nearly to her waist; that must be her veil tucked into her girdle. With her plain light brown gown and uncovered hair, she looked like a simple country girl.

The first woman he had ever made love to had been a dairymaid.

God's blood, it had been years since he'd thought of Elise, and the passionate excitement, unique to youth, to be found in her welcoming arms. That must explain the sudden heating of his blood and the rush of desire in his loins.

Whatever Lady Mathilde looked like and whatever she aroused, she was no milking maid eager to instruct him in the ways of love.

"My lady," he said, bowing in greeting as he waited for her to reach him, glad his shirt hung loose to midthigh.

She ran a puzzled gaze over him. "Have you been in the water?"

"It's a warm day," he replied, "and I thought I'd save your servants the trouble of preparing a bath. Cerdic challenged me to show my skill and I obliged. Afterward I wanted to wash more than my face and hands."

Her brows knit with concern. "I hope he didn't hurt you."

He couldn't help smiling a little. "He was the one left lying on the ground."

"You defeated Cerdic?" she asked incredulously.

He shrugged with chivalrous modesty. "As I said, I can wield more than a sword."

She started walking toward the castle, her strides betraying her agitation.

He'd better keep quiet about the wager, he decided as he fell into step beside her. "Would you rather I let him hurt me?"

"I don't know why you had to involve yourself at all," she snapped, her full lips turned down in a peeved frown.

"I had nothing better to do. Neither you nor your sister were in the hall to offer suggestions as to how I might spend my time while I was your guest."

He let the implication that they had been remiss in their duty hang in the air between them.

"I thought Giselle would be in the hall when you finally deigned to get out of bed," Lady Mathilde replied, her voice betraying some slight remorse. "She usually does her sewing there, and there was no need for her other skill today."

"Other skill?" he asked, curious as to what that might be and trying not to get annoyed with Lady Mathilde's less-than-ladylike tone.

"She tends to the sick in the castle and the village."

A most excellent quality in a knight's wife, Henry reflected. His recent recovery would surely have been aided, and made all the more pleasant, had he been cared for by such a physician. "And you, my lady?" he inquired politely. "Are you similarly skilled?"

"The smells of the sickroom make me ill and the sight of a bloody wound turns my stomach."

Blunt and to the point, as always, and should he

ever require another reason that this lady would not make a suitable bride, there it was. "I take it you weren't visiting the sick in the village then," he remarked, nodding at her basket.

"No," she curtly replied. But then her lips curved up in a secretive and surprisingly intriguing little smile. "I was visiting one of my tenants whose wife just had a baby."

He suddenly noticed a little beauty mark on the nape of Lady Mathilde's neck, like a target for a kiss—a light kiss, no more than the brush of a moth's wing. A caress of the lips before they traveled toward her full mouth and...

God's wounds, what was the matter with him?

"You shouldn't have gone out of the castle by yourself," he said, sounding not a little annoyed, although he wasn't angry with her.

"Why shouldn't I go by myself?" she demanded. "This is my home, after all."

Obviously, since she couldn't really read his mind, she'd taken his tone of voice to imply criticism and condemnation rather than anger at himself. Yet even though he shouldn't have spoken so brusquely, he did think she'd taken a risk. "You and I both know Roald is without scruples or honor. I can well believe he'd stoop to abduction to get what he wants."

Which was perfectly true.

When Lady Mathilde faced him, her expression

was as stern as that of any man. "Even if Roald did something so stupid, it would avail him nothing."

"You think not?" Henry replied. "You don't think your sister would give in to any demands he might make if your life depended on it?"

For one instant, her gaze faltered, but in the next, she boldly, defiantly declared, "No."

She wanted to believe her sister would be strong and resist, but Henry knew otherwise.

"I think she would, not because she's a woman and a woman is supposed to be weak, but because I've seen how love can make even the strongest man vulnerable," he said. Merrick had beaten him nearly to death when he believed Henry had attempted to abduct his wife.

"I will not cower in the castle like a frightened child," Lady Mathilde retorted, intense and resolute. "I will not live in fear of Roald."

"I'm not suggesting that you cower, my lady," he replied, finding it difficult to imagine this woman being afraid of anything. "I'm not suggesting that you stay within the castle walls. What I *am* suggesting is that you take a guard with you when you leave the castle. That's not so much, is it?"

"No," she answered, sounding suddenly weary as she again started toward the castle.

"I can appreciate that you don't want anyone to think you're afraid," he said as he caught up to her.

"But my old teacher, Sir Leonard, used to say there's bravery and then there's bravado, and bravado can get you killed. I would rather you be safe, my lady."

She bowed her head. "Forgive me," she said, her voice much more like her sister's dulcet tones than her usual confident declarations. "Once again, I have let my feelings get the better of me. I should not have gotten so upset when you sought only to offer well-meaning advice."

Henry himself hated being offered advice, well-meaning or otherwise, and he had to admit he had been rather domineering—an attitude he usually never took with women. But then, Lady Mathilde more often seemed his equal than a mere woman. Not now, though. Now he was forcibly reminded she was a member of the weaker sex, and a young one, at that. "No, my lady, forgive *me*. I shouldn't have let my temper get the better of me. It must be the heat, or perhaps the fight with Cerdic momentarily addled my wits."

That brought a smile to her face. It wasn't the most joyous he had ever seen, but he was pleased nonetheless. "When we return to the castle, my lady," he said, offering her his arm, "I shall regale you with the story of my impressive defeat of your brawny friend. It's very exciting, I assure you."

She lightly laid her hand on his arm, and he considered that something of a triumph, too. "I will ask Cerdic for his version of the tale, as well," she said, sliding him a wry, sidelong glance that implied friendship between them was a distinct possibility, if not yet a certainty. "I suspect the truth will lie somewhere in the middle."

He laughed, happy that they had made peace. "You wound me, my lady—but you're probably right."

CHAPTER FOUR

SINGING SNATCHES of a dirty little ditty, Sir Roald de Sayres staggered down a street poorly lit by flickering flambeaux. Fortunately, the moon was full and bright to light his way, and this was Westminster, home of the king and court, not the slums. A man like himself, well dressed, well armed and obviously noble, need not fear being set upon and robbed.

"Say what you like, I'll like what you say," he sang, his voice wavering and off-key.

Not that he cared what he sounded like. He was happily thinking about the brothel he'd just left. If only he could have stayed longer. If only he'd brought more money. There had been that one glorious creature with the full breasts and long legs ready to pleasure any of them. And the dark-haired lovely who would do anything if you paid enough. God's blood, if only he were richer, he'd spend every night he could there.

Then, with a sigh of satisfaction, he remembered that he *was* rich. Well, almost. All he had to do was claim Ecclesford. He should go there soon. It had been, what—five…six days since he'd killed Martin? Maybe he had enough in his purse for one more night before…

Suddenly a man shrouded in a long cloak, with the hood pulled over his head, stepped out of the shadows to block Roald's way. He seemed huge in the darkness, like an ogre or other supernatural creature.

"Sir Roald de Sayres?" a low, rough voice rasped.

Not an ogre or devil, Roald told himself as he felt for the hilt of his sword. Just a man. A very big man, but a mortal man nonetheless, and men could be killed or captured and imprisoned by the watch.

The fellow laughed, a sound more ugly than his voice. "Don't bother calling for the watch. They can't help you. I'd be gone before they get here."

As he spoke, the blade of a broadsword flashed out of the man's cloak, the tip pressing against Roald's chest.

"My purse is empty!"

"All the worse for you, then."

Nudging him with his sword, the man backed Roald against the nearest wall, then threw back his hood, revealing his face—and a horrible face it was, heavy and brutish, and scarred from several wounds. His nose had been broken at least twice, and he was missing most of one ear. A jagged scar ran down his cheek in a puckered, red line. "You owe a lot of money to some of the Goldsmiths' Guild."

"This is about a *debt?*"

The sword moved close to Roald's heart. "A big one, or so they say. Big enough they're willing to pay me to make you honor it."

Those stinking, money-grubbing merchants. "I will repay them," Roald said haughtily, now certain this blackguard wouldn't kill him. "They have my word."

Still the sword remained where it was. "They don't seem to think your word counts for much. That's why they sent *me.*"

"Haven't they heard my uncle's died?" Roald retorted, sounding only a little desperate. "I've got an estate in Kent now, so of course I can pay."

The tip of the sword flicked upward, touching Roald's chin. "That news reached their ears, but if the estate's yours, why haven't you gone there, eh?"

"Because I saw no need," Roald replied with all the dignity he could muster, very aware of the blade so close to his face.

Suddenly, the man's powerful left hand wrapped around Roald's throat and he shoved him hard against the wall. "You've got a fortnight to come up with the money, or I'll be taking a finger. Then a hand." His sword moved lower, pressing against Roald's groin. "Then something else, until your debt's paid. Understand, my lord?"

"Yes!" Roald hissed, fighting the urge to cup himself protectively.

"Good."

The man let go and, gasping, Roald fell to the ground on his hands and knees, the cold cobblestones cutting his palms, his knees bruising. He looked up at the figure looming over him. "Who the devil *are* you?"

"Can't you guess?" the man said with a snort of a laugh. "I'm Sir Charles De Mallemaison."

Roald felt the blood drain from his face. Charles De Mallemaison was the most notorious, vicious mercenary in England, possibly even Europe. He'd appeared in the service of a lord in Shropshire, claiming to be a knight from Anjou. The one man who'd questioned De Mallemaison's nobility had been found hacked to small pieces on the side of the road; no one had questioned it since.

"A fortnight," De Mallemaison repeated as he disappeared into the shadows, his cloak swirling about him. "The whole amount. Or you start losing bits."

As ROALD was staggering back to his lodgings, no longer drunk but shaking with the aftermath of fear, Giselle slumbered peacefully in the large bed she shared with her sister. Mathilde, however, dressed in a shift and bedrobe and, with soft leather slippers on her feet, paced anxiously by the window.

No terrible dreams troubled Giselle's sleep, Mathilde reflected. No remorse kept her awake. No shame disturbed her rest. No lustful yearnings robbed her of peace. Giselle was good and honorable and free of sin, whereas she....

What else could she be feeling for Sir Henry but lust? That day by the river, simply seeing him with his damp hair and loose shirt unlaced to reveal his chest, had been enough for her to recall, with vivid clarity, the sight of him in that tavern bed—his back, his taut buttocks and long, muscular legs. Thinking of him swimming, gliding through the water like an otter, had kept her awake for hours.

When he'd described his mock combat with Cerdic, she'd laughed harder than she had in months. He'd been both entertaining and self-deprecating, claiming that he'd managed to defeat the other warrior only by luck and the skin of his teeth.

She'd read another reason for his victory in his animated features, seen it in his sparkling brown eyes—Sir Henry was confident of his skills, and determined to win. It was a heady combination.

Aware of her own weakness, she kept reminding herself that this merry knight, whose very appearance could excite her, would not always be there— unless he won Giselle's heart. So, determined to keep him at a distance, she'd made certain he had activities with which to amuse himself and that kept him away from both her and her sister for the past few days, such as hunting and riding about the estate. She'd insisted that he take a guard whenever he rode out. As she'd told him, he was vulnerable to attack, too.

He'd taken no offense, but simply laughed in that appealing way of his. Then he'd said he was pleased she had so much concern for his person.

And she did—too much. He was so handsome and well built, she could hardly stop from staring at him as he sauntered through the hall, or spoke to Giselle or Father Thomas.

Now every night she lay awake, restless and uneasy, and prayed to forget the memory of his body and his smiling face. She prayed for the strength to ignore the lust she couldn't control, the feelings she thought forever destroyed by her past mistake, only to discover that they rose, strong and almost overwhelming, when she was with Sir Henry, and away from him, too. How could she be tempted when she knew where giving in to desire might lead?

Yet she *was* tempted. She'd nearly kissed Sir Henry that first night, until the fear and panic had come, overpowering her and making her act like a frightened child.

Sighing, Mathilde went to the arched window and looked into the quiet courtyard. The sentries' torches burned on the wall walk, little flickers of light in the darkness—darkness that even now might cloak Roald's progress toward Ecclesford.

Had she done enough to prepare for his eventual arrival?

They had as many soldiers as they could afford and Cerdic had to be a better commander than Martin, who she would have sent away even if he hadn't immediately declared he wouldn't take orders from a woman. If her father had been stronger this past year, she would have asked him to select a new garrison commander months ago, but he'd been ill, and she'd thought to spare him any more trouble.

If only he had lived! If only she'd been stronger. If only Roald had not come last year and brought disaster with him.

Rubbing her hands up and down her arms for warmth, she tried not to think about Roald or Sir Henry anymore as she went to pour herself some water in which to bathe her face.

The ewer was empty. No matter. She would get more water from the kitchen.

Opening the door, she peered down the corridor toward her father's bedchamber, temporarily Sir Henry's. A torch burned in a sconce on the wall, providing some light, although it was dark near the door to her father's chamber. To her surprise, a shaft of light spread out from below the door.

Sir Henry was still awake? Or had he fallen asleep with the candle lit? A guest had once set his bedding aflame by leaving a lit candle too close to the bed curtains.

Even so, she was not about to enter that room now,

in the dead of night, and with him abed and perhaps…
naked. Commanding herself not to think about that,
she headed for the stairs leading to the hall.

When she passed the door to the lord's chamber,
a low moan came from within. God help her, did he
have a woman with him? Was he as lustful as Roald?
Was it Faiga?

As long as he helped them as he'd promised, did
it matter if he bedded a servant? Faiga would have
gone to him willingly; she'd seen the way the serving
woman had looked at Sir Henry. There would be no
force or coercion.

Mathilde prepared to continue on her way, until
she heard a groan from inside the chamber, as if Sir
Henry was in pain.

What if he was sick? What if he had brought some
illness to Ecclesford?

What if he had knocked the candle over and the
bedclothes had caught fire and the room was filling
with smoke—

She put her hand on the latch and opened the door.
There was no smoke, and a single lit candle stood
upon the table beside the bed, its weak flame
wavering. Sir Henry was alone, the sheets twisted
around his lower body, his hair damp on his forehead
and his naked chest beaded with sweat.

Moaning again, he rolled onto his back, one arm
flung across his eyes.

Perhaps he had the ague, with its chills and fever that came and went. Maybe he'd traveled to the south of Europe and contracted it there. She'd heard that sickness could come and go for years.

Or perhaps he was only having troubling dreams. How many times had she awakened from a nightmare to find her shift clinging to her sweat-soaked body?

For the sake of the household, she should find out if he was feverish or not. She would be risking more illness if she didn't.

She crept slowly, carefully closer. He didn't make any noise, or move again, so with the same cautious deliberation, she took hold of his wrist and eased his arm away from his forehead before placing her palm lightly there.

No fever, thank God.

Sir Henry's eyes flew open. He grabbed her wrist in a vicelike grip and sat up abruptly. "Constance!" he cried, staring at her. "Is she safe?"

Mathilde's heart seemed to stop, then began beating rapidly when she realized that this was not a true awakening. He was still in the hold of his dreams.

"Yes, she's safe," Mathilde whispered, wondering who Constance might be as she tried to extricate her wrist from his grasp and push him back down. "Rest now, Sir Henry."

Instead of relaxing, his grip tightened. He

blinked, his eyes coming into focus and she realized he was waking.

She yanked her hand free and turned to run to the door before he found her there.

"Oh, no, you don't!" Henry cried, grabbing her bedrobe to tug her back, nearly pulling it from her body as he tugged her down onto the bed atop him.

Panic seized her, giving her strength as she struggled to get away.

He threw his leg over hers and grabbed hold of her hands, so that they were lying face-to-face on their sides. "I'm not going to hurt you!" he said softly, but firmly. "My lady, I'm not going to hurt you!"

Sir Henry's words finally penetrated through the grip of her fear. Panting, she stilled, and his face came into focus.

"I assure you, I won't hurt you," he said, his gaze intently searching her face.

"Then let me go!"

"Gladly," he said, releasing her hands and moving his leg.

She was on her feet in an instant, turning again to go, but again he grabbed hold of her robe. "We are not finished, my lady," he said, his voice stern and commanding. He rose, and stood before her, and to her relief, she saw that he was wearing breeches.

He followed her swift glance and a devilish smile bloomed upon his face. "This time I took precautions."

She saw nothing amusing about this. "Sir Henry, let me leave," she demanded, although inside, she was humiliated and ashamed as the vestiges of her fear departed.

He shook his head. "Not until you explain to me why you came into this chamber. I don't think it was to assassinate me, or I fear I would be already dead. Or is sneaking into men's bedchambers your rather odd manner of amusing yourself?"

Trying to regain her shattered dignity, she wrapped the bedrobe about her and ran a hand through her disheveled hair. "I heard you groan and feared you were sick. I came to see if you had the ague or some other illness."

"I see."

Watching her, and still half-naked, his skin glowing in the candlelight, he held out a goblet that he took from the table near the bed. "Wine, my lady?"

"No, thank you," she replied, although her throat was dry. But she could feel her body trembling with the aftermath of her terror, and she would not show him an unsteady hand for the world.

"Then pardon me, for I am parched," he said, tossing back a gulp.

She sidled toward the door. "Now that you know why I came and since you are not ill—"

"I'm sorry if I frightened you," he interrupted, his

gaze pinning her in place, "but then, you nearly scared the liver out of me."

She was shocked he would admit that. "I did?"

"I fear little when I'm awake, but when I dream…" He shrugged. "I wish I never dreamed."

"So do I."

The words came out before she'd thought, and when she saw the expression on his face, she wished she'd been more circumspect.

"Was it a bad dream that awakened you tonight?" he asked, finally reaching for his shirt that was lying on the back of her father's chair.

"No, I had not yet gone to bed."

"Too worried about Roald, I suppose," he replied. "If I might make a suggestion, my lady, regarding your garrison?"

He was a trained knight, learned in battle techniques and strategy. She would be a fool not to hear what he had to say about the garrison. "Please."

"Your garrison lacks discipline, more so than any I have ever seen. I fear chaos and defeat should Roald attack."

She bristled at the implication that her men were going to lose. "Cerdic is one of the finest, bravest men in England."

"I don't doubt his courage, my lady," Sir Henry replied as he leaned back against the table and crossed his arms. "In fact, you could have some cause to wish he were *less* stouthearted. He strikes me as the sort of fellow who will charge into the thick of the fighting with little regard for strategy. I fear he lacks the ability to stay back to guide his troops more effectively."

A sharp retort came to Mathilde's lips, but a niggling doubt that he was right stopped her. "The men like him," she offered instead.

"Which is good if he wants them to be his friends, not so good if he is to command them."

"They respect him, too," she added, certain Cerdic wouldn't let her down. "They will follow his orders."

"At once, with no thoughts of contradicting or complaining because they fear disobeying him more than they fear the enemy?"

Mathilde's brows furrowed with disapproval. "My father didn't govern with fear."

"It is not of governing I speak, my lady," Sir Henry replied. "It's commanding men in battle. Soldiers must react to orders without thinking, without protesting. A moment's hesitation, and all could be lost."

That might be true, and yet... "Must men fear their commanders as much as the enemy?"

"Sir Leonard taught us that your men should fight with all their heart because they not only fear to lose and die, but fear to face your displeasure."

"That is the Norman way, I suppose," she reflected. "But Roald is not a Norman. Nor has he ever led an army into battle, or attacked a castle."

"He can hire those who have, as you've sought my help. In the meantime, your sentries loll about as if every day's a saint's feast day. All your men behave as if their main tasks are to eat, drink and talk."

She had noted the lack of order and discipline but had assumed—hoped—that her men would pull together when the time came.

Sir Henry's gaze intensified and his expression grew more stern. "Discipline is not something that can be put on when needed and discarded when it's not," he said as if he'd been reading her mind. "What will happen if Roald brings an army here and your men are caught unprepared?"

"There is no need to keep strict watch from the battlements," she told him, seizing on one part of his observations that she could refute. "We have men watching every road, starting twenty miles away. A warning will be sent the moment Roald is spotted. We will be ready."

"I hope so, for your sake and all those in Ecclesford." He took a step closer and his expression was more serious than she had ever seen it. "Regardless of whether or not you think your men are prepared, let me take command of your garrison for the time I am here and ensure that they are."

His offer took her aback. "You would do that?"

"If you would allow me, especially since I have plenty of time on my hands. A man can only hunt so much. Why not use my knowledge, if I am willing to share it?"

Perhaps there *was* something he could teach their men, and they could certainly use a heavier hand when it came to discipline. Besides, such occupation would also keep the handsome Sir Henry busy and away from the hall, and Giselle. She hadn't seen any signs that Giselle was attracted to him, but he was a very fascinating man. "Very well, Sir Henry. Thank you."

He bowed. "Thank *you,* my lady. I shall endeavor not to disappoint or," he added with a roguish wink, "cause you to regret that decision."

He was so handsome, so cheerful, so charming, so appealing even when he spoke of serious matters. He made her feel that all would be well, the way her poor papa had.

The father her vanity and foolish desire had helped to kill.

This time, she got to the door. "Now I give you good night, Sir Henry," she said, her hand on the latch. "I hope you can go back to sleep."

"I wish a restful night to you as well, my lady," he replied.

Before she could leave, he came behind her and his hand covered hers, warm and strong. She could feel his body close, the heat of it. The scent. "Sleep well, my lady."

Already knowing she would not, she pulled her hand away and slipped out of the door, closing it firmly behind her.

CHAPTER FIVE

"THOU WOULDST put that Norman over me?" Cerdic demanded with stunned disbelief.

Mathilde had not expected him to be happy with her decision, but that didn't make this any easier. He regarded her as if she'd knifed him in the back, while Giselle, who'd arrived in the solar with him and glided to a seat, stared at Mathilde as if she'd taken complete leave of her senses.

Leaning casually against the wall, his arms folded over his chest and his legs crossed at the ankles, Sir Henry watched the confrontation as if he were only mildly involved in the scene unfolding before him, and not the one who'd suggested he be put in command of the garrison.

"It is only temporary," Mathilde assured Cerdic, trying not to pay any attention to the distracting Sir Henry. "When he leaves, of course you will resume command."

"You cannot be serious!" Giselle protested, rising

from her chair to stand beside Cerdic. "Resume command? Why should he lose it?"

"Roald may bring an army if he comes to claim Ecclesford," Mathilde explained. "We must do all we can to be prepared against that possibility. Sir Henry has offered to train the garrison to make them more capable of defending the estate, and I think we should accept his help. It is no criticism of you, Cerdic."

Cerdic's hostile gaze darted to Sir Henry, then back to Mathilde. "He told thee that he beat me, didn't he? 'Twas only luck. I'd have had him—"

"Perhaps it was luck, or maybe it was skill," she interrupted. "He's been taught by one of the most famous knights in England. Why not take advantage of that, too?"

Giselle glared at Sir Henry before addressing her sister. "How much money does he want for this extra help?" she asked, her voice dripping venom and her normally mild blue eyes gleaming with hostile mistrust.

"I require no payment," Sir Henry said with suspicious placidity, for Mathilde remembered how angry he'd been in the inn when she'd made the mistake of offering to pay him for his help. Either he had been uncharacteristically enraged then, or he was keeping a very tight rein on his temper now. There was something in his eyes that told her it was the latter. If so, she was both impressed by his self-control and relieved. She didn't want him arguing, too.

"I don't trust him," Cerdic defiantly declared.

"Neither do I," Giselle said, as if daring Mathilde to contradict her.

Mathilde was disappointed, but not surprised, by their responses. After all, she had felt the same at first, and even now was loath to trust him completely.

Sir Henry shrugged his broad shoulders and said, "You need only trust my hatred for Roald."

Ignoring him, Giselle clasped her hands like a nun at prayer and fixed a pitying, pleading gaze on her sister. "Oh, Mathilde, how can you be so credulous after all that you've been through?"

For a terrible moment, Mathilde feared Giselle was going to proclaim her shame to Sir Henry.

"I am *not* greedy, and when I say I require no payment, that is precisely what I mean," Sir Henry said with more than a hint of indignation, and preventing Giselle from saying more. "I must say, my lady, that I find it interesting that you can leave all the work of running the household to your sister, and apparently all the preparations for defense, and then have no qualms about questioning her judgment and criticizing her decisions."

Now it was Mathilde's turn to be stunned. And, secretly, pleased that he had come to her defense.

Giselle flushed, but didn't back down. "Mathilde

is in charge of the household not because I am lazy, Sir Henry. After what happened the last time Roald was here, I thought if she was busy, she would not think so much about...she would not dwell so much upon his villainy."

Guilt stung Mathilde. Giselle had indeed left more and more of the daily duties to her after Roald had gone, and it had never occurred to her to question whether Giselle really enjoyed all that sewing and tending to the minor ailments of the household and village while leaving the other matters of the household to her younger sister—and at the same time, giving away the respect that went with those duties. "Giselle, I didn't—"

"Never mind that now," her sister interrupted. "It's more important for you to realize that Sir Henry should *not* be in charge of the garrison. It is an affront to Cerdic, if nothing else."

"You would let this castle be taken by Roald de Sayres because you don't want to insult Cerdic?" Sir Henry demanded. "I regret having to insult your intelligence, my lady, but have you *looked* at your garrison recently? They may fight well individually, but they're undisciplined, and their armor and the condition of their weapons is a disgrace. I doubt they'll listen to orders in a battle. They'll do as they choose, and they'll get themselves slaughtered in the process. If that's what you want, by all means, refuse my help, but if not, you'll agree with your sister that I should be in command until Roald returns."

"And if he does not, how long will this Norman linger here, eating our food and drinking our wine?" Giselle asked, as if she'd forgotten Sir Henry was not ten feet away from her.

"He should stay until we are certain of what Roald intends to do, or Sir Henry decides to leave us," Mathilde replied, even though she and Sir Henry had not discussed this.

He didn't disagree.

"The men will not accept him," Cerdic growled.

Despite his harsh observation, Mathilde realized the worst of his anger had passed, giving her hope that he would accept Sir Henry's leadership after all.

"They will if you will," she replied. "Be the leader I know you can be, Cerdic, by taking the lead in this. Accept Sir Henry as your commander."

Giselle, however, was still unconvinced. "How can we be sure he won't try to steal Ecclesford for himself?"

"How would he do that?" Mathilde retorted, embarrassed by her sister's suggestion and its implication. If Sir Henry declared he wouldn't stay another moment, she wouldn't be surprised. "Even if he were such a dishonorable man, he has no right to it by law, and no men to help him. The only other way would be if he marries *you.*"

Giselle's face reddened with a blush, but not as if

she yearned to be Sir Henry's wife and had been found out too soon. It was as if she'd never heard anything so unwelcome in her life. "I have no intention of marrying Sir Henry."

"Then you need not fear he will try to steal Ecclesford."

Still Giselle was not appeased. "You, of all people, should know that an unscrupulous man will find a way to get what he wants."

"I am *not* an unscrupulous man," Sir Henry finally interposed, his stern voice and severe mien forcibly reminding them all once again that he was a noble warrior who fought for a living, not merely a smooth-speaking courtier who sought only pleasure.

Now he was insulted. Now he would surely go, and they would lose not just his presence and the power of his social position, but his help with the garrison as well.

Cerdic stepped forward and put his hand on Giselle's arm. "There may be something this Norman could teach us. It is the safety of you and your sister and Ecclesford we must put first."

Mathilde could have wept with relief. If she had Cerdic on her side…

"Oh, very well!" Giselle declared with a toss of her head. "Let him be the garrison commander. You both know better than I."

And with that, she swept out of the room.

Ignoring Sir Henry, Cerdic addressed Mathilde.

"I will try to appease her," he said before hurrying after Giselle.

Letting her breath out slowly, Mathilde leaned back against the table.

"Well, that went better than I expected," Sir Henry noted from his place by the window.

"Better?" Mathilde repeated incredulously. "That was terrible. Giselle *never* loses her temper or argues with me."

"Really?" he replied, strolling closer. "My brother and I quarrel all the time."

His relationship with his brother might not be good, but she and Giselle had always gotten along. If he was used to anger and conflict, she was not.

"I'm sure she'll get over it, my lady," he said soothingly. "After all, we're right, and she's wrong— a loyal friend to Cerdic, of course, but wrong none-theless. At least he agreed with us in the end."

"Yes, there is that," she said, taking some comfort in Cerdic's acquiescence.

"And if I don't make any improvements, you're free to send me on my way."

He spoke lightly, cheerfully, as if he hadn't just had his honor and abilities questioned. "I'm sorry they insulted you," she said.

"Oh, that," he replied with a smile and dismissive wave of his hand. "This isn't the first time I've been slighted."

Slighted was a mild way to put the things Giselle and Cerdic had said. He was an amazingly amiable and forgiving man, especially for a knight, as well as kindhearted and generous….

Feeling the need to put some distance between them, she pushed herself off the table and went around behind it, and the heavy chair. "Nevertheless, you have my apology."

"Gratefully accepted," he replied, his tone and his voice making her feel…as she should not.

She gripped the back of the chair, tempted to tell him to leave the solar. She might have, had her sister and Cerdic not just insulted him. She could go, except to do so might betray her discomfort in his presence, and that she was loath to do. She didn't want him—or any man—to think her weak or afraid. "As garrison commander, what will you do first?" she asked instead.

As he considered, he rested his hand on the top of the table and leaned against it.

His strong, sinewy hand, with its long fingers. A powerful hand. A warrior's hand, calloused and sun-browned.

A lover's hand, for surely he'd had many. How could he not, with that face and form?

She would never know what it would be like to be wooed by such a man.

"First we should have a muster of the men to announce my new responsibility."

"Of course," she replied, sounding brisk and businesslike despite her wayward thoughts.

"I should check their armor and mail, and the weapons in the armory—you do *have* an armory?"

Even the way his brow rose when he asked a question was attractive. "In the keep."

"After that, I'll have to see what skills they possess and which they lack. And then," he concluded with a devilishly delightful grin that nearly undid her, "there will be running. Lots of running."

"Running?" she repeated—sounding like a dumbstruck fool, she silently chided.

He smiled brightly. "Oh, yes. How they'll hate it—and me."

He had said a garrison commander should be feared, but she found it hard to believe that a man this friendly and amiable would actually seek to be disliked. "You really want them to hate you?" she asked as she came around the chair, the better to read his expression.

He laughed, apparently amused by her question. "Oh, yes." He lowered his voice to a dramatic whisper and leaned closer, his brown eyes alight with glee, like a little boy sharing a secret with his best friend. "You see, my lady, the more soldiers hate the men who train them, the better they treat each other. They become united against a common foe."

"I never realized..." She hadn't realized he was quite that close.

Tantalizingly close.

Frighteningly close. Her heart started to pound and she started to feel dizzy.

"What is it?" he asked, all traces of amusement gone from his face. "Are you ill?"

She put her hand to her head, willing away the memories, and the panic, and the fear. He was Henry, not Roald. "No, no, I'm fine."

"The hell you are," he declared. "Sit down. I'll fetch your sister."

"No! No," she repeated when he halted and turned back. "It's nothing. I'm just a little tired. I haven't been sleeping well."

"Ah, yes, I remember," he said softly, with compassion and sympathy that was even more appealing and unsettling than his smile. "Let's have the muster of the men right now, and save the armory for another time, when you are not so fatigued and haven't just quarreled with your sister."

She wanted to protest the implication that she was upset, but she didn't. The last thing she wanted right now was to be alone with Sir Henry in the dim confines of the armory. Or anywhere else.

He politely held out his arm. "Shall we, my lady?"

"Thank you," she said, rising and putting her hand on his muscular forearm, and fighting to ignore the feel of his flesh beneath her fingers as he led her from the room.

FROM HIS PLACE on the hall steps where he stood at Lady Mathilde's side, Henry looked out over the men assembled in the yard. Most were not pleased with what she had just announced. Several exchanged wary glances. One or two were openly hostile, and these he would have to watch carefully. If they would not accept his command, they would have to go. Dissent in the ranks was like a disease that could spread until the whole garrison was infected.

As for the lady at his side, he wondered what she was really thinking. That she was pleased by his offer, he didn't doubt. Or that she had been upset by the argument with her sister and Cerdic. Otherwise, she was a cipher, more difficult to understand than any woman he'd ever met.

"So you will obey Sir Henry as you would Lady Giselle or me," Lady Mathilde concluded. "If you will not, you will leave Ecclesford at once, with the pay owed you until today."

He had not expected that, and he waited, wondering who would accept her offer.

"What of Cerdic, my lady?" one of the Celts called from the back of the group. "Does he accept this?"

"He will be second-in-command to Sir Henry."

Cerdic stepped forward from the side of the building, where he'd been in shadow. In spite of his apparent acquiescence in the solar, Henry was half prepared for him to resist this change of command,

and if he did, Henry's leadership was likely doomed to fail.

"Aye, I accept this," Cerdic declared, his deep voice filling the yard, and to Henry's vast relief. He glanced at Lady Mathilde, and thought her shoulders looked a little less tense. Perhaps she'd been worried about what Cerdic would say, too.

"I accept it because it is my lady's order, and I am her loyal servant," he continued. "I will fight to the death for the ladies of Ecclesford, as I have pledged. If any man here will not follow this Norman as they would me, he should leave here at once. If thou wouldst have this Norman think thou art fools or cowards, go. If thou dost not want to learn the Normans' skills or their ways in battle, there is the gate. For my part, I do. We will show this Norman, aye and Sir Roald, too, if he returns, that we are a match for any force any man can bring against us."

"Aye!" the men cried with one voice, raising their fists in the air. "Aye, aye!"

Henry stifled a delighted smile. He doubted there could have been anything better Cerdic could have said that would have guaranteed their obedience and willingness to learn.

Cerdic came to stand beside Henry. As the men continued to cheer, he clapped a beefy hand on the Norman's shoulder and smiled as if they were now friends for life. But through his teeth, he said, "I will never trust a Norman."

Although he was inwardly disappointed, Henry knew he shouldn't have been surprised. After all, he had just usurped the man's position.

So Henry buried his disappointment, likewise smiled and answered without moving his lips. "Then don't. Just learn and obey."

In the distance, the village church bell tolled. It rang three times, then stopped, then three more, followed by a silence as still as death. No one in the courtyard moved, or seemed to breathe.

Baffled as to the meaning of the bells, a shiver of dread nevertheless ran down Henry's spine as he turned to Lady Mathilde. She was as pale as if that sound had heralded her doom. "What is it? What does it mean?" he asked warily.

"Roald has come."

CHAPTER SIX

ROALD FROWNED as he rode into the village of Ecclesford with his escort of ten soldiers behind him, followed by a creaking baggage cart holding his clothes and several items he considered necessary for his comfort.

The whole place looked deserted, except for a few chickens scratching in the dirt, and the occasional dog barking. It was as if a plague had swept through the village and killed everybody.

That gave him a moment's sickening pause, until he realized if that were so, the fat innkeeper and his equally fat wife and dolt of a son at the Fox and Hound would have packed up and gone, too. The villagers must simply be hiding. Stupid peasants. What did they think he was going to do, kill them? Who would work his lands if he did that?

The men behind him started muttering under their breath about the quiet. Roald glanced back sharply. "You're not getting paid to talk."

Facing forward again, his annoyance lessened a

little as he beheld the castle he would soon command. To be sure, it was smaller than many, yet it was comfortable enough. Besides, the great value of Ecclesford lay not in its fortifications, but in the fertile land surrounding it, and its location near the road between the coast and London. And the coins his uncle must have stored there.

The outer gate was closed. That was odd. The late lord of Ecclesford usually left it open. Maybe, Roald thought with abhorrence for feminine weakness, that shrew Mathilde and her beautiful sister wanted to mourn their father in peace.

Mathilde could mourn him all she liked once she was esconced in a convent, well out of his way. As for Giselle…he had other plans for Giselle.

When his cortege reached the gates, a voice Roald recognized called down from the wall, "Friend or foe?"

That stupid oaf. "Open the gates at once!" he shouted.

"Oh, 'tis thee, Sir Roald," Cerdic replied. "I didn't recognize thee in thy fine new feathers."

Roald did not look down at the embroidered surcoat he had yet to pay for. "Fool, open the gates!"

"Gladly, my lord—to thee alone. The ladies of Ecclesford have ordered that thy men may not pass."

Roald half rose out of his saddle. "I demand that you open these gates at once and let us enter!"

"Those are my orders, Sir Roald," Cerdic calmly

answered. "Surely thou wouldst not counsel me to disobey the ladies."

"I am the heir of Ecclesford!"

"Not according to my late lord's will."

That brute probably only understood money, or a strong backhand blow. "Summon the ladies."

The blond warrior crossed his powerful arms. "I think not, my lord. Their orders are plain. They have said thou art to be allowed entry, but their courtesy does not extend to thy men who caused much trouble before."

Roald couldn't dispute that. Nor did he wish to quibble any longer like a beggar at the gates of his own castle.

He signaled for the leader of his escort, a tall, thin fellow, to ride closer. "Dismiss the men," he ordered. "They may entertain themselves in the town."

"Aye, my lord."

Duly released, his escort turned and rode back toward the village.

"Now open the gate!" Roald commanded.

The bossed wooden doors finally swung open, but before Roald could ride through, a guard of ten men came jogging out and surrounded his horse. For the first time it dawned on Roald that wishing to avoid trouble might not mean that the ladies would do as he ordered.

Surely they wouldn't dare...

Cerdic appeared on the other side of the gate, his shield on his arm, his battle ax in his hands and a smug smile on his face. "As I said, the ladies wish no trouble."

One day he'd wipe that self-satisfied grin off that lout's face, Roald silently vowed, as he kicked his horse into a trot and entered the courtyard.

He was no prisoner, but the rightful master here. This was his estate, his castle, and the money in his uncle's strongboxes was his, too.

This had to be Mathilde's doing—how he'd make her pay!

There was nobody in the courtyard, either; it was as deserted as the village. Roald dismounted and tossed his horse's reins over a nearby cart, then marched toward the hall.

His cousins were going to regret this insolent reception, Mathilde most of all! He would find the most spartan, barren convent with the sternest mother superior he could in which to imprison her. Giselle, he would enjoy making beg for forgiveness before—

No one opened the hall door for him. He shoved it open himself and, immediately upon entering, spotted that bitch Mathilde glaring daggers at him from where she stood on the dais, as proudly impertinent as if she were a queen.

She hadn't been so proud the last time he'd seen

her, he recalled as he walked forward, that memory slightly mollifying his rage.

The beautiful, blushing Giselle stood beside her, dressed in a gown of soft burgundy that hugged her shapely body. It was skillfully embroidered around the cuffs and hems, no doubt the work of the lady herself, who was forever at her needle or tending to some minor wound or scrape.

He looked at the man standing next to her—and bit back a curse. Where had D'Alton come from? No doubt he'd come nosing after a beauty who stood to inherit an estate and a fortune. But Henry would have to be mad—or even more arrogant than Roald had long assumed—if he thought Roald would agree to an alliance between their families.

Roald reached the dais and gave them a nominal bow. "Good day, Giselle. Mathilde. I give you my sympathies on your father's death."

"Do you, indeed?" Mathilde replied with a lift of her brow.

By God, who did she think she was? Had she forgotten his last visit? The things she'd said. And done. "Of course I'm sorry he's dead, although he was old and ill and all men must die."

"Yes," she agreed. "All men must die, and some deserve to die sooner than others."

He hadn't come here to bandy words with her. "Mathilde—"

"I believe you know our guest," she interrupted, nodding at the Norman at her side.

"I don't think your cousin is very pleased to see me," the Norman rogue noted, mockery in his voice and in his eyes.

"No, I'm not," Roald retorted, mounting the dais. "Why is he here?" he demanded of Giselle.

She didn't answer; she only blushed and sidled back behind her sister and the landless Norman.

"Sir Henry is visiting at our invitation," Mathilde replied.

"I don't know what this villain told you to receive an invitation to my castle—"

"I invited him, Roald, and this is not *your* castle."

Roald's rage burned hotter. "Don't play the fool, Mathilde. Ecclesford is *mine*. I am the only male left in the family. That makes me the rightful heir. So I order this Norman scoundrel to leave—now!"

Mathilde folded her hands in the cuffs of her long beige gown. "No."

His anger seething, Roald gripped the hilt of his sword. "I am master here and I say—"

"No, you're not," that lout D'Alton said, stepping between them.

A mutter of discontent reached Roald's ears and he half-turned. Where in the name of God had all those soldiers come from?

Turning back, he glared at his insolent cousin.

"Will you dare to attack or imprison me after luring me here without my men?" he charged, sickeningly certain he'd walked into some kind of trap.

D'Alton's eyes glittered with animosity, and his tone was as arrogant as always when he replied. "These men are here to ensure that you do not draw your sword, Roald, and offer violence to these ladies."

Roald ran another contemptuous gaze over the Norman. "My cousins are obviously ignorant of *your* reputation at court."

"I have ever conducted myself as a gentleman with women, whether high born or low, and you will not find one person who will say otherwise."

Roald sniffed with disgust. "I can think of a few cuckolded husbands who would disagree." He smiled at his cousin's obvious discomfort. "What's wrong, Mathilde? Didn't he tell you how many men's wives he's seduced?"

"I am well aware that Sir Henry is not chaste," Mathilde replied. "He made that very clear the first time I met him. But his past liaisons are none of my concern."

"His past should be of great concern to you," Roald replied. "I don't suppose he told you about being charged with treason for conspiring against the king."

Mathilde's eyes betrayed her surprise.

"Since I'm here now, those accusations were obviously baseless," D'Alton coolly replied, and he then had the audacity to regard Roald as if he were a bug he'd like to squash.

"Yet even your best friend believed you capable of such treachery," Roald sneered. "You used to be considered a clever woman, Mathilde. What happened? Can't you see he's an untrustworthy, dishonorable rogue who seeks to marry for gain? Why else would he agree to come here?"

"What happened to me?" she demanded. "I ran afoul of *you*. You taught me about dishonor and deceit, Roald, and if there is an untrustworthy man here, I am looking at him."

"Harsh words, my dear. You break my heart."

"You have no heart—as you have no right to Ecclesford! My father's will is clear about that, and as you can see, we are not without influential friends."

Roald's nostrils flared, and his face reddened. He wasn't about to let this shrew think he was afraid of her, or the lord of Dunkeathe's wastrel brother. "Influential? Is that what he's told you? That man has no more influence than the king's groom."

"His family—"

"His brother may have some power in the Scottish court, but not the English, and his sister is married to some Scot of no account."

"Her husband is a clan chieftain," Mathilde said.

"So he has some standing—among savages."

D'Alton laughed. "Your ignorance astonishes me, Roald—not that I ever considered you a font of wisdom."

"Your audacity astonishes *me*," Roald jeered in return. "You dare to stand here and pretend to have any influence?"

Mathilde had had nearly all she could stand of Roald—his scorn, his lies and his very presence. The sight of him was enough to sicken her, while the stench of his perfume made her want to retch. It took every ounce of her will not to bolt from the dais. "You may be the only male in our family, but my father left Ecclesford to Giselle and me."

"You know as well as I your father was too ill when he changed his will for it to be valid," Roald returned. "His wits were addled, and his older testament that names me heir should prevail."

Mathilde came forward, glaring at him as if she would strike him dead with her eyes. "You know my father had good reason to change his will, and that he was well enough to know *exactly* what he was doing."

"If your father had been in his right mind, he would have turned you out for whoring."

She gasped and Roald knew he had struck home— and there was more to gladden his heart. The Norman had given Mathilde a look that told Roald he'd had no notion of the kind of woman she really was.

A triumphant smile blossomed on his face. "She

didn't tell you about our little rendezvous, did she? Or why she wants to have her vengeance on me? I refused to marry her, you see, in spite of all her efforts."

Mathilde knew what he was about to do, the truth he was about to reveal. She wanted to scream at him to stop, to be silent, but her throat felt too tight to breathe, let alone speak.

"And quite the efforts they were, too, weren't they, Mathilde?" Roald continued, making a mockery of her shame and his crime. "But I wouldn't marry her even after she came into my bedchamber and gave herself to me."

Her chest clenched like her throat while Roald further destroyed her honor and her life.

"She wept and wailed and tried to force me to take her for my wife, but I had no desire to tie myself to a woman of such low morals. Why, she would have her husband a cuckold in a month."

"Liar!" The word burst from Mathilde's throat with the force of a dam bursting in the spring flood, her whole body tense as a drawn bowstring, her hands balled into fists. "Lying, villainous cur!"

"Ah, now we see the real Mathilde," Roald taunted. "The harpy, not the soft and gentle lover. You'll notice, my dear Henry, that she doesn't deny she came to my bed. Because, of course, she can't. Tell me, has she come creeping into your chamber at night, too, looking vulnerable and sweet as she never does in the day?"

Delight flashed in Roald's eyes at the sight of Henry's obvious shock.

Mathilde wanted to howl with anguish and humiliation and shame. What must Henry think of her? That she was no better than a whore? That she'd connived to bring him here under false pretenses? That she was a liar and deceiver, as Roald said?

If only Roald *was* lying. Of all the impetuous things she had done in her life, going to his chamber, stupidly believing his tender words, telling herself that what she felt was love, was the worst.

And more than she had suffered for it.

Even so, now that he had spoken, she would have the truth known. Yes, she had gone to his chamber, but in innocent naiveté, believing that he loved her. She had thought he would kiss her, and perhaps offer a proposal of marriage—and nothing more. "What happened that night was not of my will," Mathilde declared, hating him and herself for her stupidity.

"Of course you wanted me to take you, or why else would you come to me at night in my bedchamber?" Roald taunted before he again addressed the expressionless Sir Henry. "And then, when I refused to marry her, she went crying to her father, claiming it was rape."

"It was!" she cried as her gaze swept over the rest of the people assembled there—Giselle, white to the lips but her eyes full of compassion, for she had always known the truth. She had been the one to tend Mathilde after Roald had attacked her. She had washed the blood from her sister's thighs and bound her wounds. She had listened to Mathilde's wracking sobs and heard the whole truth told in a choked whisper.

Cerdic, tall and strong, stood immobile, aghast with shock. Behind him, the other soldiers muttered and whispered, but did not meet her eyes, as if she had ceased to exist. In their eyes, perhaps the noble Lady Mathilde was as good as dead. Dead because of desire. Killed by shame and weakness.

"Stop playing the martyr, Mathilde," Roald sneered. "We all know that any woman who goes to a man's bedchamber can hardly claim to be virtuous. Isn't that right, Henry?"

"It would depend upon her reason," the Norman replied, his voice grim and cold as his face.

Although he hadn't condemned her outright, he must think the less of her. If he only thought her shameful and weak, that would be bad enough, but if he thought her no better than a whore…

"What other reason could there be but to make love with me?" Roald inquired. "That was certainly Mathilde's reason. She didn't pull away or protest when I kissed her."

"Because I was a fool—ten thousand times a fool!" Mathilde cried, determined to make Sir Henry and everyone else in the hall understand that while she had made a horrendous mistake, based on pride and Roald's flattering lies, he had vilely taken her virginity against her will. "I believed you when you spoke of love and marriage. I thought we would kiss and then you would ask me to be your wife."

"Based on what? A few commonplace compliments? You see how she is, Henry," Roald said, turning to the Norman and speaking as if she were not there. "You should bless your lucky stars I arrived to tell you the truth about Mathilde—although I grant you, Giselle is very beautiful and tempting." His lips curved up and his eyes gleamed. "I may marry her myself."

Giselle's hand fluttered to her breast. Her eyelids closed and she would have fallen, except that Henry moved quickly and caught her as she lost consciousness. Kneeling, he gently laid her on the dais.

"You beast! You loathsome, despicable monster!" Mathilde cried as she rushed to her sister's side. "She will never marry you, never!"

No matter what Roald did, what threats he made, he would never have Giselle, even if she had to die protecting her.

As Faiga hurried forward with a goblet, the Norman regarded Roald with coldly sardonic eyes. "I must say, Roald, this looks most unpromising. The very thought of being your wife seems to make the lady ill. Not that I blame her, of course."

Looking murderous, Cerdic shoved his way

through the soldiers. For a moment, Mathilde thought he was going to attack Roald with his bare hands, but instead, he pushed Roald roughly out of his way and knelt beside Giselle.

"I will carry her to her chamber," he said, lifting her as easily as if she were a goose down pillow.

Her whole body trembling with rage and shame and despair, Mathilde faced Roald. "Get out, Roald, before I have these men drag you out like the dog you are."

Henry's hand moved to the hilt of his sword. "You heard her, Roald. Go."

Roald's nostril's flared, but otherwise, he didn't move. "Stay out of this, Henry. This business should be no concern of yours."

"As a knight, I am sworn to protect women, and I perceive that these ladies are in very grave danger." He took a step closer to Roald. "Will you go, or must I run you through?"

His back straight, Roald stepped back. "You think I don't see what you're up to? You want Giselle for yourself."

"What I *want* is for you to leave here and never trouble these ladies again."

The angry muttering of the men behind Roald grew louder. Blinking back tears, Mathilde realized that she might be disgraced in their eyes, but they would still protect her, and Giselle.

"You'll regret this, Mathilde," Roald snarled, backing off the dais. "By God, you will—and your sister and that Norman knave and that big oaf, too." He pointed his finger at Henry. "I would not risk the king's enmity if I were you, not even for the beautiful Giselle. You are nothing but a landless knight and while your family may have some power in Scotland, it will not be enough to spare you when I return. Will you risk your life for these women? Will you embroil your brother and sister in this, too?"

"What are *you* risking?" Henry countered. "A threat to me is a threat to the lord of Dunkeathe, close friend of the Scots king. I'm also the boon companion of the lord of Tregellas, most favored friend of the king's brother. Do you really think the king will risk their enmity for *you?*"

Emboldened by Henry's presence and counterthreats, as well as her men's loyalty, Mathilde stepped forward. "We hold Ecclesford by right of law, Roald, and we will keep it. If you try to move against us, it will be a mistake."

"Brave words, my lady," Roald mocked as he continued to back away. "You are truly one for vows and fierce resolve. I recall you once swore you would love me till the day you died."

"I will *hate* you till the day I die!"

Roald laughed coldly. "Passionate as always, eh, Mathilde? What a pity you are such an ugly creature, or I might have been persuaded to marry you—for a considerable dowry, of course."

Mathilde grabbed the circlet of silver holding her veil in place and threw it after him, while Henry leaped down from the dais, rage twisting his handsome features into a frightening mask.

"You'll be sorry for these threats," Roald vowed, a hint of fear tinting his voice as he drew his sword and backed away more quickly. "I'll go to the king. He'll stand by me and see that I get what I deserve."

"No, Roald," Henry said, his voice almost a purr—a low, frightening purr, like that of a great cat sighting a delectable prey. "I'll see that you get what you deserve."

"No!" Mathilde commanded. As much as she detested Roald and would like to see him dead, he was an excellent swordsman and this was not Sir Henry's fight. It had never been his fight, or his family's, or his friend's. It should not be their fight now.

She never should have asked him here. She wished she'd never met him. Most of all, she wished she'd never seen the look that came to his face when Roald proclaimed her shame. "Let him go."

Henry hesitated, and in that moment, Roald ducked out the door.

"Coward!" Henry cried, rushing after him, but before he reached the door, they heard the sound of hooves striking swiftly against the cobblestones.

Bleakly aware that her life was forever changed, Mathilde stood still as a statue as Henry turned back. His eyes stayed firmly focused on her face as he strode toward her. "I think, my lady, that there are some things we should discuss, preferably in private."

CHAPTER SEVEN

IF SIR HENRY was going to denounce her for a duplicitous, dishonorable creature who'd lured him here under false pretenses, she would prefer privacy, too. "Come with me to the solar."

He nodded, and followed as she led the way. She felt him behind her, and her whole body burned with shame and regret.

From the moment she felt Roald rip her maidenhead, her hopes for a happy marriage had ended. She had known it even as she lay crying, bleeding, on his bed. She had seen the truth of it reflected in her father's sorrowful face, and heard it in Giselle's soft sighs. She had thought she had accepted it, and that while she would keep the secret of her shame, she had vowed she would not lie to a man who offered her honest marriage believing her a virgin.

Yet, in spite of everything, she'd kept some spark of hope alive that the past and her mistake had not completely tainted her future.

Until now.

If only she had not been so vain, so eager to believe a young and comely man could love her. If only she had been stronger! If only she had resisted from the moment his expression had altered from querying to lustful, instead of being so bewildered by the change and then his sudden brutal actions that she didn't move until her shift was up around her waist and Roald...

If only she had resisted Roald's flattery and soft words, she would still have her honor, her father might yet be alive and all this trouble and pain averted.

When she reached the solar, she crossed the comfortable room with its tapestries and fine furnishings to stand behind the trestle table. Her hands clasped, she watched as Henry came to stand opposite her and she waited, like a condemned prisoner, for him to denounce her, steeling herself for the words that would be like lashes of a whip.

Before he said a word, Cerdic appeared on the threshold and for a moment, Mathilde forgot her misery. "How is Giselle?"

"Better," he answered. "It was the shock of what that villain said that disturbed her. A little rest and she will soon be well."

Mathilde searched Cerdic's face, seeking to discover what he thought of her now that he knew what Roald had done, for the only people in the household who had known the truth about Roald's abrupt departure had been her father and Giselle. "I am glad to hear it."

He nodded. There was a new reserve in his manner, which added to her pain.

"Roald is a great liar, my lady," Sir Henry said, interrupting the awkward silence and speaking as casually as if he were discussing the weather. "I wouldn't be inclined to credit his words, except that your reactions seem to suggest he might be telling the truth about what happened between you."

She marveled that he would give her the benefit of the doubt, although that didn't ease her anguish. "I went to his bedchamber, as he said," she admitted, "because I believed myself in love with him, and that he loved me and wished to marry me. I thought we would kiss and he would say sweet words to me, and ask me to be his wife—and nothing more."

How silly that sounded now, how naive. But she had been innocent and naive then, raised by a father who kept them from the court and the society of supposedly chivalrous knights.

Her throat tightened as she went on, but she would have him and Cerdic know what had happened and why she had not fought back until it was too late. "Roald would not let me go. He held me tight and smiled when I told him he was hurting me. I grew frightened, and then he threw me onto his bed. It was so unexpected, I could scarce believe…"

"Enough, my lady," Sir Henry said quietly, his eyes glinting like sparkling water. "I don't believe you oppose him out of spite as he claims." He glanced at Cerdic, who was studying the floor. "You didn't know about this, either, did you?"

Her friend's head shot up and, glaring at the Norman, he growled an oath, then said, "If I had, he would never have left here alive."

The Norman nodded. "That's what I thought." He turned his cool gaze onto Mathilde. "This crime was kept a secret, then?"

She nodded. "My father sought to prevent my name from being shamed and I agreed. Like that serving girl, I feared people would believe Roald and not me, because I had gone to his chamber."

"Your father was quite right," Sir Henry said. "Opinion would probably have gone against you, at least among noblemen. Under similar circumstances, many of them would have made the same assumption and done the same thing if you'd gone to their bedchambers in the night, regardless of your motive."

He had not, she thought. Sir Henry had not made such an assumption that first night.

"As for why you went to his bedchamber…" Sir Henry shrugged. "I daresay Roald can be persuasive, if he tries."

"Yes, he can," she agreed. "And I was very stupid."

"We have all been stupid in our day, my lady."

Not the way she had been. Even so, she appreciated his effort to make her feel less of a fool.

"The question now becomes, what will happen next?" Sir Henry mused aloud.

"You go, we fight," Cerdic said with grim resolve.

Sir Henry's brows rose. "Go? I have no intention of leaving."

How she wished that he could stay! Everything he had said about the garrison she believed, and they could use his help, but… "Roald also threatened you and your family, and your friends. You must not stay on our account."

Sir Henry's expression grew stubbornly determined. "My family and friends can defend themselves against Roald de Sayres, but I fear your garrison will be in dire straits without an experienced knight to lead them. You need me."

"What of this charge of treason against thee?" Cerdic demanded.

Although like Sir Henry, Mathilde believed Roald a great liar and didn't give credence to his accusations, she couldn't help wondering about that, too.

Sir Henry made a dismissive motion with his hand, as if to wipe Cerdic's question from the air. "A misunderstanding on my friend's part and as I said to Roald, there was nothing to it, or I would not be free. I would be imprisoned or executed."

"We can beat Roald and any men he sends against us without thee," Cerdic said stubbornly.

"Can you?" Sir Henry demanded before Mathilde could answer. "Has something changed since Lady Mathilde first accepted my offer to assist you? Are you more certain of the skills of those undisciplined men in the hall below? You can guess how Roald will attack and where and when? You've become more familiar with siege techniques than I?"

Cerdic's cheeks reddened.

"We have already accepted Sir Henry's aid and I, for one, am grateful," Mathilde said, now certain that they needed the Norman's aid, or all would be lost.

Cerdic, however, continued to glare at Sir Henry as if he took his presence there as a personal affront.

No doubt he did. But surely he could see that they would be foolish to refuse whatever counsel and advice Sir Henry had to offer, especially now.

Unfortunately, he didn't. "I say we don't need this Norman sniffing around your sister's skirts," he growled. He walked up to Sir Henry and shoved him hard in the chest. "Keep away from Lady Giselle."

The Norman grabbed Cerdic's hand, twisting it back and away from him. "Even if I did want her," Sir Henry said through clenched teeth, "what is more important—the fact that I might try to woo and wed her, or that I can help you defeat Roald?"

Even if he wanted her? What man would not?

Cerdic's face flushed and the veins in his neck stood out, but he would not give ground either. "She will never marry thee!"

"Are you her father or brother to dictate who she may marry?"

"Stop!" Mathilde cried before they came to blows. "We have enough trouble without fighting over Giselle!"

Sir Henry immediately let go. "Forgive me, my lady," he said with a courtly bow. "You're quite right."

Cerdic, meanwhile, rubbed his arm. "I am sorry, too, Mathilde," he muttered, although he continued to glare at the Norman.

"Cerdic, you said you would accept Sir Henry's command," Mathilde said sternly. "I expect you to hold to your word."

Once more he flushed, and then he curtly nodded. "Aye, I will."

It might not have been an enthusiastic response, but it was enough to content Mathilde.

"Good," she said briskly. "Tell the men Sir Henry will be inspecting the barracks and their armor." She looked at the Norman. "Is that not right, Sir Henry?"

After he inclined his head in agreement, Cerdic nodded once more, then marched from the room.

Mathilde sank down into her father's chair. Now that Roald had come and gone, and Cerdic had left the chamber, she was bone weary and all her doubts and uncertainties about the future, all the shame and humiliation of her past, came flooding back, threatening to overwhelm her.

"He's certainly a proud fellow," Sir Henry remarked, once more standing by the window.

And he was not?

Although the look in his eyes remained grave, he gave her a small, rueful smile and spread his hands. "I regret I alone was not enough to strike fear into Roald's black heart. Perhaps if I were bigger or had a nasty scar…"

She appreciated his attempt to lighten her dismay, even if it was hopeless. "I was wrong to think he could be so easily dissuaded, yet I hoped…"

Her words trailed off in a sigh as she laced her fingers in her lap.

"You hoped he would see sense."

"Yes," she replied, raising her eyes to look at him.

"What was this business about your father's will?" he asked. "He had more than one?"

Mathilde nodded. "Before Roald attacked me, my father intended to leave Ecclesford to him, with provisions for dowries for Giselle and me. We were to be under Roald's guardianship, too, because my father trusted him then, as did we all. But…afterward…my father wrote a new will, for he would not leave his daughters or his land in that man's hands. My father was ill, his sickness brought on by what had happened, but I assure you, he was not addled in his wits, as Roald claims. The new will is perfectly legal and must take precedence over the old."

Mathilde went to the aumbry standing against the opposite wall. She opened the wooden doors of the cupboard and drew out an ebony box inlaid with silver. She unlocked it with a small key from the ring of household keys at her waist and pulled out a rolled parchment. "This is my father's will, marked with his seal. You may read it for yourself and see that my father's wishes were clearly, competently stated, and witnessed by Father Thomas."

She handed Henry the will, then hesitated to let go of the precious document. "Can you read?"

"Yes. Sir Leonard made sure of that, too."

As Sir Henry took it from her, their hands touched. It was only for a brief moment, but it was enough to make her feel as if her fingertips had caught fire. She didn't dare look at him to see if he noticed, or felt the same thing as he took off the riband binding the will and unrolled the scroll.

It seemed forever until he finished reading it and handed it back to her. "This was written in August," he noted.

"Yes."

"When did your father die?"

"The fifth of September."

"How long had he been ill?"

"Since last year. Yet his mind was not affected by his illness, not even at the end."

"I believe you," he answered simply, "but Roald will certainly argue otherwise."

Careful not to touch him again, Mathilde returned the will to its box and began taking writing materials from the aumbry—a quill, a vessel of ink and a roll of parchment, which she sat upon the table.

"What are you doing?" Henry asked.

"I am going to write to the bishop. He will surely agree that the new will is valid."

Henry's brows furrowed with puzzlement. "The church has no authority over who inherits land. That is for the king's court to decide."

"I am well aware of that," Mathilde said as she settled in the chair to write, "but they do have some authority over wills. If I have the bishop's agreement that my father's second will rightly overrules the first, Roald will have less of a case to take before the king's court." She slid Sir Henry a sidelong, questioning glance. "Roald seems convinced that the king will support his claim, no doubt believing that means he will triumph in the courts, as well. You have met the king and queen. Do you think it likely Roald is right to seek their aid?"

Sir Henry shrugged his broad shoulders. "I believe that if the king offers his support to anyone, his choice will depend upon who will be of more use to him. But Roald is also related to the queen, as you must be."

"My father never sought close ties with her family, as Roald's did."

To his dismay, Sir Henry's expression did not change. "Unfortunately, I fear Roald won't be content to wait for judgment. I can more easily see him raising an army of the most battlehardened mercenaries he can find and trying to take Ecclesford by force."

Mathilde tried to subdue her increasing dread. "We have heard he is deeply in debt. How could he pay for such an army?"

"I'm sure he could find moneylenders willing to gamble that he'll win, or that the queen will back his claim, and once the estate is his, he'll be able to repay them."

"Oh, God!" Mathilde cried softly, rising, for she could well believe this, too. "He cannot take Ecclesford and if he tries, we must fight him. We *will* fight him—and we will win!"

Sir Henry's lips curved up in an approving smile that was more threatening to her self-control than any threat of Roald's. "I thought you were a brave, determined woman," he said quietly. "Now I *know* you are."

She couldn't meet his steadfast gaze. "I am also a ruined woman who will never marry."

Query flickered across his face, but it was just as

quickly gone. What else could she expect—that he would disagree?

"I am glad you are staying to lead the garrison," she said. "I do not know what we would do without your help."

"Oh, Cerdic and your men could probably manage," he replied, apparently studying the pattern of the stone at his feet. "But you could lose more men than you need to."

"I had hoped to avoid losing any."

"I trust they appreciate your concern, and I will do all I can to see that they're prepared, should Roald attack," he said, raising his head. "Even if he rides to London today, Roald isn't important enough to get an audience with the king and queen at once. And if he has decided to raise an army, that will take some time, too. Nevertheless, we have no time to waste. I shall leave you to your letter and go to inspect the state of your men's armor and their weapons."

She nodded and bent to her letter writing as he went out the door.

AS HENRY STRODE across the courtyard toward the barracks, he felt more resolute and determined than he ever had in his life. He was going to make Roald de Sayres pay for what he'd done, to Lady Mathilde, to that little serving girl and God knew how many others. The man was a beast, a lout, a plague and Henry was going to destroy him.

No wonder Lady Mathilde had shied away from him that night. No wonder she seemed so tense when they were alone.

God save him, he could barely stand the scent of wet stone after his days in the dungeon and the slightest scratching sound reminded him of the rats and made him shiver. For her, being alone with a man must be like being locked in a small dark room would be for him—nearly unbearable.

Yet she'd not just overcome her fear when she was with him, a man who had done her no harm and never would; with defiance and courage she'd faced the man who had so vilely used her.

Now he understood why she had looked at him as she had when he'd told her about that girl and challenged him about letting Roald go.

He came to an abrupt halt, suddenly sickened. If he'd had Roald imprisoned that night, if he'd summoned the watch and had him charged with rape, Mathilde would have been spared. She need not have suffered.

His resolve even stronger, his expression grim, he started toward the barracks again. He owed it to Mathilde to help her defeat Roald. He owed it to her to kill the bastard.

He ran up the stairs leading to the large chamber

above the stables full of rope beds and stools and wooden boxes for the soldiers' belongings. He threw open the door, and as the men scrambled to their feet, he put his hands on his hips and shouted, "All right, you lazy curs, your days of leisure are done. I'm in command now, and by God, you're going to wish I wasn't."

CHAPTER EIGHT

"How many more carts?" Mathilde asked as she watched the alewife's son unload the casks of ale into the buttery seven days later.

Around them other villagers and servants bustled, toting, moving and carrying bundles and baskets of food and provisions, wooden chests of clothing and household goods in preparation for a possible siege.

Voices rose and fell in discussion and argument, and above them all, keeping an eye on the surrounding countryside, were the sentries on the wall walk, their weapons newly forged and sharp, their mail mended and cleaned, and their attention firmly on their duty.

"Two, my lady," Balwyn replied. "Mam says that's nearly the whole lot. The innkeeper wants to keep some in the taproom in case Sir Roald don't come after all. He says it would be a terrible thing to have no ale to offer because it's all here."

Mathilde nodded her agreement. "As long as he is willing to lose it should Roald return and lay siege to Ecclesford."

"Aye, my lady," Balwyn replied, sliding her the sort of sidelong, curious glance she had received many times in the past se'ennight, ever since Roald had publicly proclaimed her shame.

Ignoring his curiosity, she said, "You and your family must come here when you hear the church bells sound the alarm."

"Aye, my lady."

"Good." She looked over her shoulder at the miller, who was standing in the middle of the yard, shouting about spilled flour.

She had spent hours going through the storerooms attempting to find as much space as possible for the incoming food, ale, wine and fodder for the animals. She had set the maidservants to clearing out any place a family might be housed, including the stables. Other men had been sent to find stones and carry them up to the wall walk, in preparation for throwing them down on any enemies who tried to scale the walls. The smith had built large iron pots and tripods, now set on the battlements, in which to boil water or pitch to rain down upon invaders. The village smith and castle armorer were busily repairing and sharpening the weapons they had, and making new swords.

She would never forget the look on Sir Henry's face when he went to the armory with her. He had run a disgusted gaze over the weapons stored there. Yet when she had, with regret, remarked upon their poor condition, he had shrugged and simply said, "It is more important to have loyal men."

He always spoke that way to her now, brusquely and succinctly, and rarely smiled. She asked herself again what else she could expect now that he knew—

"My lady!"

She looked up to see Father Thomas hurrying through the throng, a very worried expression on his face.

"Bishop Christophus is coming," he said. "He and his acolytes are in the village now."

Her heart started to race as it did whenever she was near Sir Henry, but for a very different reason. "Could he have made his decision already?"

Father Thomas looked doubtful. "I think not. Perhaps he comes to question you about your father and his will."

She put her hand on Father Thomas's arm. "I hope he has, and then he'll learn that everything was legally done."

"You have never met the bishop, have you, my lady?" the priest asked quietly, and in a way that filled her with even more trepidation.

But she would not betray any dread in the yard, where there were so many people who could see her. "If you will wait in the hall, Father, I should find Giselle and prepare to greet him."

She scurried off to find her sister and change her

gown to something more appropriate in which to greet such an important visitor. She wished Sir Henry hadn't taken the men to train in the woods today, and Cerdic gone with him. She would have welcomed their company when she met the man who could have a hand in deciding their fate. Now she and Giselle would have to greet the bishop without their support, unless she wanted to keep the bishop waiting, and that she couldn't do.

Unfortunately, and although she searched the hall, the kitchen and the bedchambers, she couldn't find Giselle. She asked all the servants she met if they had seen her sister, but no one knew where Giselle was, and before Mathilde could locate her, the noise of an even greater commotion in the yard announced the arrival of the bishop.

Muttering an oath, Mathilde looked down at her plain dark blue gown. Where on earth was Giselle? She was always the one who greeted visiting nobles or clergy. She was the one who was always impeccably attired, modest and polite.

There was no time to change now, so Mathilde tucked an errant lock of hair back beneath her simple linen scarf, brushed any stray bits of dust and chaff from her skirt with her hands and hurried to the courtyard, pausing a moment to ask Faiga to bring wine to the hall for their guests. She would see to chambers for them later.

The bishop's cortege was unexpectedly large and well armed, led by the tall, stately clergyman wearing a very fine purple cloak as befit his rank, and a purple zucchetto on his white-haired head. Beneath his cloak she could see an equally fine black robe and a wide purple belt across his ample middle. The various jewels in his golden pectoral cross winked in the fall sunlight.

In addition to the bishop, there were several more plainly attired priests, as well as soldiers in matching tunics armed with swords and pikes. Behind them came carts of baggage and, it seemed, enough food and wine for a small army. Clearly the bishop traveled in comfort and didn't take his chances with his host's provisions.

Her father had had as little use for high-ranking clergy as he did for most noblemen, and looking at this man's expensive clothing and the jewels of his cross, Mathilde shared his aversion. Had not Christ said it was easier for a camel to go through the eye of a needle than for a rich man to get into heaven? Did that not extend to His supposed holy servants here on earth?

Whatever she thought of Bishop Christophus, however, she had to be polite and act as befit a woman so, taking a deep breath, she walked out to greet him, gesturing for Father Thomas to join her.

"Greetings, my lord bishop," she said, bowing low. "Welcome to Ecclesford. I am the lady Mathilde, and this is Father Thomas."

The bishop took off his glove and presented his ring for her to kiss, which she did. She felt his measuring scrutiny and tried not to betray anything, either shame or anger or dread.

"Bless you, my lady," Bishop Christophus intoned as she stepped back, his voice deep and soft as ermine.

"I have refreshments awaiting in the hall," she said, "if you will follow me."

"With pleasure," he replied.

Mathilde hurried ahead, chewing her lip and anxiously hoping he wouldn't find fault with anything. He would undoubtedly realize something was afoot by the commotion in the yard, and the goods that had been stored even in the hall.

His gaze roving over the yard, the buildings, the battlements and the servants, the bishop followed at a more leisurely pace, trailed by the priests who'd arrived with him like so many holy beetles.

Once on the dais, the bishop lowered himself onto her father's chair with the air of a man used to deference and respect. His holy underlings sat on stools her servants hastened to provide. Father Thomas remained standing to the left of the dais while, at the bishop's request, Mathilde sat on another chair facing him.

Out of the corner of her eye, she saw Father Thomas give her an encouraging smile that was quickly squelched by a sharp glance from the bishop.

Faiga, more subdued than Mathilde had ever seen her, arrived bearing a tray with a silver goblet for the bishop, one for Mathilde which she set on the arm of her chair, and several other, smaller vessels for the visiting priests and Father Thomas.

The bishop took his goblet with a regally benefi-cent smile. "Thank you, my child," he murmured, putting his hand on Faiga's head in a way that seemed more like a caress than a blessing.

Faiga seemed to think so, too, judging by the shocked look she gave the bishop before she lowered her eyes and backed away.

After sipping some wine, Bishop Christophus set the goblet on the small table near his chair, steepled his plump fingers and regarded Mathilde over their tips. "We are grieved, my child, very grieved, that there should be any conflict over this estate between you and your noble cousin."

"If there is a conflict, my lord bishop," she replied, firmly but politely, "it is Roald who makes it. My father's wishes regarding his estate were very plain in his will, as I am sure you realized when you read the copy you were sent."

The bishop laced his fingers together and brought his index fingers to his lips. His gold ring of office with its immense purple stone glistened in the light from the candles on the stand nearby. "Your cousin does not dispute that the will is genuine. However, he is quite certain your father was too ill when he wrote it for it to be valid under the law."

How did he know what Roald thought? "You have had a message from my cousin regarding our dispute?"

"He came to our abbey and explained his position to me."

Mathilde silently cursed herself for not foreseeing this and writing to the bishop sooner. Roald was evil, but he wasn't stupid. "So he may claim, my lord, but Father Thomas will tell you my father was not sick in his head when he changed it."

The bishop's glance flicked to Father Thomas. "Sir Roald also told us that Father Thomas is much devoted to your family."

Mathilde could not, and would not, deny it. "He has ever been a kind and true friend to us, my lord, but he is an honorable man of God who would never lie."

"Of course," the bishop smoothly answered. "Father Thomas is a most excellent shepherd of his flock, and kindhearted almost to a fault."

"He does not support us because he is kind-hearted," Mathilde shot back, forgetting for a moment that she was addressing a bishop and Father Thomas was close by. "He does so because it is right."

The bishop's white brows lowered.

"Forgive me," she said quickly, "but I would not have you think Father Thomas guilty of being less than truthful to help a friend."

"If he did so, he was misguided by affection, I'm sure," the bishop replied, his expression serene once again.

Even so, Mathilde knew she had erred. This man expected deference as his due and would not forget her outburst.

Father Thomas gave her another smile, but Mathilde did not have the heart to return it.

The bishop's expression became less mild and his voice lost its dulcet sweetness. "Your cousin spoke of other things, my lady, things it shocked me to hear. I regret to discover a noble lady could behave so wantonly."

Mathilde clutched at her skirt, bunching it in her fists as she struggled to remain calm. She should have guessed Roald would make what had happened between them all her lascivious fault. Even so, did the bishop have to speak of it here in the hall, in front of his acolytes? "He is no innocent Adam. He spoke words of love to me and I believed him. It was a proposal of marriage I dreamed of when I went to him, and when I begged him to stop and let me go, he refused until he had satisfied his lust."

Bishop Christophus regarded her with undisguised disdain. "You may be able to fool a man like Father Thomas with such claims, my lady, but you are a woman, a creature of the flesh, like Eve. A sinner, like the Magdalen. And despite your lack of beauty, a temptress, like Salome. Roald confessed his sin most humbly, begging absolution. But you— proud, debauched woman that you are—have the audacity to cast the blame for your sin unto another."

Anger rose in Mathilde, hot and strong. Trying to stifle it, she moved abruptly, knocking her goblet to the ground. Faiga darted forward to pick it up while the wine soaked into the rushes on the floor. That gave Mathilde some time to calm herself before she spoke.

"I know I am not without guilt," she said. "I freely admit that I was guilty of desire and wrong to go to him. I have confessed to Father Thomas and done penance."

The bishop's frown grew pained. "You do not sound penitential."

This was what he considered most important? What of Roald's crime against her? Obviously she could expect little understanding or sympathy from this man, so she gave up trying to explain what had happened. "I have begged God's forgiveness and mercy, my lord bishop, and now I beg yours. Do not let this sin color your judgment, for if you do and you rule against us, more than I will suffer at Roald's hands. He will not be a kind and generous lord."

"Will you tell me you are cursed with unnatural foresight, my lady?"

Worse and worse! It could be one step from this question to a charge of witchcraft. "Not at all, my lord. That is what I *fear.*"

"Roald is your only male relative. It is God's plan that women be subject to men. Or do you dispute that, too?"

Mathilde willed herself to think and answer carefully. "Is it not also a child's duty to be subject to their parents? Should I not then fight for what my father wished above the demands of another? Should I concede to a cousin and defy my father?"

Bishop Christophus laced his fingers and studied her in silence. She forced herself to wait for him to speak, which he soon did. "Your cousin claims he is being robbed of his rightful inheritance. He further claims you act out of rage and spite, and that he is the victim of a lustful woman's vengeance. You have accused him of a most despicable act—even though you admit you went to his chamber and you brought no charges against him in the king's court. I would say that was wise, because I doubt there is a court in the land who would condemn your cousin when you freely, shamelessly admit going to his bedchamber."

Shamelessly? Did he think she felt no shame? "I assure, my lord bishop, I am ashamed of what I did. I regret it every day, every hour, every minute. I will regret it, and be ashamed, for the rest of my life. But although I cannot and will not deny I went to his chamber, I can and do deny that I willingly gave myself to him. We didn't accuse him publicly because my father hoped to keep my dishonor a secret."

"Sins of the flesh will always make themselves known," the bishop said primly. "It is one way God punishes the sinners and sets an example to the rest of us."

As if he were spotless. Judging by his girth, and the fine cloth of his cassock, he was guilty of gluttony and vanity—and pride, too, she was sure.

"That is not all your cousin had to say to me," the bishop continued. "I gather there is a knight here, one whose reputation may bring some stain to that of your dear sister."

Not to *her*, Mathilde noted. But then, in the eyes of this man, she was little better than Jezebel. "This man Roald is so swift to condemn chivalrously came to our aid when we sought his assistance. He is acting as our garrison commander because ours deserted us after my father's death."

The bishop frowned. "That is not the explanation for his presence your cousin gave."

"There is bad blood between Roald and Sir Henry, my lord bishop. An old quarrel—over a woman, I believe." She would give no details; let the bishop assume what he would about Roald's motives for mentioning Henry.

"It isn't seemly to have a young knight here when there are no male relatives to watch over you."

"I appreciate that *my* honor is besmirched," she

replied stiffly, "but I beg you not to malign that of my sister, or Sir Henry, without just cause."

The bishop's face flushed, and for a moment, he actually looked contrite. Yet whatever contrition the bishop may have felt, it was short-lived. "Surely it's understandable that your cousin is most upset by this situation and the conflict between you. Indeed, he's so dismayed, he's asked us to pray for him and promised us a new chapter house in humble gratitude for our efforts, as befits a dutiful son of the church. Such men deserve forgiveness, and the support of the church as they seek God's holy guidance."

There was an undercurrent in the bishop's tone her ears were quick to catch. No doubt Roald had promised the bishop more than a chapter house if the bishop declared her father's later will invalid—something more personal, such as gold or jewels.

Roald had outmaneuvered her with this thinly disguised bribe, and although it sickened her, if Roald had sought to influence the bishop this way, what choice did she have but to do the same?

"A chapter house is most generous, and something the lord of Ecclesford could well afford to provide," she observed. "We, too, plan to honor our father's memory with a gift to the church— provided my father's second will is honored. Otherwise, everything belongs to Roald." She frowned as if innocently baffled. "But I do not understand how Roald can promise any gifts to the church until his debts, which we have heard are quite considerable, are paid."

The idea that Roald was deeply in debt didn't seem to come as a complete shock to the bishop. Perhaps he, too, had heard things about Roald and his financial difficulties, and had wondered the same thing.

She hoped so.

The bishop tapped his foot as he continued to study Mathilde. "Tell me, my child, have you ever considered taking the veil to prove your remorse and redeem yourself in the eyes of God?"

She had not anticipated that question, but it was in keeping with the way this man's mind worked. If she became a bride of Christ, her inheritance would go to the church. He was probably already thinking of the glory that would come his way when he could claim he had convinced a wealthy woman who was almost a Magdalen to repent and give herself to God.

Unfortunately for the bishop, he was bound to be disappointed. She would rather live and die a spinster in the village than submit to the strictures of a holy life. She must be in the world, not out of it, and she believed God would prefer it that way, too, or He would not make it so difficult for her to be quiet and demure.

The door to the hall banged open and Sir Henry strode into the hall, heading straight for the dais, his sheathed sword slapping his muscular thigh with every rapid step.

The bishop's acolytes stared as if they'd never seen a knight before, or perhaps it was Sir Henry's disheveled appearance that took them aback, as it did her. He looked as if he'd been riding at breakneck speed, his hair tousled, his clothes and boots splattered with mud.

The bishop's displeasure, however, seemed decidedly more personal as he regarded Sir Henry. "Is *this* the knight of whom your cousin spoke?" he demanded.

Obviously, he knew Sir Henry—and didn't like him. She got a horrible sinking feeling in the pit of her stomach, as if Ecclesford had slipped from her grasp the moment Sir Henry came through those doors. She tried to salvage the situation, or at least prevent it from becoming any worse, by ignoring the bishop's animosity. "Yes, this is Sir Henry D'Alton. His brother is a lord in Scotland and his sister—"

"My most excellent and portly bishop, what an expected surprise!" Sir Henry interrupted as he came to a halt and, with a mocking smile, made a sweeping bow. "I never thought to see you in England again. I was sure your ambitions would take you to Rome."

The bishop's face reddened. "And I thought your wastrel ways would see you jailed or dead."

"Yet here we are, both wrong," Sir Henry genially replied, throwing himself into a chair at the edge of the circle.

Despite his tone and attitude, Mathilde saw the very real animosity in the knight's eyes, and wondered at its cause.

It could merely be that Henry was a worldly man who lived his life with exuberance and pleasure, and apparently little concern for the future, whereas a clergyman must—or should—lead a more exemplary life and think of his eternal soul.

At least, she hoped that was the source of conflict between them and not something that might cause the bishop to support Roald's claim. "I didn't know you were acquainted with Bishop Christophus," she said to Sir Henry, wanting the bishop to understand that she had been ignorant of any quarrel there might be between them.

"I wouldn't call us acquaintances," Sir Henry calmly explained as he plucked a goblet from the tray Faiga held out to him. "It was his son I knew better."

His *son?*

As Mathilde took in that shocking declaration, the bishop's cheeks reddened even more. His priestly companions exchanged looks that told her they were both scandalized and thrilled, as if someone had openly spoken of what they all knew to be true, but didn't dare discuss except in private.

"Sir Roald was correct to question the motives of this man," the bishop declared.

Sir Henry ran a coolly measuring gaze over the

irate clergyman as he set down his wine. "I suspect *your* motives for coming here are not unselfish."

Ignoring him, the bishop addressed Mathilde. "I suggest, my lady, that you send this fellow on his way. He is a most worldly man and not fit company for ladies who have no male protector."

Then he rose with haughty majesty and swept his cloak behind him. "We shall return to the abbey at once. Good day to you, my lady."

This was a disaster! If the bishop decided that her father was too sick to know what he was doing when he made a new will, Roald's claim to Ecclesford would be strengthened, and theirs…theirs could be totally disregarded.

Mathilde jumped to her feet to ask the bishop to stay, but before she could open her mouth, Sir Henry coolly remarked, "Surely if you're so concerned for the safety and honor of these ladies, you ought to stay."

The bishop's only answer was a disdainful sniff as he started toward the door, trailed by his anxious acolytes.

Mathilde started to go after him.

"Let him leave, my lady," Sir Henry advised from his seat on the dais. "Once the bishop calms himself, he'll realize that it would be to his advantage to side with you and not Roald. If you and your sister inherit and marry, he could have two powerful allies instead of one. Trust me, Christophus judges all things by the value to himself."

Mathilde hesitated, until the last of the bishop's priests left the hall, the door banging shut behind him like the door of a prison cell, final and condemning.

By the time she reached the door and looked into the yard, the bishop was mounted on his horse, cursing the grooms and stableboys in a most worldly manner, and generally giving every sign that he was far too angry to listen to reason as he turned his horse toward the gate.

Sighing, she closed the door, to find Father Thomas behind her.

"Do not despair, my lady," the priest said. "God will reward the just. And as Sir Henry says, once the bishop has calmed himself with prayer and meditation, he will surely reason wisely."

Mathilde doubted Bishop Christophus spent much time in meditation or prayer, or wise reasoning, for that matter.

"At least I will pray to God that it be so," Father Thomas added, betraying his own doubts.

"Let us hope so, Father," she fervently replied. She gave him a smile, for he had tried his best to cheer her. "Will you join us for the evening meal?"

"Bless you for asking, my lady, but no. Old Evans is near the end of his time on earth, and I have promised to sit with him tonight."

"Of course, Father," she said. "Tell him I shall be praying for him, too, although I am sure there is already a place in heaven prepared for such a kind and generous man."

Father Thomas smiled. "I will, and he will be glad to hear that you have him in your prayers, I'm sure. God be with you, my lady."

"And you, too, Father," she said, opening the door for him.

The mention of Evans had momentarily pushed the bishop and their troubles from her thoughts, but when she turned and saw Sir Henry still seated on the dais as if he were the lord here, her worries returned with even greater force.

"Why didn't you tell me you knew the bishop and that you were enemies?" she demanded as she marched toward the dais.

He rose and gestured for her to sit, still acting as if this were *his* hall. However, since she wanted to hear his answer, she made no comment on that, but plopped down on the nearest chair and raised a pointedly querying brow.

"I didn't tell you I knew Christophus," he said with infuriating calm, "because when you told me you were writing to the bishop, you never mentioned his name, and as I told that arrogant fellow, I never expected that he would be in England, let alone in Kent or involved in your dispute with Roald."

Was that possible? "I never mentioned the bishop by name?"

Henry shook his head. "No."

She could not fault him for this particular trouble then. With her elbow on the arm of the chair, she rested her cheek in her palm. "I wish I had."

"So do I," Sir Henry admitted, throwing one long leg over the arm of his chair and slouching down into the seat. "If I had known *he* was the bishop you were talking about, I would have stayed with the men rather than rush here when I heard a bishop had come. It was my intention to help you, not make things worse. Did he ask for a bribe?"

"Not precisely, but as good as," she confirmed. "Apparently Roald had already offered him something." She shook her head. "It seems a terrible thing to bribe a man of God."

"Not all clergymen are as holy and good as Father Thomas," Sir Henry replied. "Christophus is a man of large appetite, for many things. Most ambitious men of the church keep their offspring a secret. Unfortunately for him, his son was too much like him not to brag that his father was an important man."

"You've met his son?"

Henry smiled, but it was the closest thing to a smirk she'd ever seen him make. "His father sent him to Sir Leonard, too. James did not take kindly to instruction, to put it mildly. He complained morning, noon and night. Worse than that, he was a braggart and a bully, and one day, when I'd had enough of the way he teased Merrick for his silence, I hit him."

The smirk became a disgusted frown. "All I did was bloody his nose, but you'd think I'd cut it off. Christophus arrived a week later. I gather he wanted Sir Leonard to send me home in disgrace, as if I had a home to go to."

This was the first time he had ever spoken of his childhood, apart from tales of training with Sir Leonard, and it hinted at troubles and sorrow he never spoke of—and perhaps wanted to forget, as there were memories she would banish forever if she could.

"I don't know what Sir Leonard said to him," Henry continued, oblivious to her sympathetic reflections, "but the bishop was pale as a lamb's wool when he left, and took James with him, to the regret of no one."

"He condemned *me* for sinfulness," she muttered with disgust.

"Whatever he said to you, forget it. That man's a greedy pig."

While she appreciated Henry's ire for her sake, it would be impossible for her to forget the bishop's words or the pain they inflicted. He had said to her face what so many others would be whispering behind her back.

Sir Henry sat up straight and reached out to lightly lay a hand on her arm. "Please don't let that man's words upset you, my lady. He's a fool and a weakling. His own acolytes detest him. You're clever and strong, and your people justly love you."

He smiled at her, and his eyes that could harden like flint when angry, were now gentle and full of compassion. Her gaze roved over the sharp, attractive planes of his cheeks to settle on his full, enticing lips.

Her body warmed with desire and her heartbeat quickened. Yes, she was a weakling, or she would send him away from Ecclesford, because if they were alone now and not in the hall, who could say what she might do?

She didn't even have the strength to get up from her chair, but sought a way to keep him here in the hall, if only for a little while before he returned to his duty, or went to his chamber to wash. "How goes the training? Are you pleased with the men's progress?"

Sir Henry's hand slipped from her arm, and she told herself she was relieved.

"They're fast learners, I'll give them that," he said. "Some of them are a bit foolhardy and keen to show off, but a few bumps and bruises quickly teach them to be more careful."

"And Cerdic? He obeys your orders?"

"Without qualm or question, thank God. He's determined to learn all he can, and the men certainly respect and look up to him, although he has a long way to go when it comes to using a lance. He took quite a tumble today. I'd feared he'd broken his leg, but he was up and hobbling about quick enough. Nevertheless, I sent him to your sister to make certain his ankle was only sprained, and not more seriously injured."

That must be why she hadn't been able to find Giselle; she'd been in the barracks tending to Cerdic.

Henry leaned a little closer, nearly as close as when he'd almost kissed her.

She tried not to panic or act as if his proximity affected her at all, whether for good or ill. "If I might make a request, my lady?"

Her heart was pounding so hard, she thought he must be able to see it. A swift, sidelong glance told her he was looking at her neck, and she wondered if he could tell that she was agitated. So she struggled to keep her voice steady and make him doubt what he was seeing when she replied, "Of course."

"I've been thinking you should give an ale in the next few days, as a reward to your men for working so hard to learn new skills, and to the villagers for… well, in case there are hardships ahead. I gather the innkeeper sent quite a quantity of ale here already, enough to withhold a three month siege and more." His grin was devilment incarnate. "I asked."

That intimate grin was nearly impossible to resist, although she realized he would not be paying for the ale. Even so, the men *had* been working hard and the villagers could be facing hardships to come, whether they won or lost. "I think that's an excellent idea. I wish I had thought of it myself." Something else about his proposal made her heart a little lighter. "So you don't expect Roald to attack soon?"

"He might, but if he doesn't, such a celebration would do much to lift the people's spirits."

"Then there is no more to be said," she replied, briskly getting to her feet. "My sister and I will host an ale in three days' time."

He rose, took her hand and pressed a gallant kiss upon it. "You are a most kind and generous lady. Excuse me, then, while I go and spread the news."

She watched him hurry away, his pace swift, his long strides strong and purposeful.

Even if what she felt for him was not wrong—and it was—she must remember that one day, he would leave, perhaps with that same firm purpose. The only reason he would stay would be to court Giselle.

That would be even harder to bear than watching him go.

CHAPTER NINE

THREE DAYS LATER, on a cool afternoon in October, Henry patted the strong neck of Apollo, his battle-trained destrier, attempting to calm the excited animal as they waited their turn. This contest involved trying to catch an iron ring suspended on a thin rope between two poles at the end of the field with the tip of a lance.

Cerdic was taking his last turn now, his horse galloping down the field, his lance waving a bit too much. Cerdic was leaning a bit too far forward, Henry thought as he kept an instructional eye on the man and fought the urge to look at the spectators—Mathilde in particular.

It was getting more and more difficult to ignore her, and not just today. As his time here had passed, he'd come to admire her resilience, strength and resolve, as well as her ability to organize and run a large household virtually by herself. He had grown to respect her for her concern for everyone under her protection, right down to the lowliest spit boy. He was impressed by her goodness and generosity, and the ease with which she addressed all and sundry, whether well-to-do or not.

Most of all, though, he admired, respected and appreciated her astonishing courage and determination. How many other women could so boldly, bravely face the man who had done such a degrading, disgusting thing, and demand her rights? He knew what it was to be attacked and humiliated, and his experience had been easy compared to hers. He had been beaten and scorned, but not violated as she had been.

How could he not think her worthy of a man's highest regard? What had *he* ever done that could compare with her confrontation with Roald?

Nothing, came the answer. Nothing at all. Compared to her, he was the feckless wastrel his brother always claimed he was. Compared to her, he wasn't even worthy to command her garrison, let alone think of—

So he wouldn't think of that, he told himself, and he'd keep his distance, knowing that even the touch of her fingers was enough to ignite his passionate yearning. Every time they sat together at table, he wanted to kiss that little beauty mark on her neck and he was nearly overwhelmed with desire whenever he saw her bustling about the hall or in the yard. He kept imagining her in *their* hall, or in *their* bed, making love, sometimes tenderly, with gentle restraint, sometimes ardently, with thrashing excitement. He wanted her in a way that was both primal and different from anything he'd ever felt for a woman before. He desired much more than a few nights in her bed.

So in spite of his determination to keep his attention on Cerdic, he was well aware that she was standing beside Father Thomas, that she had on her gray cloak and wore gloves on her slender hands, and that a lock of waving chestnut hair had escaped her wimple.

A cheer went up and his gaze flew to the end of the field where Cerdic's horse pranced. Cerdic held up his lance, a ring around its shaft.

"Damn," Henry muttered. Everyone in this contest had missed once, except for Cerdic, and him. If he missed on this pass, Cerdic would be the winner.

The exultant Cerdic trotted past the spectators, a wide grin splitting his face. He had every right to be pleased, and Henry didn't begrudge him his triumph. But that didn't mean Henry didn't intend to get his lance through a ring, either.

Turning away, he saw Lady Giselle watching Cerdic. A moment's fleeting expression crossed her face—and it was one he recognized at once.

God's blood, was *that* the way the wind blew? Lady Giselle and the proud blond warrior? How had he not seen this before? How could he, justly known for his perception in such matters, have been so blind to that mutual attraction?

Did Mathilde know? If she did, she must approve, or her displeasure would hardly be a secret. Perhaps she'd been too distracted by her trouble with Roald to see love blooming right beneath her nose.

When she did find out—for such things invariably came to light, no matter how one tried to hide them—would she, could she, approve of their liaison? Would she be able to accept a marriage between her sister and a man without birth, without wealth, without an estate? A marriage that would see Cerdic the lord of Ecclesford?

"Are you ready, Sir Henry?"

Henry started and regarded Toft standing beside him. The soldier held up a lance for Henry to take. "Yes," he replied, reaching for the weapon.

Since this was a friendly competition, and his "opponent" nothing more than a ring on a rope, Henry wasn't wearing any armor or even heavy padding. The worst he could expect was a tumble from a horse and while that could be dangerous, he was at far less risk than he would be in a battle or a melee in a tournament. Nevertheless, the tip of his lance had been covered to blunt it as a precaution.

Gritting his teeth, determined to succeed, Henry kicked his heels lightly against his horse's sides. That was enough to set the huge horse cantering.

Urging Apollo to a gallop, Henry put everything else from his mind and concentrated on the ring. It seemed miniscule in the distance, although it was a good ten inches wide. He had chosen a relatively easy target for his men, so more would have a chance of getting their lance tips through it.

Closer he came to his target, and closer still. He gripped his horse hard with his knees, keeping his spurred heels out. His mount was already going fast enough; more speed would be unnecessary, and indeed, would make it harder for him to get the ring.

Nearly there. He held his lance against his body, ready to think of it as an extension of his arm.

Suddenly, a crow flew up from a nearby tree, its harsh caw taking Henry's attention from the target for one brief moment, and he turned his lance slightly in that direction. He realized what he'd done in an instant, but it was too late. They had passed the rope and he had missed the ring.

There were a few muted cheers, but more groans. After his initial disappointment, Henry took some comfort from the fact that some in the crowd had been hoping he would win, and reminded himself that this was intended not for his glory, but for his men's reward.

All things considered, this loss was little to him. He could think of something he'd be far more loath to lose.

He wondered what she thought of his failure, then

dismissed that question. His lance raised and resting on his booted foot, he nudged Apollo into a trot back to the other end of the field. He handed his lance to Toft and slipped from his saddle, then gave the reins of his horse to one of the grooms before he went to join the ladies and the still grinning Cerdic.

Since this was the final competition of the day, the other spectators began drifting toward the green, and the benches set up there and, of course, the ale. Some of the people of Ecclesford hadn't left the benches at all, preferring to watch the various contests from afar—and keeping a closer eye on their brew.

None of these were Henry's men. They'd been strictly warned that he would not be pleased if any of them imbibed too much, even if the ale was free and plentiful. Fortunately, it seemed his order was being obeyed, and his men afraid to risk a sharp reprimand from him tomorrow.

"Well done, Cerdic," he said as he joined the others. "I thought you weren't going to keep your seat during the last pass, though. You were leaning too far forward."

Cerdic frowned, and so did Lady Giselle, but Mathilde smiled her rare and pretty smile. "Surely we can have one day without a lesson," she chided, her eyes shining with laughter in a way that delighted him, for her laughter was rare. "Did you not say this ale was to celebrate all that the men have already accomplished?"

"You're right," Henry readily agreed. "If I don't take care, I may wind up like Sir Leonard. He makes everything a lesson, even to eating." He lowered his voice in gruff imitation. "Mind how you hold your knife, boy. You could take out your eye if you're not careful."

He was rewarded by another burble of laughter from Mathilde, the sound more lovely and welcome than a lavender-scented bed at the end of a long, hard day.

"I thought you admired your old teacher," she noted as they all started toward the green.

"I do. He's the best at what he does. However, riding herd on a bunch of youths who think they're the equal of grown men, or better, is not a future I covet."

Giselle turned to Cerdic. "They've started dancing on the green. Dance with me, Cerdic?"

Henry nearly burst out laughing when he saw how her request discomfited him.

"I don't know how," he muttered, sounding for all the world like an embarrassed little boy.

"Of course you do," Giselle indignantly replied. "We taught you years ago."

"I think you had best dance with her, Cerdic," Mathilde said, apparently without sympathy for his plight. "Otherwise, she may pester you all night."

"I've forgotten how," Cerdic mumbled in protest.

"I'm sure you'll remember," Giselle persisted.

"I think you ought to surrender, my friend," Henry said. "These ladies appear to possess a streak of stubbornness against which we men are powerless."

"It's Cerdic who's being stubborn," Giselle complained with a very pretty, and attractive, pout.

Cerdic gave in, but not without some remaining reluctance. "Very well, my lady," he said glumly, "but should I step on the hem of thy gown or mash thy toes, thou art not to complain."

Giselle merely laughed with happy triumph and took his arm to lead him to the green.

Henry turned to Mathilde. "Will you dance, my lady, or would you be ashamed to be seen with a man who did not win one competition today?"

Smiling, she slipped her hand in the crook of his elbow, delighting him yet more, and warming him more than any dance on this chilly afternoon.

"I think you faired poorly on purpose, Sir Knight," she said pertly.

"Alas, my lady, I did my best and failed," he confessed with mock despair. "Sir Leonard would be most ashamed of me today. Later I shall go and mope by the river, contemplating my dismal failure."

"No one would have won anything if you hadn't suggested the contests," Mathilde pointed out.

As they got closer to the green, he put his hand over hers for an instant, then just as quickly withdrew it. He didn't want to frighten her, or arouse bad memories, as the scent of damp stones could remind him of that dungeon. "Thank God I know how to dance, so I'm not an utter disgrace."

Mathilde thought she had never met a man who had less cause to consider himself disgraceful. He had performed admirably in every competition that day, and despite his claim that he hadn't purposefully lost, she didn't think he had particularly exerted himself to win, either.

Nevertheless, she enjoyed his wry, self-deprecating comments. He was so pleasantly different from most men of her acquaintance, and nothing like the few arrogant knights who'd come to Ecclesford, usually seeking shelter. And usually, once they'd seen Giselle, they'd wanted to stay, until her father sent them on their way.

"Cerdic does know how to dance—or at least, he did," she amended. "Giselle and I spent hours teaching him when we were younger."

"He must have enjoyed your company very much."

Mathilde smiled, thinking of those happier, more innocent days. "He enjoyed Giselle's more. I teased him too much."

"Does he still prefer Giselle's company to yours?"

There was something in Henry's tone that gave her pause and made her look toward the green where Giselle was gaily instructing Cerdic. Their friend no longer looked disgruntled. He was laughing with her sister, letting Giselle guide him, their heads intimately close—

By the saints, was it possible? Had she been blind to something so important happening between them?

Maybe she had. When their father had died, Giselle had fallen into Cerdic's comforting arms, and he had stroked her hair. The Christmas before that, they had sat together by the Yule log for the whole of Christmas Eve, whispering and laughing. At May Day, they had gone into the woods together to gather flowers and been gone the whole of the morning.

God save her, she *had* been blind.

"You see it now, too?" Henry asked softly, his voice close to her ear. "I don't think I have any chance of winning your sister's hand, should I wish to try."

He didn't sound the least bit disappointed. She thrilled to realize that, because surely he would be upset if Giselle had been his object.

But that didn't mean he would then want her. Indeed, to think that would be as foolish as…

"I hope their liaison doesn't upset you."

"Why should it?" she asked, surprised by his apprehensive tone. "If she wants him for her husband, she should marry him. I certainly won't object. He's a good man. My father liked him, too."

"Although he has no rank or wealth?"

"He is a descendent of kings, if not Norman ones. And if he loves Giselle and she loves him, that is more important than wealth. Besides, Giselle will have enough wealth and land for both."

"If you win your dispute with Roald."

"*When* we win."

A gaggle of children ran by, giggling and calling to each other. Henry took her hand to pull her out of their boisterous way, bringing her close to the trunk of the oak beside the smithy.

The blacksmith had banked the forge's fire so he could join the ale. Even so, it was warmer here beside the building and in the shelter of the massive tree. It was secluded, too, far from the bonfire being kindled as the sun set, and far enough from the festivities that when night fell, they would be in darkness, virtually invisible from the merry-makers dancing on the green. It was dark here already, in the shadow of the smithy, in the shelter of the tree.

She could feel Henry's presence close beside her, and smell him, too—the heady, masculine, earthy odor of leather, horse and ale.

"You aren't disappointed Cerdic cares for your sister?" he asked, his voice low and intimate.

Did he think that she…? "Not at all," she honestly admitted. "I've never cared for him that way. He's like a brother to me."

"I'm glad," Henry said softly, taking her hands in his.

The sensation of his strong grasp seemed to travel from her fingers to the crown of her head and the tips of her toes, warm and throbbing. Once she'd thought she'd never be able to endure a man's touch; now, she never wanted Henry to let her go.

She was no longer a virgin. She did not have that prize to lose anymore. It was gone. Gone forever.

Taken. Stolen.

What did it matter if she gave her body to another man?

She could get with child.

For a moment, she felt that same dread that she had lived with for days after Roald had fled, waiting and fearing and hoping for her menses. She would not, could not, go through that again. But to embrace? To kiss?

Why not?

She gently pulled her hands away, then put them on his upper arms and leaned toward him. His hands slid around her waist. Her breathing quickened, but not with fear or panic.

"I want to kiss you, Mathilde," he whispered, his breath warm on her cheek. "May I?"

Her answer was a sigh. "Yes."

Although need and desire raged through Henry like tinder bursting into flame, he held himself back as he brought his lips to hers. He must not hurry this; he must let Mathilde lead the way. She must be the one to decide how much and how far, lest he kindle fear and panic instead of yearning.

But oh, it was not easy when she relaxed into him and moved her lips over his. It wasn't a simple thing to ignore the growing urgency within his own body.

Never, ever, in his life, had he craved a woman as he did Mathilde, and not to simply satisfy the needs of his body. He wanted to love her as she should be loved, with tenderness and compassion as well as desire. To give his body to her, not take hers with rough and selfish lust.

She drew back and her voice held hurt when she softly said, "I thought you wanted to kiss me."

He nearly groaned out loud. "I did. I do—very much, but I don't want you to fear that I'll go too far. I want you to feel safe with me."

He held his breath as she cupped his face in her hands. "I have never felt safer, or more happy," she murmured, brushing her mouth across his—and nearly driving him mad with desire.

Thrilled, delighted, relieved and eager, he gathered her into his arms and revealed more of his need, kissing her deeply, letting some of his pent-up passion free, although he was still tender and cautious. When she parted her lips yet more in response, he dared yet more, gently thrusting his tongue into the moist warmth, until he touched her teeth.

Still she did not pull away. He insinuated his hands

beneath her cloak and gathered her into his arms, warm and welcome. He could feel her hips against his, arousing his manhood, so he focused on their kiss. The softness of her lips. The taste of ale lingering there. Her body molding itself to his.

She arched her back and instinctively, his hands moved lower, toward her buttocks.

His mind commanded him to take care. To be careful, lest he inadvertently alarm her.

His body would not listen and he shifted, bringing more of her into contact with him. Even through the layers of clothing between them, his flesh responded as if they were naked.

She broke the kiss and put her hands on his chest as if to hold him back. "Stop. I can't—" Her voice caught as if her very heart were broken.

Then she burst into tears, great rasping sobs, her shoulders shaking.

"Oh, God, Mathilde!" he cried softly, feeling helpless, even cruel, although he had meant to be anything but. He shouldn't have touched her. He should have been stronger, waited longer. "I'm sorry. I didn't mean to—!"

"It's not your fault. I am not angry or afraid. I'm sorry. I wish…if only I…"

The realization that she was trying not to cry, to be brave once more, nearly shattered him. He didn't know what to do or what to say. He felt completely, utterly powerless. He yearned to put his arms around her and hold her close, to offer her some comfort, yet that might only upset her more.

But he couldn't simply stand here and do nothing, listening to her anguished weeping, so he very gently, very slowly, eased his arms around her. If she'd made the slightest move in protest, he would have stopped at once, but she didn't. Nor did she shy away when he stroked her back. She leaned her cheek against his chest and continued to cry, the sound a torment to hear.

How long she wept, he couldn't say, but he would have stayed there all night rather than leave her alone and in such pain.

Finally, she wiped her face with her hand and drew in a shuddering breath. She pulled away and he let her go.

"Forgive me," she said, wiping another tear as it slipped down her cheek. "I have not cried like that since…"

He expected her to say since Roald had attacked her.

"Since I found out I was not with child," she confessed. "I was so relieved, I burst into tears and fell to my knees and thanked God over and over again."

He had no words, could think of none, except curses to heap on Roald de Sayres's head. If God was just, that man would burn in hell for all eternity.

"I suppose it was like a wounded man being told

he would live and not die," she said. She looked up at him then, shy and so very vulnerable. "Or like that girl when you came to her aid. She was very lucky to have such a champion and so are we."

Henry had been given many compliments in his life, some of them deserved. He had been admired and his body craved, and his martial skills occasionally acknowledged. But never had any words of praise made him feel both proud and unworthy at the same time as Mathilde's did tonight.

"I would I were a better one," he said quietly, and sincerely. He knew well what he was, and that he wasn't deserving of such admiration. "I'm no paragon, Mathilde, or even that fine a knight. I may have some skill in battle because I was well taught. Otherwise, I'm vain and arrogant, proud of my looks and my body, just as you realized that first day. I've been envious of my brother's accomplishments, and bitter that my friends were so quick to believe I would betray them. I've lusted after many women. I've cuckolded husbands and told myself that if their wives were willing, it was no sin of mine, although in my heart, I knew better. I'm not worthy to be anyone's champion, Mathilde."

And in his heart, he felt the truth of what he'd said. He'd wasted too much of his life, spent too much time in frivolous pursuits. For the first time in his life, he looked at himself with brutally honest eyes—her eyes—and saw himself for what he truly was, what his brother had always said, a merry wastrel.

"Who does not feel envy?" she asked in a gentle whisper, her voice a balm. "I've long been envious of Giselle's beauty, and bitter that no man looked at me as they did at her. I was even jealous when I realized you were right, and that Cerdic loves her, even though I don't love him. Is that not the height of selfishness?

"And you speak of your lust. What did I feel for Roald but lust? I know now it wasn't love. And I was vain and foolish, too, believing his empty flattery."

Henry put his finger against her lips to tenderly silence her. "You wanted to be loved. Who does not?"

"Other women do not put themselves in harm's way as I did."

"That was a mistake, and you have suffered the most for it. I could name other women who had sinned far more grievously than you, Mathilde, and never been punished, except perhaps by their conscience, if they possessed any."

"Roald—"

He pulled her close and embraced her. "Is a coward and a base, despicable villain. Mathilde, I cannot erase what happened to you that night and I would give much to make you forget, but in my eyes, you are not the lesser for what happened. You are not tainted, or stained—*he* is. I've known many women in my life, Mathilde, and made love to more than one, yet I swear to you on my life I've never felt about a single one of them as I feel about you. It's more than desire, more than affection. I've never respected another woman as I do you, or admired one more. Mathilde, I've never told another woman I loved her. I—"

She put her hands on his chest and pushed him away. "Say no more, Henry!" she cried as if he'd struck her instead of being about to tell her that he loved her.

Then she turned on her heel and fled.

KEEPING TO the shadows, skirting the green, Mathilde ran back to Ecclesford. She could hardly see for her tears, breathe for her sobs.

She never should have stayed with Henry in the dark. Never should have kissed him. Never should have listened to his words of love.

Henry mustn't love her. He deserved a virgin bride with wealth and a vast estate, the best England had to offer.

Not a woman who'd been raped by Roald de Sayres.

HOPING SHE'D simply been caught off guard by his admission and unsure what to say or do, Henry ran after Mathilde. But she disappeared in the shadows and he lost her. He studied the people around the green in the light of the bonfire and didn't see her.

A sliver of fear lodged in his heart. Roald was an evil man, and it was very dark.

Picking up his pace, he ran to the gate. "Has Lady Mathilde returned?" he demanded of the guards who'd snapped quickly to attention when they saw him approach, and at a run.

"Aye, my lord," the older of them replied. "A little while ago."

Henry nodded and started through the courtyard, determined to follow her and... What? Demand an explanation? Ask her why she'd fled? She was a free woman and not bound to him by family tie or betrothal. Surely following her and pestering her with questions was not the way to proceed.

So instead, Henry went to his bedchamber, noting that the door to Mathilde and Giselle's was closed. He disrobed, except for his breeches, and lay down upon his bed, the candle lit as always, wondering and more than half hoping she would come to him tonight.

But she did not, and when he broke the fast in the hall the next day, it was as if those kisses beneath the oak tree had never happened, and his words had gone unspoken. She was as briskly businesslike as always, and nothing in her eyes gave him any sign that things had changed between them.

He told himself that perhaps she needed time to accept that he cared so much about her, or maybe she wanted to ensure he was no fickle, faithless cad. If so, and as before, he would have to be patient and wait for her to speak.

No matter how long that might take.

CHAPTER TEN

As HENRY was riding down the field aiming for an iron ring, Roald was kneeling before the thrones of the king and queen, who were seated in their hall in Westminster. It had taken him several frustrating days to be admitted to the royal presence, despite his family connection to Eleanor and even the offer of bribes. But he was here at last, and although this wasn't a private audience, there were only a few courtiers present. They were talking quietly among themselves at the far end of the paneled chamber heated by a roaring blaze in the massive fireplace, and lit by candles in polished brass holders that shone like gold.

"Your Majesty!" Roald cried, apparently enraptured as he addressed his distant cousin the queen.

"Roald," she said sweetly, "it is always such a pleasure to see someone from home."

"Not so much as it is a pleasure for me to see you," he replied, rising in response to her graceful gesture.

Her husband, however, was looking at Roald as if

he'd never been more bored in his life, or perhaps it was only the effect of that slightly drooping eyelid.

"We understand you have some important business to discuss," the king said.

"Yes, Your Majesty, I do, concerning the estate of my late uncle." Ignoring the other courtiers, and mindful not to overtax the royal mind, he quickly told them of his uncle's illness, the illegal change to his will and his cousins' subsequent outrageous behavior.

"And thus, Your Majesty, my cousins refuse to relinquish the estate, although it should be mine," he concluded.

He was pleased to note that the king, as well as the queen, was now regarding him with interest. "We have heard of this estate," the king remarked. "Well situated, prosperous, although the late lord was rather…eccentric."

"Indeed he was," Roald confirmed.

"And his daughters…one of them is quite a beauty," the queen added.

Roald guessed where this was headed. He also noted that several of the courtiers, who'd been paying little heed to the conversation, suddenly turned their attention toward the throne.

"Lovely, but not so beautiful or gracious as Your Majesty," Roald replied. "Her dowry is considerable, however. Of course, I fully intend to abide by my uncle's original will, in which he made ample provision for his daughters' dowries."

"There is more than one daughter?" the king asked, raising the royal brow.

"Yes, Majesty, but I fear the younger would be no reward to anyone in marriage. She is a shrew, and ugly, too, and I'm certain she is the one who came up with this contemptible scheme to rob me."

"Yet she will be well dowered?" the queen inquired.

"If any man could be found to take her," Roald replied. "I should mention that their father also allowed that should either of his daughters decide to become a bride of Christ, their dowry would go to the church."

The queen's eyes gleamed at that, no doubt contemplating the amount of ecclesiastical influence she could wield with such a sum at her disposal to be dispersed as she decided. At the moment, she needed all the ecclesiastical influence she could get if she was to get her rogue of an uncle confirmed as archbishop. "Is this girl likely to follow that course?" she asked.

"When I possess Ecclesford, my lady, I would most strongly urge her to do so. It could be either that, or a marriage that she will not find to her liking."

While the queen didn't look at all nonplused by that suggestion, the king's brows furrowed. "We do not like to hear of women being threatened into marriage."

Roald spread his hands in supplication and gave them a wide-eyed, innocent look. "On my honor as a knight, I would never force her into a marriage or the church, Your Majesty. But she is as stubborn as she is shrewish, and thus may require some extra… guidance."

"This other sister—the beauty," the king remarked, leaving the subject of Mathilde mercifully alone. "She's never been to court?"

"No, Your Majesty," Roald replied, noting the queen's sharp glance at her young husband. "Her father lived almost a hermit's life."

"Perhaps we should meet your cousins."

"I think not, my love," the queen said softly, putting her hand on her husband's knee and smiling sweetly. "We have enough to do here. We must arrange your brother's marriage, for one thing. And this beauty might be too distracting to the young men of the court. You don't want to have any wars breaking out over a woman."

"No, we don't," he agreed.

Roald had to admire the ease with which the queen manipulated her husband.

"The only woman in England capable of being a second Helen, Your Majesty, is yourself," he said with a courteous bow.

The queen darted him a glance, as if he should have kept his mouth shut. Roald flushed, and decided he'd better be more careful. His royal relative's temper was not something to be roused without risk.

"While we agree there is good reason for you to dispute your late uncle's will," the king said, "these matters are for the courts to decide. You must await their judgment."

The queen shifted with agitation, and Roald could guess why. She would rather the distribution of land and estates belonged to the king alone, assisted by the helpful advice of his queen, of course.

In this instance, so did he. He didn't trust the English and their laws, and certainly not their courts.

Nevertheless, that was the way it was in this barbarous land, so he had best proceed cautiously, careful lest he anger the king. "I am aware that the courts have such power, Majesty," he said, "but if it is known you support my claim to the estate, that will surely carry great weight with those who will stand in judgment."

"And we do think you should possess it," the queen confirmed, much to Roald's delight.

"Yet even so," the king said firmly, "we cannot be too open with our favor. The barons are looking for anything they can use against us to foment rebellion."

Roald could well believe that, especially after the king's recent foray in France. It had been a disaster, and the king had been forced to agree to a five-year truce.

It was also no secret that many of the English nobles didn't like the queen, believing that she was too eager to reward her relatives at the expense of England.

The clergy also held the queen in low esteem, for she seemed equally determined to reward her ecclesiastical relatives with power and influence. And if the church courts decided to make him pay for her sins by decreeing that his late uncle's second will took precedent over the first—

Damn the law and all who practiced it! Damn the English and their courts! Damn everyone who stood in the way of his rightful inheritance!

The young monarch rubbed his chin and regarded Roald thoughtfully as he spoke. "We point out that when it comes to matters of law and property, possession is more important than words written on a parchment, even in Latin. Therefore, Sir Roald, if you should, by chance, come to possess the castle of Ecclesford, so much the better for you. We will always be ready to support the claim of a faithful courtier."

Roald nearly shouted for joy. The king had as good as given him permission to take Ecclesford by force.

Oh, that shrew Mathilde was going to be sorry she ever tried to refuse him! Giselle was going to pay, too, for siding with her sister and always treating him as if he had ringworm. And D'Alton was really going to regret sticking his nose in something that didn't concern him.

Thinking of that arrogant bastard, Roald assumed a mournful expression and didn't hesitate to use the king's dread of conspiracy to his advantage. "I fear my cousins have managed to find themselves an ally—the brother of the lord of Dunkeathe."

Roald eagerly watched the king and queen's reactions to that information. As he'd expected, they weren't pleased. The lord of Dunkeathe had been given his estate by the king of Scotland, not England, and Lord Nicholas made little secret of his lack of respect for the rulers of England. Henry, too, had sometimes been less than judicious in his comments about the monarchy.

"I would hate for something...unfortunate...to happen to Sir Henry because he's interfered in matters in which he should have no interest," the king said slowly.

Roald was sure, from the gleam in the king's eyes and the look in the queen's, that if D'Alton should die, they would not be sorry. However, it was also true that Henry and his brother were not without allies at court, so they had to be cautious with their enmity.

The king rose. "We are fatigued," he declared, gazing down at his wife. "We shall retire."

"I, too, am weary," she said, likewise getting to her feet, although the look she gave her husband was anything but indicative of fatigue. "Good day and good luck, Roald," she said, bestowing a cool smile upon him.

He bowed deeply. "Your loyal servant, Your Majesty."

"So I would hope," she said before she turned and departed with the king.

Roald didn't care if they started rutting behind the throne. Now that he had royal approval to take Ecclesford, he was more concerned about where he was going to find the money to raise an army. It would take more than ten men to capture the castle.

ROALD WAS STILL deep in thought when he reached the small room he had rented in Southwark, across the London Bridge. In this crowded, stinking part of the City given over to entertainment and the vices that went with it, a man could hide more easily.

He was not expecting to find Charles De Mallemaison awaiting him in the murky shadows of his windowless room, with his sword drawn.

Roald instantly reached for his weapon, but before he could grab the hilt, De Mallemaison's blade flashed like a striking snake, slicing Roald's sword-belt from his body. It and his sword fell to the floor, striking the bare boards with a clatter.

Roald turned to flee, but De Mallemaison hauled him over the threshold and kicked the door closed

YOUR PARTICIPATION IS REQUESTED!

Dear Reader,

Since you are a lover of fiction – we would like to get to know you!

Inside you will find a short Reader's Survey. Sharing your answers with us will help our editorial staff understand who you are and what activities you enjoy.

To thank you for your participation, we would like to send you 2 books and a gift – **ABSOLUTELY FREE**!

Enjoy your gifts with our appreciation,

Pam Powers

SEE INSIDE FOR READER'S SURVEY

What's Your Reading Pleasure...
ROMANCE? *OR* SUSPENSE?

Do you prefer spine-tingling page turners OR heart-stirring stories about love and relationships? Tell us which books you enjoy – and you'll get 2 FREE "ROMANCE" BOOKS or 2 FREE "SUSPENSE" BOOKS with no obligation to purchase anything.

Choose **"ROMANCE"** and get **2 FREE BOOKS** that will fuel your imagination with intensely moving stories about life, love and relationships.

FREE!

Choose **"SUSPENSE"** and you'll get **2 FREE BOOKS** that will thrill you with a spine-tingling blend of suspense and mystery.

FREE!

Whichever category you select, your 2 free books have a combined cover price of $11.98 or more in the U.S. and $13.98 or more in Canada.

And remember. . . just for accepting the Editor's Free Gift Offer, we'll send you 2 books and a gift, ABSOLUTELY FREE!

YOURS FREE! We'll send you a fabulous surprise gift absolutely FREE, just for trying "Romance" or "Suspense"!

® and ™ are trademarks owned and used by the trademark owner and/or its licensee.

Order online at
www.FreeBooksandGift.com

YOUR READER'S SURVEY
"THANK YOU" FREE GIFTS INCLUDE:

- ▶ 2 Romance OR 2 Suspense books
- ▶ A lovely surprise gift

PLEASE FILL IN THE CIRCLES COMPLETELY TO RESPOND

1) What type of fiction books do you enjoy reading? (Check all that apply)
- ○ Suspense/Thrillers   ○ Action/Adventure   ○ Modern-day Romances
- ○ Historical Romance   ○ Humour   ○ Science fiction

2) What attracted you most to the last fiction book you purchased on impulse?
- ○ The Title   ○ The Cover   ○ The Author   ○ The Story

3) What is usually the greatest influencer when you <u>plan</u> to buy a book?
- ○ Advertising   ○ Referral from a friend
- ○ Book Review   ○ Like the author

4) Approximately how many fiction books do you read in a year?
- ○ 1 to 6   ○ 7 to 19   ○ 20 or more

5) How often do you access the internet?
- ○ Daily   ○ Weekly   ○ Monthly   ○ Rarely or never

6) To which of the following age groups do you belong?
- ○ Under 18   ○ 18 to 34   ○ 35 to 64   ○ over 65

YES! I have completed the Reader's Survey. Please send me the 2 FREE books and gift for which I qualify. I understand that I am under no obligation to purchase any books, as explained on the back.

Check one:

☐	**ROMANCE** 193 MDL EE4W 393 MDL EE49

☐	**SUSPENSE** 192 MDL EE5L 392 MDL EE5W

FIRST NAME

LAST NAME

ADDRESS

APT.#

CITY

STATE/PROV.

ZIP/POSTAL CODE

The Reader Service — Here's How It Works:

Accepting your 2 free books and gift places you under no obligation to buy anything. You may keep the books and gift and return the shipping statement marked "cancel." If you do not cancel, about a month later we'll send you 3 additional books and bill you just $5.24 each in the U.S., or $5.74 each in Canada, plus 25¢ shipping & handling per book and applicable taxes if any.* That's the complete price and — compared to cover prices starting from $5.99 each in the U.S. and $6.99 each in Canada — it's quite a bargain! You may cancel at any time, but if you choose to continue, every month we'll send you 3 more books, which you may either purchase at the discount price or return to us and cancel your subscription.

*Terms and prices subject to change without notice. Sales tax applicable in N.Y. Canadian residents will be charged applicable provincial taxes and GST.

If offer card is missing write to: The Reader Service, 3010 Walden Ave., P.O. Box 1867, Buffalo, NY 14240-1867

BUSINESS REPLY MAIL

FIRST-CLASS MAIL   PERMIT NO. 717-003   BUFFALO, NY

POSTAGE WILL BE PAID BY ADDRESSEE

THE READER SERVICE
3010 WALDEN AVE
PO BOX 1341
BUFFALO NY 14240-8571

NO POSTAGE
NECESSARY
IF MAILED
IN THE
UNITED STATES

behind him. Then he stood in front of it, blocking Roald's escape.

"I'm here for the money—or something in lieu," he said in his low, raspy voice.

Roald's blood turned to ice. He couldn't pay his debts; indeed, he would have to borrow more if he was to gain Ecclesford.

De Mallemaison's blade hovered lower, near Roald's manhood. "What's it to be?"

As Roald regarded the man reputed to be the most cold-blooded mercenary in England, an idea came to his tumultuous mind—one so astonishingly brilliant, one that also offered the perfect solution to all his troubles, it was a wonder he hadn't thought of it before.

"It seems you've come down in the world, De Mallemaison, if you've taken to collecting debts of tradesmen," he said, no longer afraid in spite of the sword blade still close to his body.

A scowl darkened De Mallemaison's features. "Don't have it, eh?" He added a completely piti- less, "Too bad."

Roald held up his hand. "I know a way you can earn more than the goldsmiths are paying you." Not that he knew how much that was, although it was likely a considerable sum. De Mallemaison wouldn't come cheap.

De Mallemaison's eyes gleamed with greedy interest. "The goldsmiths pay well and you're already in debt up to your neck. If you know a way to get money, how come you haven't got it?"

"Because my cousins are stubborn fools who refuse to give me my rightful inheritance. However, I've just come from the king, who's given me leave to take possession of my estate by any means necessary."

He left out the complication of his uncle's will. "It occurs to me that you're just the man to help me raise a suitable force with which to do that. Once we've defeated my cousins, I'll be rich and very able to pay for your assistance."

De Mallemaison didn't look impressed. "I don't work for free."

"You wouldn't be. I assure you, you'll be paid when—"

"*If,*" De Mallemaison growled, his sword flicking up again. "I don't work for *ifs,* either."

"I give you my word you'll be well compensated."

De Mallemaison snorted. "You expect me to gamble on your word?"

"I'm a knight of the realm," Roald haughtily replied.

De Mallemaison had the most vile chuckle Roald had ever heard. "Oh, I know exactly what you are, Sir Roald, and *I'm* no fool. I either see half the money before I start, or I don't start at all." He lifted his blade so that it was between Roald's eyes. "I don't think you've got a half a penny, for me *or* the goldsmiths."

Roald tried to think of another inducement to get De Mallemaison to help him. Why, one look at his scarred visage and half the garrison of Ecclesford would probably throw down their weapons without a fight. "My cousin—one of those opposing me—is a very beautiful woman, more beautiful than the queen. Help me defeat them, and you can have her."

He didn't like giving up Giselle, but if he must, he must.

"One woman's as good as another in the dark."

Good God, was there nothing he could say... offer...promise...?

That scar on De Mallemaison's cheek... He'd heard a story once, years ago, about how he'd come by it. It was worth a try. "My cousins have the brother of the lord of Dunkeathe helping them."

"I know the lord of Dunkeathe." The mercenary pointed at the scar marring his cheek. "Bastard gave me this."

"Really? Then no doubt you'll be happy to give his brother a few scars, too."

De Mallemaison sheathed his sword. "I'd be happy to kill the bastard's brother and send him his head in a basket."

Roald nearly collapsed with relief. Thank God he'd been told years ago that Nicholas of Dunkeathe had once nearly killed Charles De Mallemaison by slicing open his cheek.

De Mallemaison's lips twisted into an evil smile. "How many men do you need and when do we leave London?"

A FEW DAYS LATER on a sunny autumn morn and humming a ballad about two star-crossed lovers, a lone mounted knight trotted along the road toward Ecclesford. His slender yet muscular body was attired in mail, including a cowl pushed back to reveal a head of ruddy hair and a face that reminded many of a fox. His mail hauberk was covered by a forest-green surcoat and he wore a sword at his waist. He had no other obvious weapons, and there was a small pack tied to his saddle.

Despite his seemingly lax attitude, the knight's gaze darted about like that of a particularly alert hawk or, given his visage, a fox seeking its next meal. And although he was alone, there was that in his bearing and his watchfulness that would have given any but the bravest or most foolhardy of footpads cause to let him pass unmolested.

And wisely so. The garrison commander of Tregellas was no man to meet in a fight, unless you wanted to lose.

Sir Ranulf's shrewd gaze took in the workers digging trenches and otherwise preparing the fields for winter, the livestock grazing on the stubble and, especially, the village and castle in the distance.

Ecclesford. Where Henry—merry, impetuous Henry—was reported to be.

Several of the peasants looked up at Ranulf as he passed, then quickly returned to their work. No one challenged him, but they were unarmed, so that was not surprising. He was more curious about his reception at the castle.

As Ranulf drew near a fork in the road, he heard a sound like low drumbeats. He recognized it at once—many men marching at a quick pace.

Considering he was alone, uncertain if Henry was here or not, or if this force approaching would be friendly, Ranulf had no qualms about dismounting and leading his horse behind a small thicket of brambles, some still bearing leaves, where he could hide while watching the road. Not for him the foolish bravado of issuing a challenge when he might be outnumbered.

In the next few minutes, a group of soldiers came trotting into view along the rutted road. They weren't wearing chain mail, but only the padded gambesons generally worn beneath. They carried shields and spears, and had conical helmets on their head and swordbelts around their waists. Their faces were streaked with sweat, their gambesons stained with it. Their feet barely rose from the road, and their breathing was labored. They'd obviously been at this a long time.

"Pick up those feet!" a familiar voice shouted, giving Ranulf one of the greater surprises of his life. "Anybody falls back, they'll feel the tip of my spear in their backside!"

So Henry *was* here—and apparently, astoundingly, training a group of soldiers. That hadn't been included in the news that had reached Tregellas from Scotland.

The men, although clearly exhausted, quickened their pace and lifted their feet higher.

Since he would surely be safe if Henry was in command, Ranulf led his horse out from behind the trees, until he was standing in the road directly in the path of the column of men, who came to a shambling and stunned halt.

"Who told you to stop?" Henry bellowed from the rear before he came into view. He, too, wore a gambeson and sword belt, carried a spear and shield, and even had on that ridiculously small helmet.

Ranulf wouldn't have believed it if he wasn't seeing it with his own eyes. "Henry!" he called out over the grunts and panting of the soldiers, his usual sardonic manner missing.

"Ranulf?" his friend exclaimed, breaking into a smile and hurrying forward to greet his friend. "God's blood, what the devil are you doing here?"

"I could ask you the same thing," Ranulf answered as he walked toward him. "I thought you were bound for Scotland."

"I was," Henry replied with his irrepressible grin. "I thought you'd still be at Tregellas. What brings you to Kent?"

"As a matter of fact, I've come looking for you."

Concern furrowed Henry's brow. "Trouble at Tregellas? Does Merrick need my help?"

"Everyone is quite well, and as for our boon companion Merrick, you never saw such a changed man. I actually heard him singing to himself one morning. I nearly swooned from the shock."

Henry grinned, then glanced at the exhausted men. "We were on our way back to the castle. You'll stay awhile, I hope?"

"With pleasure, as long as I don't have to endure a forced march. I had quite enough of that with Sir Leonard."

Henry laughed in his merry, carefree way, then called out, "Cerdic, take them back to the barracks."

A tall, blond fellow appeared from the midst of the men and barked at the men to get moving.

"Toft," Henry called out to a small, dark-haired fellow. "Take charge of Sir Ranulf's horse and see that it's properly stabled."

The soldier did as he was told and took hold of the bridle of Ranulf's horse, then led it away, following the soldiers.

Meanwhile, Henry slapped Ranulf on the back. "Come on," he said, starting toward the castle. "I'm in command of the garrison of Ecclesford, just as you're in command of the garrison of Tregellas."

Ranulf fell into step beside him. "That's a bit… unexpected."

Genuine and unusual annoyance came to Henry's usually merry eyes. "Don't you think I'm capable of being in charge of a group of soldiers?"

It wasn't at all like Henry to lose his temper so quickly. "Of course you are. It's just a surprise, that's all. I seem to recall you chastising Merrick when he asked me to take over his garrison. If I recall correctly, you thought I should be insulted."

"Yes, well, I was wrong about that." Henry suddenly gave Ranulf a quizzical look. "How long have you had that beard? I nearly didn't recognize you."

Ranulf self-consciously stroked his short reddish brown beard. "A few weeks."

"Makes you look old."

"Does it? All that sweat makes you smell."

Henry barked a good-natured laugh. "I daresay it does. I promise I'll wash right away." He slid his friend a wry, sidelong glance. "I don't suppose you came all the way to Kent from Cornwall to show me your beard."

"No, I didn't," Ranulf replied. "Merrick got a letter from your brother asking about you. A friend at court sent him word that you'd gotten yourself mixed up in some trouble between Roald de Sayres and his relatives over an estate in Kent. Nicholas wanted to know if you were still at Tregellas or not."

A noncommittal "ah" was the only response Henry made before Ranulf continued. "Merrick wrote back that you had left Tregellas intending to journey to Dunkeathe. He suggested that you might have met with some kind of distraction, and then sent me looking for you to make sure you hadn't gotten into any trouble."

Henry laughed again, but there was a bitter undercurrent to the mirth. "No doubt Nicholas now imagines me lolling about in a brothel somewhere. Thank you very much, Merrick, my good friend, for giving him that idea!"

Ranulf sighed with patient forbearance. "Merrick still feels badly about what happened, Henry. And what was he supposed to do? He could hardly let your brother's letter go unanswered."

"Granted, but there was no need to send you haring after me—or does Merrick think I need a nursemaid?"

"He was worried when he got your brother's letter, and I must say, so was I. What are you about, getting mixed up with Roald de Sayres's family?"

"I'm fulfilling my obligations as a knight," Henry said, kicking a stick out of his way. "I'm coming to the aid of ladies in distress."

"We heard it's a dispute about an inheritance."

"That and other things."

"Did you know Roald's been to the king?"

"I expected that. Do you know what happened?"

Ranulf clasped his hands behind his back. "Apparently Roald and the king and queen spoke quietly together, and afterward Roald seemed rather pleased. Rumor has it he's hiring mercenaries—and not youths just out from behind a plow, either—so apparently *he* believes he has the king's support for his claim."

Henry cursed with soldierly crudity. "How long has it been since Merrick got the letter from Nicholas?"

"Three days," Ranulf answered.

"So Roald was at court…?"

"A se'ennight ago."

Henry muttered another filthy epithet and quickened his pace.

"How did you come to be involved in this at all?" Ranulf asked as he broke into a jog to keep up. "I know you hate Roald, but this is a bit extreme, isn't it?"

"Roald's trying to steal his cousins' estate and they're women. Do I have to tell you what sort of fate two women under Roald's rule might suffer?"

"These ladies…I gather neither of them are married or betrothed?"

"No—and before you assume I'm here because I have matrimonial designs upon either one of them, I don't."

Ranulf didn't reply. For one thing, he was indeed

acquainted with Roald de Sayres, at least by reputation, so he could only agree that no woman should
have him for a master.

For another, since he had on full mail, he was
getting rather winded.

WHEN A HOT, tired and sweating Ranulf entered the
hall of Ecclesford Castle after Henry, he was fairly
certain he'd discovered another reason Henry was so
keen to help these previously unknown ladies.

The woman working at some sort of embroidery
and seated near one of the windows was the loveli-
est woman Ranulf had ever seen—so lovely, the
normally self-possessed knight very nearly gasped
aloud. As she rose and walked toward them, he
realized that she was graceful and, judging by the
blush that pinked her cheeks, modest, too.

It was an intoxicating combination.

After the men bowed in greeting, Henry said,
"Lady Giselle, this is my boon companion, Sir
Ranulf, from Tregellas."

Lady Giselle held out a slender white hand.
"Welcome to Ecclesford, Sir Ranulf." Her voice was
soft and sweet, too, just as one would expect. "I'm
delighted to meet any friend of Sir Henry's. You must
stay and visit a while, if you're able."

Smiling the smile he reserved for beautiful ladies,
Ranulf took her hand and pressed a kiss upon it. Her

hand was soft, too, and cool to the touch, and as lifeless as a dead fish on a platter.

Another face came to his mind, a lively, vivacious face belonging to a young lady who talked too much—but this was hardly the time to think of Beatrice. "You are most kind, my lady."

"If you'll excuse me, I should wash and change before the evening meal," Henry said. "May I leave Ranulf in your care?"

The lady blushed again. "Of course." She gestured toward a maidservant who was hovering nearby, a well-built comely wench who hurried toward them and eyed Ranulf in a way that brought another sort of smile to his face as Henry hurried up the stairs.

GOD'S BLOOD, Henry thought as he took the steps two at a time. Why did Nicholas have to get his breeches in a knot now? He had enough on his mind without having to deal with his critical brother.

"Back so soon, Sir Henry?"

He looked up to find Mathilde on the steps above him, as calm and inscrutable as a cat.

"A visitor has arrived, my lady," he replied, going up the last few steps until he was one step below her. "My friend, Sir Ranulf, the garrison commander of Tregellas. I regret he brings bad news. Roald is indeed hiring an army, and after speaking with the king."

She swayed and, fearing she might fall, he

leaped forward and grasped her about the waist. She put her hands on his arms to steady herself—and she didn't pull away.

It was the first time he had touched her since the ale, and he was instantly alert to the feel of her soft body against his.

"Roald has the king's backing?" she asked with quiet dismay, her thoughts obviously totally occupied with Roald and the king.

"Of some kind," he replied. "From what Ranulf says, the king was subtle about it, which tells me the king isn't as committed to Roald as he might hope, or assume."

Her eyes brightened, and still she didn't pull away. "Do you know when Roald and his men will get here?"

"Soon, I fear," he answered, watching the play of worry and determination in her expression, and loving her even more.

"We'll be ready for him," he assured her, believing that with all his heart, too. "Your men are loyal and courageous, your castle provisioned for a siege. If we can't beat his men, we can hold out for a very long time."

She moved back at last, and he reluctantly let her go. Then she looked up at him—shy, vulnerable, brave and resolute. "I have faith in you, Sir Henry," she said softly. "And I cannot bear to think what might have happened if you had not agreed to help us."

Abashed, he couldn't meet her steadfast gaze. He no longer felt like a bold, proud knight, but merely like a man who hopes his beloved's trust is justified and fears that he will fail.

Mathilde reached out to caress his face. "If only we had met before Roald."

If only they had met when he had earned an estate. If only he had already proven himself worthy of such a lady.

Before he could do or say more, before he could take her in his arms and kiss her as he yearned to do, she was gone, running down the steps and leaving him alone.

As he deserved to be.

CHAPTER ELEVEN

LATER THAT NIGHT, Ranulf studied his friend in the flickering firelight as they sat near the hearth. The ladies had long since retired, and the maidservants had disappeared. Close by, several of the soldiers and male household servants had bedded down on their straw pallets, their sighs and snorts a familiar chorus. Even the dogs had given up foraging in the rushes and were sleeping, too.

During the evening meal, Henry had told Ranulf that most of the soldiers and servants here in Ecclesford were English or Celts. That was unusual, but it also meant that he and Henry could converse without being understood by those nearest them, should they awaken, and if Henry would deign to speak.

Ranulf was used to silence from Merrick; indeed, that was Merrick's natural state. Henry, however, was usually talkative and entertaining, especially after a fine meal in the company of a beautiful woman. Tonight, though, he'd barely said ten words during the evening meal.

It could be that he was so grave because Lady Giselle was not overly friendly. Perhaps whatever hopes Henry had harbored regarding the lady had been dashed, yet he still felt obliged to remain. Or perhaps that was typical behavior for her. After his first meeting with her, Ranulf reflected, she'd grown distinctly aloof toward him, too. Or maybe she was simply quiet and modest in company.

Then there was the enigmatic Lady Mathilde. Henry had described her as spirited as they washed before the evening meal, and while there was a certain mobility to her plain features, she had not been what Ranulf would call vivacious. Whatever was afoot here, he was certain Henry had no amorous intentions regarding that particular young woman, either.

"The ladies set a fine table," he finally ventured, knowing that to question Henry too bluntly might not yield the answers he sought.

Henry merely nodded, then lapsed back into his uncharacteristic silence.

Obviously, casual conversation was not going to help achieve his goal. Perhaps the thing to do was to be more direct. "When you agreed to help these ladies, did you give any thought at all to the greater ramifications?"

That got Henry's attention. "What did you say?"

"Have you given any thought at all as to how being here will affect your future?"

Henry's brow furrowed. "I care only about protecting these ladies from Roald."

One of the hounds lumbered closer to Ranulf's chair. The beast sniffed at the knight, then settled himself at Ranulf's feet.

"It's not that simple," Ranulf said, hiding his exasperation by bending down to scratch the dog behind its ears. "By involving yourself in this business, you've put yourself in danger of a charge of treason."

"Again?" Henry scoffed, straightening. "Have you gone mad?"

"If the king takes Roald's side, that's what he might call it."

"You said the king conferred with Roald in private. That hardly sounds like a firm alliance."

"Granted—but it could be. And Roald's related to the queen, as are these ladies. You've always professed to dislike and distrust Eleanor."

"So I do. The ladies' relationship with Eleanor is a distant one, much less close than that of Roald."

Ranulf stopped petting the dog and looked at his friend. "Even if there's no overt sign of enmity from the king, you do realize you'll probably never be given an estate by our sovereign after this?"

Henry slouched further down in his chair. "A knight should not concern himself with personal gain."

"I appreciate that's how it's *supposed* to be," Ranulf replied. "Knights who are already wealthy and have estates can afford to take such a high road, but you and I are not rich, nor do we possess estates—and now, it seems, you've made it doubly difficult to get one."

Henry regarded his friend with a critical expression that was new to Ranulf, although it wouldn't have been to the soldiers slumbering nearby. "I don't see you trying very hard to win one."

"Because I don't particularly care. I'm quite comfortable at Tregellas, for the time being, but you—"

"How's little Lady Bea?" Henry interrupted. "Still mooning over you?"

Ranulf's jaw clenched. "We are not talking about Lady Beatrice. We're talking about the trouble you're causing by being here."

"So I don't get an estate from the king," Henry replied with a casual shrug of his shoulders. "I've managed without one so far."

Some of Ranulf's impatience made itself manifest. "All right, then. We won't discuss how this affects you. What about Nicholas, your sister Marianne and Merrick?"

Henry frowned. "What about them?"

"If the king thinks you're against him, he may think they are, too."

The worry left Henry's face. "They can claim—quite rightly—that they had no idea where I was or what I was doing."

Ranulf's patience frayed still more at his friend's nonchalant response. "No, they didn't, and you didn't consult with them before you chose to stick your nose where it didn't belong."

Henry kicked at a log in the fire, sending a shower of sparks into the air. "I'm not a child to have to consult with anyone about what I do or where I go."

"No, you're not," Ranulf retorted. "You're a grown man who should think before he does something—a concept you apparently cannot grasp. What if the king doesn't believe they were ignorant of your involvement in this dispute?"

Henry scowled—another sign that something was amiss. "The king will believe what he believes—I can't help it if he sees conspiracies everywhere, whether they exist or not. If he was really worried about rebellion, he wouldn't listen to his wife so much."

"Hush!" Ranulf chided, looking around to make sure no one had heard that fierce denunciation.

Henry got to his feet. "I won't be quiet and I won't sit here and listen to you, my alleged friend, criticize what I do. Such fine friends I have! Merrick accuses me of being a traitor and attempting to abduct his wife, and you have all but charged me with being no better than a selfish fool."

The hall was not the place to continue this...discussion, so Ranulf grabbed Henry by the arm and pulled him into the kitchen corridor, where it was relatively private. "Let's assume you don't give a damn about your own future, or your family's or your friend's," he hissed, "and talk about the ladies. What do you think will happen if you lose against Roald?"

Ranulf held up his hand to silence Henry's potential protests. "You know as well as I that Roald is vicious, cruel, and unprincipled. He won't kill them— they're too valuable for that, but it doesn't take a seer to guess they'll suffer somehow for daring to defy him."

"It's because he's already made them suffer that I'm here," Henry retorted. "And we *won't* lose."

"Oh, so you can foresee the future? You already know how the battle will go? Damn you, Henry, you ought to know anything can happen in a battle. You could get killed or maimed. Your men might be outnumbered and overwhelmed. *Anybody* can lose. The outcome is in God's hands, not yours, and we cannot know the will of God. What about the ladies then? And the garrison? De Sayres will probably kill anybody who took arms against him."

"It can't be the will of God that we lose. Justice demands that—"

"Oh, God, Henry, listen to yourself! Justice is decided by the victors."

Henry glared at him, angry, hostile—not like the man Ranulf had known since boyhood.

"Shut your mouth and leave me alone," he growled, turning toward the hall.

Roald grabbed his friend's shoulders and pinned him to the wall. *"Why,* Henry? Why are you doing this? It's obvious Lady Giselle isn't interested—"

Henry swiftly brought up his arms to break Ranulf's hold, then shoved him across the corridor so he hit the opposite wall.

"I'm not staying here because of her," Henry snarled. "I'm staying here because I'm an honorable knight. I've told these women I'll help them, and by God, I will! So you can take yourself back to Tregellas and leave me to do what I must." His lips curled with a sneer. "And have no fear. I won't call upon you, or Merrick, or my brother to come to my aid. After all, it might be too *dangerous.*"

Just as angry, Ranulf returned his glare. "Now you'll insult me?"

"Why not?" Henry demanded, his hands balling into fists. "You've insulted me by implying my only reason for being here is greed or lust—and you've insulted me plenty of times before this. You've always treated me like I'm your jester. Here's Henry, good for some laughs. Oh, Henry said it, so of course we won't take it seriously. Pay no attention—it's only Henry."

"God's blood, Henry, you're the one who makes jokes about everything," Ranulf cried with exasperation. "I can count on the fingers of one hand the times you've been serious about anything."

"Count on this, then, Ranulf," Henry said, jabbing his friend in the chest with his forefinger. "I'm serious about staying here, and nothing you, or anybody else, can say to me is going to change that."

Ranulf knocked Henry's hand away. "You'll risk putting these ladies in more danger?"

"I'm going to protect them from Roald, even if I die doing it, so go back to Tregellas and tell Merrick not to meddle with me or my life again. Tell him to write to my brother, since they are on such good terms, and say the same to Nicholas—who was apparently so concerned about my welfare he couldn't be bothered to send a letter to me directly, but had to ask my friends what I was up to, like a gossiping old woman."

"It's clearly useless to try to talk some sense into you," Ranulf said, turning on his heel.

"If by sense you mean abandoning the ladies of Ecclesford and leaving them to the tender mercies of Roald de Sayres, yes, it is."

Ranulf paused at the end of the corridor and turned back to look at a man he no longer recognized. "I'll leave at first light."

"Good!"

AFTER RANULF left him without another word, Henry slumped back against the wall, panting like a wounded animal.

Leave Mathilde to face Roald without him? Never,

as long as he lived, and regardless of any problems it brought him. Nicholas, Marianne's husband and Merrick could all look after themselves; he must and would protect Mathilde.

WHEN MATHILDE entered the hall the next morning shortly before dawn, yawning after another restless night, haunted by both desire and regret that she hadn't kissed Henry on the stairs, she was surprised to find Sir Ranulf not just up and about, but dressed as if he was preparing to leave Ecclesford that very day. Not even all the men of the household were awake, and the only servants already about their daily duties were those in the kitchen.

"Good morning, Sir Ranulf," she said when he saw her and acknowledged her presence with a bow. "You're not thinking of leaving us so soon?"

She tried to keep any hope from her voice, but in truth she found this redheaded man and his shrewd gaze as unsettling as the news he'd brought about Roald. He made her feel as if he could ferret out all her secrets, all her most private hopes and fears, simply by looking at her long enough.

"Alas, my lady, I must," he replied. "My duties summon me back to Tregellas."

"Then I hope the weather holds," she said, continuing to make polite conversation. "Sir Henry will surely be sorry you couldn't stay with us longer."

Sir Ranulf smiled, but there was no joy in his eyes. "I'm sure he'll understand why I couldn't stay."

She caught an undercurrent of bitterness in the man's voice. Last night she'd noticed Henry's constraint and wondered what was wrong. He'd spoken of Sir Ranulf many times, and always as a friend, but they hadn't seemed very friendly. "My sister will be sorry you left before she was able to say goodbye."

That brought a wry gleam to Sir Ranulf's hazel eyes. "Will she?"

"Any friend of Sir Henry's is a friend to us as well."

Sir Ranulf glanced at the steps leading to the bedchambers. Was he looking for Giselle? Then he turned back to her and fixed his steadfast gaze upon her. "My lady, may I have a private word with you before I go? About Henry?"

Her curiosity and dread instantly aroused, she wondered if it had been Henry he'd been looking for—and hoping to avoid? "Of course. We can speak in the solar."

Once there, not a little worried by Sir Ranulf's request and his mysterious manner, she lit the candles in the tall iron stand near the window shuttered with linen to keep out the wind. As the candles flicked to brightness, she nodded at a chair. "Please sit down."

He did, and when she had, too, he again regarded her with his shrewd and discomfiting gaze. "My lady, how did you meet Henry?"

She hadn't been expecting that question and hesitated to answer. What would he think if she told him the truth?

She decided to give him part of it. "He was staying at a nearby inn, and as we had need of a knight to help us defend our home from our cousin, we sought him out and asked him to assist us."

"He understood exactly why you wanted his aid, and against whom?" Sir Ranulf asked.

"Yes," she replied.

Sir Ranulf put his elbows on his knees, clasped his hands and leaned closer. "Did *you* understand exactly what you were asking of him?"

She shifted and tried to maintain her dignified poise. "I don't know what you mean."

"No one here seems to have considered the broader consequences for Henry or his family or his friends if he helped you, including Henry. I can appreciate that you found yourself in dire circumstances, my lady, but Henry is not so powerful that he can risk the king's enmity. And even if Henry wins a battle against Roald and secures you your inheritance, his life may be endangered in other ways. His chances for an estate could be seriously compromised, as well.

"More, his brother could be drawn into this dispute because he has some influence, and he *will* use it if he thinks Henry is in danger. So might his sister, who loves Henry dearly.

"And then there is the lord of Tregellas, a good friend and ally to the king's brother, the earl of Cornwall. The king may see a conspiracy involving us all."

In truth, Mathilde had not considered all these things, but she resented this man's implication that she had blithely ignored the risks to Henry. She hadn't...exactly. "No one forced his hand, Sir Ranulf. It was his decision to come here, because he's a knight sworn to protect ladies. I admit I didn't think of everything that it might mean for Sir Henry, but what would you have had me do? Turn Ecclesford over to Roald and hope that he would be merciful?"

Yet even as she spoke, guilt and remorse— feelings with which she was all too familiar—washed over her. She had told herself...convinced herself... that there would be no risk of any kind to Henry, even while knowing deep inside that any knight who came to their aid would anger Roald and perhaps face the queen's wrath, too.

As subtle as the passage of the sun from dawn to dusk, Ranulf's attitude shifted from interrogator to sympathetic counselor. "Tell me, my lady, are you really willing to let him die or ruin his life for you? For his sake, and that of his family and friends, I ask you to tell him to go."

Did this man, this stranger, have any idea what he was really asking of her? "We need him."

"No, you don't, my lady," Sir Ranulf replied evenly, as if this was not a matter of life and death, sorrow and suffering. "You can leave this castle, seek sanctuary and fight for your rights through the law."

Who was this man to tell her what to do, especially when she had tried to avoid a battle every way she could, except surrender?

She rose and faced him squarely. "Roald brings the battle, not me. And if Henry wants to leave here, I will not try to stop him. But you should be proud to have such a friend, a man of honor and chivalry, and not seek to turn him into a selfish coward."

"What in God's name are you doing, Ranulf?" Henry demanded.

They both turned to see him on the threshold of the solar, his hands braced against the door frame as if he would forcefully widen the door.

Henry had never been more angry in his life, except once: when he had learned what Roald had done to Mathilde. Now, as then, fury engulfed him. Rage burned within him because this man whom he had considered a friend had presumed to chastise him like a child, then had the gall to go behind his back and upset Mathilde. Despite her glorious, courageous defiance, he could see her distress in the lines of concern in her brow and in the depths of her beautiful eyes.

"Why are you still here, Ranulf?" he demanded,

letting go of the frame and walking into the room. "Are you seeking to destroy what reputation I have left after Merrick called me Judas and nearly killed me?"

"I'm *trying* to prevent you from making the worst mistake of your life," Ranulf replied, getting to his feet.

"How kind—but you're no paragon of virtue. Your own family cast you off, or have you conveniently forgotten that?"

Ranulf flushed, and equal anger appeared in his hazel eyes. Henry knew he had struck a low blow, but he didn't care. Ranulf had struck an even lower blow by going behind his back to Mathilde.

"What happened to me in the past is not important," Ranulf said through clenched teeth. "I'm more concerned with what you're doing right now, and what it could mean for you, your family and your friends, although you don't seem to give a damn. Nicholas may be in Scotland, but the king's reach is long, and the queen's even longer. What about your sister? What about Merrick? Do you care less about them than you do about two ladies you didn't even know until a few weeks ago?"

Henry's eyes darted to Mathilde, her face pale, her eyes full of pain—but her back was straight, her gaze steady as she stood there, watching them. "I will not abandon the ladies of Ecclesford."

The church bells rang—three times and then a pause, and then three more.

"What?" Ranulf demanded, his gaze darting from Henry to Mathilde as they exchanged troubled looks. "What does that mean?"

"It means, my *friend,*" Henry said with scornful gravity, "that Roald has come back. If you're going to run home to Tregellas, you'd better make haste."

"Are *you* leaving?"

"Not until Roald is defeated or dead."

Ranulf fixed a resolute gaze on Henry. "Then neither am I. As you were so good to point out, my family has cast me off, so there's no risk to them if I stay, and thanks to you, Merrick's already entangled in this dispute. And *I* do not forget that we're sworn brothers-in-arms."

"We don't need your help," Henry said.

"A fighting force should never shun an extra man, Sir Leonard always used to say."

"I don't think—"

Mathilde stepped between them. With Ecclesford and the safety of her sister and her people at stake, she wasn't above asking for any help she could get. "If you wish to stay, Sir Ranulf, my sister, my men and I will be grateful for your aid."

His eyes bright with victory, Sir Ranulf's mouth curved up in a grin that made him look more foxlike than ever while he bowed as gracefully as any courtier to Mathilde. "Then I shall gladly stay. Use me as you will, my lady. I am yours to command."

CHAPTER TWELVE

THE COURTYARD was chaos. Wagons and carts and people seeking refuge in the castle crowded in through the gate. Chickens squawked and flapped their wings, geese honked, dogs barked and cows lowed as they were reluctantly led toward the stables.

When they reached the wall walk, Mathilde saw that Giselle and Cerdic were already there, side by side, their shoulders touching, as they looked out to the road leading to the village. She wordlessly followed their gaze beyond the walls, to see a steady stream of people and animals coming to the castle, and in the distance, Roald's army, his banner flapping in the cold October wind.

Shivering, she wrapped her arms about herself. She wasn't just cold from the biting wind; judging by the dawn light glinting on metal, Roald had brought many more men than she had dreamed even in her worst nightmares.

"How many do you make it?" Henry asked Ranulf, echoing her own thoughts, and as if he and his friend hadn't been nearly at each other's throats only a few moments ago.

"Two hundred at least," Ranulf grimly replied. "Where there's the chance for loot, one can always raise an army."

Feeling sickened, for she could guess the sort of army this would be, Mathilde clasped her hands and prayed all her people would reach the castle in time. Then she prayed that once there, all would be safe.

As Roald and his army came closer and they could distinguish the arms and armor of his men, Henry swore under his breath. "The big brute beside Roald wearing that plumed helmet," he said to Ranulf. "Is that who I think it is?"

Ranulf followed Henry's pointing finger, then hissed like a snake, and cursed, too.

"Who? Who is it?" Mathilde demanded, alarmed by their reaction.

Henry gave her a smile, yet his eyes betrayed a tension that had been absent before. "I didn't mean to frighten you. And I probably shouldn't be so surprised to see Charles De Mallemaison with Roald."

"Who is Charles De Mallemaison?" she asked.

"A mercenary," Henry said with a shrug and turning his attention back to the road, as if that was of no great import.

"A notorious one," Ranulf added. "I wouldn't have thought Roald could afford him. No doubt the rest of those men are thieves and murderers when they're not fighting for pay."

As Henry darted him a sharp and critical glance, Mathilde's blood ran cold. Out of the corner of her eye, she saw Giselle slip her hand into Cerdic's and wished she'd kept quiet, except that they should know the kind of force they faced. Giselle was no child, and Cerdic might one day be the lord of Ecclesford.

If they defeated Roald and this army he'd bought.

God help her, she had so hoped it would not come to this! She had hoped Roald would back off, unwilling to risk a battle. Then she hoped she could count on the church, only to discover that the man she thought would support their claim was far from honest.

So many mistakes. How many more would she make before this was over and how many more would have to suffer for her errors?

Henry must have seen her dismay, for he gave her a more encouraging smile, and confidence returned to his features. "It doesn't matter who those men are or what they've done. Our soldiers can beat thieves and murderers, who fight for themselves alone and don't take orders very well—something Roald likely didn't consider."

"He never trained with Sir Leonard," Sir Ranulf said, as if this were a serious detriment to success. Then he, too, smiled.

"Of course we'll win," Cerdic declared, coming

closer. "We can beat any rabble Roald brings against us."

"Naturally," Sir Ranulf coolly agreed, "especially now that I'm here to help you."

Mathilde couldn't tell if Sir Ranulf was serious or not, and neither, obviously, could Giselle, for her sister stepped forward and demanded of Henry, "Cerdic is still second-in-command, is he not?"

Cerdic stood proudly at attention. "As long as we win, it matters not to me whether I am second-in-command or not."

Sir Ranulf swiftly put up his hands as if to push away any bad feeling. "I have no wish to take any kind of command here. Henry can treat me as merely another soldier."

"Ladies of Ecclesford!" Roald shouted from the other side of the dry moat.

At the sound of his detested voice, Mathilde went to the edge of the battlement, stepping into the embrasure between two merlons so that Roald could see her, until Henry unceremoniously pushed her behind one of the them. "Have a care, Mathilde. He's probably got archers training their arrows on you right now."

She hadn't thought of that.

"Why so quiet, Mathilde?" Roald called out. "Surely you're not surprised to see me again. I told you I'd come back, and so I have, except that now

I've got the support of the king and an army at my back. Show some sense, Mathilde, and end this now. Open the gates and let me and my men enter. Surrender peacefully, and no one will be hurt."

As if anyone in Ecclesford would believe him, especially her. "You tricked me once, Roald," she called back. "Never again. In spite of the army you've somehow managed to raise, you have no hope of taking Ecclesford."

"You've got a bunch of poorly trained foot soldiers and a castle full of frightened villagers. You don't stand a chance against my men."

"I would put any one of my soldiers against any of that rabble you've bought," she declared. "The only way you will ever get inside this castle again, Roald, is if you're carried in on a plank, dead. Tell that to your men, especially that brute who sits at your horse's ass."

"Mathilde!" Giselle gasped, while the three men beside her burst out laughing.

She glanced at her sister. "De Mallemaison *is* sitting at his horse's ass."

"You stupid slut!" Roald roared. "You'll pay for that, and every other insult! You'll be sorry you denied me my rights! I'll make you beg my forgiveness on your knees!"

Henry grabbed a bit of loose stone, drew back his arm and launched it through the air. They could hear the clang as it hit Roald's shining helmet.

"God's blood!" he bellowed. "You dishonorable—"

"I'm only sorry it wasn't a spear," Henry loudly interrupted. "I used to throw stones at the birds that threatened the crops when I was a boy. It seems I haven't lost the skill."

"I'm going to kill you myself!"

"You're welcome to try," Henry replied. "And then, De Mallemaison, I'll be looking for *you*."

Charles De Mallemaison raised his visor and Mathilde saw a face that belonged in a nightmare.

"With pleasure, Sir Henry," he returned, bowing in his saddle. "I owe your brother some recompense for this scar on my face. Your body will do nicely. That blond beauty's body will do for something else."

Giselle blanched, then closed her eyes.

Mathilde went to her sister. "Giselle, are you—"

Holding tight to Cerdic, Giselle opened her eyes, which blazed with a fierce rancor. "I'm not going to faint, Mathilde. I was praying that God would strike him dead."

"If He doesn't, I will," Cerdic vowed. "You are not to kill that one, Henry. He will be for me."

"Alas, my friend, I can't promise that. If I get the chance, he dies by my hand."

"No," Cerdic replied. "I want—"

"Let me in, Mathilde!" Roald shouted, interrupting their dispute. "Let me in or by God I'll hang you from the walls!"

"Go away, Roald," she called back. "I will never let you in. I will die first."

Giselle stepped forward and shouted over the battlements, "And I would kill myself before I let your toady touch me!"

De Mallemaison laughed, but Roald's face was red as a cardinal's robes as he wheeled his horse with such a hard yank, it sat back on its haunches. He rode away through his lines of men, followed at a slower pace by De Mallemaison.

One thing was certain, Mathilde vowed as she watched. Neither she nor Giselle would be unarmed if the castle walls were breeched. She would die fighting rather than let Roald or his men touch them.

"Now, Henry, I assume you've got some sort of a plan?" Sir Ranulf asked, sounding for all the world as if he were talking about a feast.

Henry nodded and clapped his arm on his friend's shoulder. "A rudimentary one. I'm sure you'll say it needs improving and you're just the man to tell me how. Cerdic, you come, too. I've thought of a task for a few of our best men. Ladies, will you join us?"

Mathilde had been wondering if he'd forgotten them.

Giselle shook her head. "I must see that my medicines and bandages are prepared, in case they're needed."

"I will leave the battle plans to the soldiers," Mathilde said. "I should see that all have found accommodation."

"Until later, then," Henry replied. "Now come along, my friends. We have a battle to plan, and I daresay Roald will attack upon the morrow. The man lacks any kind of patience—or intelligence."

THAT NIGHT, Mathilde stood by the window in her bedchamber, looking at the surrounding land and the small, bright fires in the enemy's camp. Some of the buildings in the village had obviously been occupied, and occasionally raucous voices shouting and singing told her that they'd found the tavern and the wine and ale the tavern keeper had optimistically left behind.

She wondered if the tavern keeper heard them, too, and was sorry he'd abandoned his stock. On the other hand, he'd probably heard about the nature of Roald's army and wasn't sorry he was safely in the castle. Word had spread from the soldiers on the wall to the villagers inside of the type of force in control of the village, and she had had to reassure them all that neither Sir Henry, nor Cerdic, nor Sir Ranulf thought this fortress could be conquered.

It had been easy to say that at the time, and she'd believed it, but now, when she stood awake and alone in the dark, with her slumbering sister nearby and Roald's army outside the gates…now she feared she had been wrong to oppose her cousin. Wrong to insist they should fight him. Wrong to put her sister, her people and Henry, his friends and his family at risk. Perhaps she should have surrendered. As Sir Ranulf had said, she and Giselle could have sought sanctuary at a convent until the matter of the inheritance was decided. They could have abandoned their home.

What of Henry? Did he regret agreeing to help them? Was he awake and pacing in his chamber, cursing himself for a fool and wishing there was an honorable way he could extricate himself?

He had not given a hint of any such doubts either on the wall walk or later, as they ate the evening meal, blessed by Father Thomas, in the crowded hall. He had seemed more anxious to have the battle begin, the sooner to have a victory. Indeed, he had been excited, almost…passionate…in his anticipation.

Was he too excited to sleep? Had he even tried to rest?

He would need to be rested if he wasn't to be hurt or killed during the battle.

Surely he would not actually be *in* the battle. He was to direct her men and that would keep him out of danger.

Except that he hated Roald so much, might he not be tempted to seek him out and fight him? And if he did, and he was tired from lack of sleep....

She drew her bedrobe over her shift, belting it loosely with her girdle, then went to her sister's medicine box resting on the table. Giselle had a potion that made it easier to sleep; she'd offered it to Mathilde more than once after Roald had attacked her. At first, she'd accepted it, although even it couldn't keep the dreams at bay.

She reached into the box and found the small jar covered with waxed cloth. She lifted it and sniffed the contents. A familiar scent of poppies filled her nostrils. Yes, this was the one.

Taking it, she went to the door and quietly eased down the latch and opened it. Just as she'd suspected, a dim light shone from beneath the door of Henry's chamber. She would offer the potion to him, tell him how much to take, then return to her bedchamber and her restless vigil. She would not enter Henry's chamber and she would knock softly on his door in case she was wrong and he was already asleep.

Holding the jar, she crept quietly down the corridor. Once outside Henry's door, she hesitated, but only for a moment before she carried out her plan.

Despite the quietness of her knock, the door opened in an instant to reveal Henry on the threshold, clad in his breeches and an unbelted, open-necked shirt, his feet bare. "Have they attacked?" he demanded, her gaze anxiously searching her face.

She shook her head. "No. I feared you couldn't sleep and came to give you this."

He glanced down at the sealed vessel she held out to him. "What is it?"

"Giselle makes it from poppies. It will help you sleep."

"I notice you're still awake."

"I won't be leading men into battle tomorrow."

He shook his head. "I thank you, but it would take a heavy dose to make me sleep, and I would be sluggish come the dawn. If you really want to help me, keep me company awhile." He opened the door wider.

She hesitated. She had on only a shift and bedrobe; he was clad in breeches and a shirt loose and unlaced, exposing his muscular chest.

His brow furrowed. "I merely wish to talk, my lady. Nothing more, I promise you."

If only he knew the yearning coursing through her now, he would realize this was no simple request. Yet how could she deny him when he asked so little of her in return for all his help?

She forced her feet across the threshold and into his chamber. In the corner, a round stand with twenty candles lit the room. A heel of bread was on the table, along with a goblet and carafe for wine. His chain mail lay spread out upon the bed, his helmet gleaming dully beside it.

"I was checking my mail for tears or bent links," he explained as she came farther into the room. "Sir Leonard impressed upon us that it was best for us to check ourselves, since our lives could be at risk if our mail was damaged."

Suddenly she saw, with her mind's eye, not Roald's mocking face that usually intruded unwelcome into her waking thoughts, but Henry's handsome visage, wide-eyed with pain as he fell on the battlefield.

She put the jar on the table and spoke without looking at him. "Your life shouldn't be at risk." She clasped her hands and faced him. "You must stay out of the fighting. You must not be hurt or killed."

"Although there are those who would surely curse me for admitting this—minstrels and troubadors, especially—I have no intention of being hurt, or dying, for that matter. I plan to be very much alive when we claim the victory."

His cheerfully spoken admission acted like a balm to her heart, and when he gestured at the chair beside the table near the arched window, she wrapped her bedrobe more tightly about her and lowered herself onto the seat. He sat on the end of the bed, causing the ropes under the featherbed to creak.

"I hope you're not letting Ranulf's worries about

possible consequences upset you, too," he remarked. "Believe me, if Merrick and Nicholas and my sister say I acted without their knowledge, most people will believe it."

"Yet I'm troubled to think that helping us has made for difficulties between you and your family and friends."

Henry crossed one leg so that his ankle rested on his knee, then clasped his hands around his knee. "Oh, you need not concern yourself with that. I see little of my sister, who is busy with her husband and family, and my brother and I have never seen eye-to-eye. Indeed, he's more like a critical parent than a brother, given that he's many years older than I. As for Merrick…"

He put his foot down on the floor and stared off into the distance, as if he were no longer in that chamber at all. "It took very little to convince him that I'd betrayed him. I was imprisoned in the dungeon of Tintagel, where he beat me and told me I was going to be executed as a traitor."

He rose and crossed to the window, and began to toy with the edge of the linen shutter.

"If you would rather not speak about it," she said gently, "I understand."

He turned back. "I think you, of all people, *can* understand how betrayed I felt, how upset and lost. You can comprehend my misery and shame."

She nodded, her heart aching for him, knowing the

agony he had felt, and still lived with every day. Some days would be worse than others, but those memories and the hurt was always there, haunting waking hours as well as sleep.

"Every moment I was in that hellhole, I was in pain and despair, afraid every sound, every footfall, meant I was about to die." He ran his hand through his hair. "Even now, at night or when I smell damp stone, the fear and anguish and panic returns."

Oh, yes, she understood that, too. She knew how the memories could come, strong, unbidden, horrifying, like an ambush in your mind.

He made a helpless gesture at the candlestand bright with little flickering flames, and then a sad, self-mocking little smile. "I'm even afraid to be alone in the dark."

How could she not love him, this man who could be so strong, so confident, in spite of the secret terrors he fought every day and every night? How could she not admire his ability to still find room for humor and good cheer in his life?

She rose and went to him, wanting to embrace him, yet still fearful she might unleash the overwhelming power of her desire. And what then? What then for her, for him?

"I'm afraid of the dark, too," she admitted. "And in the day, the memories of Roald and what he did come back to me, too, like a sudden slap."

"I'm so sorry, Mathilde."

"As I am for you," she whispered as she reached up and caressed his stubbled cheek. "I don't want you to die for me, Henry. I want you to leave here."

His hand covered hers and he shook his head, his steadfast gaze resolute. "If I do die, I die as a knight should, with honor, chivalrously defending the lady I love."

She cupped his face, willing him to listen and understand. "I know you're a brave, good and honorable man. I know you will fight for us to the very death—but I couldn't bear it if that happened. I have been the cause of so much trouble, so much sorrow. If I had your death on my conscience, it would be too much." She dropped her hands to her sides. "Please go, Henry," she urged, meaning it with every fiber of her being. "Now. Tonight."

As determined as she had ever been, he shook his head. "I can't, Mathilde. I can't leave you and the others to face Charles De Mallemaison and that horde of cutthroats." He caressed her cheek, her chin. "Your men are ready for this. I don't doubt but that we'll win. And I'm here because I *want* to be. Never forget that." He tilted her chin so that she was looking directly into his dark, questioning eyes. "Will you promise me you'll not forget that?"

"I'll try," was all she trusted herself to say.

"Because I love you."

She shook her head. "No, you can't. It's impossible," she whispered, telling herself it must be so. He couldn't mean it, not after—

"You think I don't know my own heart, Mathilde?" he asked gently.

"I think you are good and kind and—"

"And stupid, that I don't know what it is I feel?"

"No, I'm sorry, I didn't mean…"

He took hold of her hands. "I do know what I feel for you, Mathilde, and that it's no mistake. Don't you think it's possible for me to love a woman whose determination and strength are more beautiful than any form or feature? That I can admire and desire a woman as brave as any knight, as shrewd as any scholar, yet whose kisses stir such a longing in me, I am nearly dizzy? Rather ask, how could I not?"

Her lips parted to try to protest again, to tell him he should go, but instead, she obeyed the command of her heart, and raised herself on her toes and kissed him. Oh, how she kissed him! With all the fervent passion she'd been trying to imprison and ignore.

This might be the last time they could be together. There might be only this night to be with him as she yearned to be. To give him her body as well as her heart. And she would. By all the saints, she would.

Yet even as Henry held her close, returning her kiss with heated ardor, she felt him holding back. She guessed he was concerned for her, afraid to upset her as he had the night of the ale, when she'd run away like a frightened girl.

She had been frightened, but not of him. She'd been afraid of the strength of her feelings, realizing that what she'd thought was love for Roald was but a pale shadow of what she felt for Henry.

Memories of Roald, the panic at being in a man's arms, threatened to return, but she willed them back. This was Henry. Henry, her beloved. Henry, who might die for her.

She would allow no other shadows to darken her thoughts, no other man's face to enter her mind. There was only *this* night. *This* chamber. *This* man.

No other man, no other night. No other kiss.

She eagerly leaned into Henry, pressing her body against his and gazed up into his desire-darkened eyes. "Make love with me, Henry, please," she pleaded in a whisper. "I want you so much."

He pulled away. "No, Mathilde. I can't. I won't."

As she stared at him with dismay, Henry's face clouded with anguish and remorse. "God's blood, I *want* to be with you. There's only one thing that I want more—something that is impossible, and because it is impossible, I have to let you go tonight." He stepped back. "I cannot offer you marriage, Mathilde."

Marriage? She'd had no thoughts, no hopes of marrying him. He should marry an unsoiled woman, untainted by another man's touch. "I've said nothing of marriage."

His brows furrowed with confusion, then rose as comprehension dawned. "You would make love with me with no promise of marriage?"

"Yes. You deserve a better bride than—"

"Oh, Mathilde, my love, my love!" he cried, pulling her into a tender embrace. "You misunderstood. Dear God, that's not it all."

Scarcely daring to hope, she drew back to search his face, his eyes, seeking the truth.

"It's I who am not worthy of *you.* I'm a knight with no estate, no wealth, no home. I have nothing to offer you."

"Nothing?" she repeated incredulously. "You call yourself nothing?"

"What am I but a merry gadabout with some skills and amusing stories?" he replied, very real torment in his confession.

She put her hands on his broad, strong shoulders. "You are not nothing, Henry. You are the man who made me feel whole again when I thought I was forever destroyed by what happened with Roald. You brought laughter and joy into my dark days. You make me feel safe. You gave me back desire. You are the man I love, Henry, with all my heart."

"You mean that?" he murmured as if he was afraid to believe it. "You love me?"

"I love you, unworthy as I am—"

He stopped her with a kiss. "What happened with Roald was not your fault," he whispered as he pressed light kisses on her lips and cheeks and chin. "He stole from you one thing, and that's all. He thought he could conquer you, but you are made of sterner stuff." His wonderful, joyful smile blossomed on his face. "And I am no virgin myself."

Nobody else could make her feel as he did, could take the burden from her as he did with one look, one smile, and the perfect words. When she was with him, she was Mathilde as she used to be, before Roald had ever come here.

"Nor should you worry about money or an estate," she said, happiness and excitement stealing over her in equal measure as he held her in his arms. "When we wed, I shall bring both as my dowry." The old dread appeared at the edge of her optimistic joy. "*If* we wed."

"Oh, it will be when, Mathilde. I want to marry you more than I've ever wanted anything. I want you as I have never wanted a woman. I need you as I never thought I'd need anyone." He went down on one knee and took her hand in his. "I've always vowed I would love my wife when I wed, and never until now have I found such a love. Although I don't deserve you, will you do me this honor, Mathilde? Will you marry me?"

Her heart soared as she pulled him to his feet. "I

should not accept. You could do better—but oh, Henry, I am too weak to say no!"

His smile was beyond glorious as he gathered her into his arms. "Weak? Not you. Never you, my love. You are many things, but weak is not one of them."

He kissed her tenderly, and then with growing passion.

"Make love with me now, Henry, please," she pleaded as his lips left hers to trail along her cheek.

He stopped and pulled back, a shadow in his eyes. "No man can say what might happen during a battle, and while I have confidence in our men and our plan, something may go wrong. I could be killed, and if I leave you with a child—"

"Nothing would give me more joy," she said, meaning it. "I would be *proud* to be the mother of your child, whether we are married or not. As for anything else, the world already knows my shame. What more can people say about me that has not already been said?"

She watched him struggle, as she had so often struggled to keep back the black memories.

"Please, Henry," she whispered, running her hands over his chest as she'd dreamed of doing, marveling at his strength and his ability to temper it. To be as tender as a youth in the throes of first love, and then as fierce as one of the Northmen of old. "Please, don't send me away tonight."

CHAPTER THIRTEEN

WITH A GROAN that was part desire and part surrender, Henry tugged Mathilde back into his arms and kissed her fervently.

Thrilled, delighted, she relaxed into him, giving herself over to the pleasure and excitement, liberating herself from worry and care, guilt and remorse. She might have only tonight to give herself to Henry, to live a lifetime with the man she loved, and God save her, how she would!

Eagerly her hands moved over his back, feeling the hard muscles shifting. He held her close and he began his own exploration while she slowly insinuated her hands beneath his shirt.

Her palms brushed over the uneven terrain of his warm skin, the myriad small scars that spoke of past hurts. She lifted his shirt over his head and let it fall on the floor in a puddle of white linen while she surveyed Henry's naked chest. There were scars here, too, some red, some white, and holding his upper arms, she bent to press a kiss on each one. He moaned softly, the sound enflaming her more as she brushed her lips over his slightly salty flesh.

She drew closer to the dark circle of one of his nipples. The dark hairs surrounding it tickled her nose. She reached up to scratch, and he laughed, bending down to kiss her forehead, then her brows, and then her eyelids as she closed them. Her cheek, her jaw and finally, lightly, her lips, as his hands parted her bedrobe and glided around her waist, pulling her back against him.

She could feel his aroused shaft through her shift and his breeches. She tensed, and the panic threatened…

"If you want to stop, my love," Henry whispered, holding her loosely, "we'll stop."

Determined not to surrender to the fear, she gave a little shake of her head. "Kiss me," she whispered. "Kiss me and make love with me and help me forget."

"I will try," Henry softly promised. "As I love you, I will try."

He loved her. He loved her, and his touch was light, gentle, exciting, thrilling. His lips brushed across hers as soft as velvet.

Too soft, for she felt his restraint. Although she loved him for his selflessness, she sought to unleash the passion he was keeping in check. She must, or he might forever treat her as fragile, afraid to express his desire freely. Constrained. Imprisoned. She would not have him a slave to fear, as she had been.

So she tugged him close and slid her tongue between his parted lips. With new urgency, she gave her own passion free rein, and surrendered fully to the desire surging through her body.

Sensing the change in her, the need, the desperate longing, Henry finally accepted that she truly wanted him to love her tonight. That even if she could not quite subdue her fear, she trusted him enough to let him make love with her.

Free of the dread that she was asking more for his sake than her own, he stopped worrying and gave himself up to enjoy what he'd been imagining since the day he'd met her.

But even so, and although his fervor increased with every moment, he was aware that he must not be too rough, too forceful.

So he didn't sweep her into his arms and carry her to the bed. He didn't do anything except kiss her for a time. Only when he was sure she felt safe and fully at ease did he slide the bedrobe from her shoulders and gathered her to him, feeling her warm flesh through her thin white shift. And her taut nipples brushing against his naked chest.

He broke the kiss and took her hand to lead her to the bed. He turned to blow out the candles, but she put her hand on his shoulder to stop him. "I want to see you. Your face. Your body."

He smiled, relieved and delighted by the boldness of her request. "I want to see yours, if you're willing."

Her hands trembled as they went to the tie of her shift; nevertheless, she undid the knot and loosened the drawstring. She pushed her shift down past her perfect breasts and wiggled her narrow hips until it fell to the floor. Then she blushed, shy as any maiden, in spite of her unabashed action.

How could any man not love her, respect her, admire her and want nothing but the best for her? How could Roald have—

Roald could wait till morning, and it would be his last morning. Tonight was for Mathilde.

Henry cupped her smooth shoulders and ran his hands down her slender arms, gazing at her body. "You are perfect, Mathilde. Perfect."

Her blush extended nearly to her nipples. "I know I'm not beautiful."

He raised his eyes and said with all sincerity, "You are the most beautiful woman in the world to me, and you always will be. Yours is the beauty that can never fade or diminish, because it shines from within." Then he smiled as only Henry could, making her heartbeat race and her blood throb. "And I must confess, it pleases me to think so many men are blind to it."

Her hands stole around his waist. "I think you were blind to it when first we met."

"Unfair, my lady! You surprised me when first we met. You had me at a disadvantage."

"You surprised me by grabbing me and pulling me down onto your bed."

He kissed the tip of her nose. "You should be glad I didn't grab my sword."

She kissed his chin. "You might have done yourself an injury, naked as you were."

"And then we would not be here, like this…."

His voice trailed off as he bent again to kiss her, more passionately this time as excitement overcame them, and he eased her back onto the bed.

"If you hadn't agreed to help us, we would not be here, like this," she murmured, smiling just as he'd imagined while she entwined her arms about his neck.

He shifted her until her head was on the pillows upon which he'd tossed and turned every night that he'd been here, at first because of his terrible memories and the nightmares they engendered, and then because he could not sleep for thinking of Mathilde.

Lying on his side beside her, resting his weight on one arm while he encircled her with the other, he kissed her first on her lips, then the curve of her jaw, then along the smooth column of her neck. Meanwhile, her fingertips brushed across his shoulders and his naked back. He sidled lower, kissing and licking lightly, arousing her slowly, gently, with tenderness, listening to the soft catch of her breath and making certain it was only pleasure that he heard.

Anything else, any fear or pain, he would stop and wait…but he heard nothing except encouragement and counted himself blessed.

He reached her nipples, the pink tips crowning the rounded peak. He swirled his tongue around the hardened nub, licking with slight pressure as she moaned softly and arched her back. As he pleasured first one, then the other, he caressed her thighs, moving slowly upward, toward the place where they met. Gently, cautiously, as she squirmed and sighed, he skimmed the milky white skin with his palm, first up, then back a bit, then up a little more, teasing with all the patience he could muster even as his shaft swelled and pushed against the confines of his breeches. Only when she was ready would he strip them off. Only when he could wait no longer would he take her, and then only if she was still willing.

Up again and down he moved his hand, as she instinctively spread her legs open to his touch. Then up again and down once more before he moved his hand up over her stomach. He thrilled to hear a little sound of disappointment breaking in her throat.

But he wouldn't enter her yet. Not until he was certain she was moist and relaxed, anxious for him and not afraid.

If he was patient, if he took his time and made

certain, she should feel no pain. Pain was what that lout Roald had given her; he would give her only pleasure, as well as the choice as to whether or not they continued until the zenith, or stopped when she willed.

He rose to kiss her mouth again, his hands stroking her flat belly. How eagerly she locked her lips to his and accepted his tongue into her mouth!

And then she was stroking his chest, lightly, teasing his body to new heights of tense expectation. Her fingertips swept over his stomach, then up to his nipple, making him gasp while they kissed.

He could not wait…he must wait. She must be ready, and willing.

He gently fondled her breasts before he again bent to use his mouth and tongue. She whimpered with need, arching again to meet his lips. He pushed with gentle pressure on the rise below her navel before ever so carefully sliding his hand lower, seeking the moistness that would tell him she was ready.

To his relief and delight, she was—or nearly. He took her mouth again with passionate need and shifted, moving until he was between her legs.

He felt her stiffen then, and her eyes opened wide, dazed and frightened, too. Disappointment swept through him and his ardor began to cool, until she focused on his eyes, and smiled.

"Mathilde?" he whispered softly.

"I want you to love me, Henry," she answered,

tucking a lock of hair behind his ear. "I am willing and not afraid. I trust you. I love you."

Looking at her, there could be no doubt that she meant what she said.

Loving her, cherishing her, desiring her, he sat back on his heels and undid the drawstring of his breeches. Then, to his surprise, she sat up and put her hands on his waist. For a moment, he wondered if she had changed her mind, but instead of asking him to go no further, her voice dropped to a sultry, incredibly arousing whisper. "Let me help. I would have you naked as I am."

Henry moved off the bed and stripped off his breeches. "With pleasure, my lady."

Mathilde didn't look away. She studied his face, the planes made more striking by the play of candlelight that made his skin glow bronze. His long hair that made him seem like a warrior of old, in the days when the Gauls were ruled by the Romans. His muscular body....

She looked up at his face. His loving, lovely face. Then she rose on her knees and reached out for him, bringing him back onto the bed with her. Where he would love her. Where he would take her not with force and brutality and pain, but with love and tenderness.

She was ready for him. Ready for his love. Ready for everything as he kissed and stroked her, exciting her and making her pulse race.

He positioned himself between her legs and kissing her deeply, he gave one small push.

Instinct told her to clamp shut. To push her legs together. To protect herself. Her heart overruled that momentary panic and reminded her this was not Roald, but Henry, the man she loved, and who loved her.

The fear drained away as he paused, and she opened to him, encouraging him. Wanting him. Needing him.

Then he pushed again, more deeply, easily, without pain.

Without pain. Sweet heaven, without pain!

His bottom lip clenched between his teeth, he thrust again.

Was he holding back for her?

He must not. The worst—if worst it could be called—was over and it had not hurt. Now there was only a glorious, wonderful fullness, his body joined with hers. This was no invasion, no taking of her worth. This was giving, loving and exciting and wondrous.

To show him all was well, she kissed him fervently, with all the passion he inspired.

He responded in an instant, deepening their kiss, stroking and caressing her body, quickening the pace of his thrusts as he made love with her.

It didn't hurt. It felt good. And right. And wonderful.

She wrapped her legs about him to hold him closer still. He was Henry, her lover. Her savior, in so many ways. Her beloved.

Tension climbed. Her body stretched taut with anticipation, like a drawn bowstring. Her blood pulsed through her body as if she had run for miles, her breathing panting gasps of expectancy.

Then the tension snapped. She let out a cry of release as her hands clutched at Henry as if she was about to fall.

Above her, Henry threw back his head and groaned. As the glorious throbbing slowed, he kissed her on the lips, her eyelids, her cheeks, her delightful ear, before he pulled free to lie beside her.

He put his arm around her shoulders and held her close. She nestled in his arms, her head on his chest. Brushing her forehead with his lips, he reached around to pull the bed coverings about them.

"We should get under the covers," he noted with a lazy, sated smile, "lest we get a chill."

"I'm warm enough, and I don't want to move."

"I suppose you're going to have to, eventually."

"Eventually," she murmured, tracing the edge of the areola of his nipple with her fingertip.

He caught her hand, and his look was sober when she glanced up at his face. "Before the household stirs. What will Giselle think if she wakes and realizes you aren't there?"

Mathilde laughed softly, enchanted by his concern. "I'm never there when she awakes. I'm always
dressed and gone before she opens her eyes." She
grew a little more serious. "And I have no reputation
to protect anyway."

He raised himself on his elbow and regarded her
gravely. "You are an honorable woman, Mathilde, in
the truest, best sense of the word."

"And you are the honorable man I love," she whispered as she drew him down to kiss.

"DID YOU SLEEP?" Mathilde asked as the stars
began to dim in the coming light of dawn, and after
spending the night in Henry's arms. She had dozed
off once or twice, but no more than that. Although
she was tired and comfortable, she was too aware
of what might happen come the morning to even
try to sleep.

"A little. More than I thought I would. I usually
never sleep before a battle, or a tournament, either.
Too anxious." He lightly kissed the top of her head.
"Something must have tired me out."

Marveling that he could sound so cheerful even on
such a morning, she rolled on to her side. "You're not
too tired, I hope."

He rose from the bed. What was left of the candles
in the stand still flickered, casting their feeble light
on his magnificent body. "Never before a battle." He

looked over his shoulder as he went to the ewer and basin. "Afterward, I used to sleep like the dead."

She inwardly cringed at that final word even as she sat up and watched him wash, her hungry eyes roving over him like a starving man's a loaf of bread. "Used to?"

"I haven't been in a battle or tournament since... recently."

Since the days in the dungeon, she suspected.

"Don't worry, my love," he said as he dried off. "I won't fall asleep in the middle of the fight. I'll be very wide-awake.

"And don't worry about the battle, either," he added as he came to sit beside her on the bed. "The men are prepared, and we've got a good plan." He nodded at the window. "Cerdic and fifty of the men should already have gone out the postern gate under cover of night. When Roald attacks the main gate, they'll circle around behind him and come at his men from behind."

"That sounds like an excellent plan."

"Ranulf was all for having them go over the wall, but I said why go to all that trouble and risk having them picked off by archers? Send out a few of the Celts who can move as if they're invisible to deal with any men Roald's got watching the gate, then go out that way."

"That does sound less risky," she agreed.

"That's what I thought. Now, my love, are you going to stay in bed all morning, or will you act as my squire and help me dress? I can't manage all the ties and buckles by myself."

"Gladly," she lied. In truth, it felt like he'd asked her to help him put on his shroud.

Trying to shake that grim, foreboding feeling, she got out of bed and put on her shift, and pretended to be as cheerfully unconcerned as he. "Why don't you have a squire?"

"Can't afford it," he replied as he put on his linen undergarment and tied it at the waist. "The food alone would cost me a fortune."

She helped him into his shirt, and couldn't resist running her hand down his chest as she pulled it in place.

He gave her a wry grin. "Now that's something no squire would ever do," he said, bussing her on the cheek. "At least, not one in my service." He waggled his eyebrows suggestively. "Care to help me with my hose?"

"I think you can manage that by yourself," she pertly replied as she went to find his gambeson.

The padded garment, stuffed with wool and quilted, should have been easy to find.

"Where's your gambeson?" she asked as she continued to search through his clothes in the large wooden chest in the corner.

He held up something. "I've already got it."

Feeling rather foolish, she said, "Do you need my help with it?"

"Need? No." He grinned with sly devilry. "Would I *like* it? That's a different question."

"You, Sir Knight, should have been a jester," she said with mock displeasure. Even though dread gnawed at her, she simply couldn't resist his merriment.

He'd put on the quilted jacket by the time she reached him, so it only required to be tied closed. He stood with arms outstretched, chin up. "Tie me, my lady," he said majestically.

"Perhaps I'd rather *untie* you," she murmured, reaching into his breeches.

"God's teeth," he cried, jumping back when she touched him. "Now I *know* you're not my squire."

"I'm your lover," she agreed, sidling closer.

"Soon to be my wife," he agreed, reaching out and pulling her into his arms.

"I may not be the best knight in the realm," he said as he rained light kisses on her upturned face, "but I'll be the most loving. And the most entertaining."

She laughed softly. "I daresay you will."

He glanced out the window again, and the jollity left his face. "Alas, my love, we have no more time for games. Unless my ears deceive me, Roald's men are on the move."

She had feared it would come to battle and had

been dreading it for days, but the terror that gripped her now was as strong and sharp and sudden as if Roald's attack was a complete surprise.

Henry chucked her lightly under the chin. "No need to look so distressed, my love. I've been in battles before."

"Not for me," she whispered, not willing to speak louder lest her voice tremble.

"No," he agreed. "For far less important causes. Now help me with my hauberk and surcoat, and send me on my way with kisses and your blessing."

He smiled, and she knew he was trying to be light-hearted for her sake, and loved him all the more.

Yet despite his efforts, her heart was heavy with worry as she helped lift the heavy mail hauberk over the gambeson, then tied the opening tightly. She had to fight her foreboding as she did the same for the armor that covered the front of his shins.

His surcoat of scarlet and gold, slit for riding, came next, and she tried to keep her hands steady as she pulled it into place and buckled his swordbelt around his waist. She bit her lip to keep from sighing as she helped him don his mail coif, the metal link hood with the neck guard that went below his chin and then up to be tied beside his brow.

After she put his helmet over the coif, she stepped back to look at him, her lover, her friend, her savior. With his visor down, he could have been an imposing stranger standing before her, a warrior sheathed in metal, and with a metal heart.

Then Henry raised the visor and revealed his smiling face. "No need to look so frightened, Mathilde," he assured her. "I'm very well trained, you know."

She buried her fear for him as deeply as she could and smiled. "I know, just as I know that because you command the garrison, we shall win today."

With a look in his eyes that wiped the trembling smile from her lips, he held his arms out wide. "Will you kiss your champion once more, for luck?"

She eagerly stepped into his embrace and passionately brought her lips to his—for luck, and with gratitude, and in the ardent hope that she could kiss him again when the battle was over.

CHAPTER FOURTEEN

A SHORT TIME LATER, after Mathilde—wonderful, glorious, Mathilde who would be his wife when this strife was over—had left him, Henry stood on the battlements of Ecclesford Castle with Ranulf beside him.

The very air seemed imbued with tense expectancy, like the men waiting with Henry on the wall. The villagers huddled in the buildings below. Giselle and the servants who would tend the wounded were in the hall, while Mathilde was in the kitchen supervising the heating of water for the wounded, and the preparation of food for when the battle was over. From the chapel came the muted responses of the people praying for victory.

Henry said a silent prayer for success and hoped God would understand that he didn't dare stray off the walls, not even for mass. He was sure Roald would attack as soon as it was lighter. He was also sure Roald would assume they would huddle inside the castle walls and only defend themselves, and so they would—until they attacked.

Foot soldiers on the wall walk and in the yard stood ready to douse any flaming balls of pitch Roald's catapults or trebuchets might throw into the castle. Stones were piled by the merlons and pots of water were being boiled, to be thrown or poured on men who tried to scale the walls. Holly bushes and brambles had been uprooted and thrown into the moat to impede their enemies' progress.

"You really think he'll attack today?" Ranulf asked, now likewise dressed and armed for battle.

"Yes, and I wish he'd get on with it," Henry replied, for although he was attempting to be patient, waiting like this tried him sorely. He hoped that once Roald's band of mercenaries realized the competent garrison of Ecclesford was going to put up a fierce fight, they would decide the personal risk wasn't worth the possible reward and abandon Roald.

"Do you think Roald's got any siege engines?"

"I'd like to believe he's spent all his money on mercenaries," Henry replied just as he spotted some movement in the open ground between the green and castle road. He pointed. "There," he said to Ranulf.

Ranulf let his breath out slowly. "Ah, yes. Here come his archers with their pavises."

They watched in silence as men bearing the large wooden pavises ran out and positioned the protective guards, larger than the shields men carried into battle, on the ground to form a makeshift wall. Behind them other men, with quivers on their belts and short bows of yew in their hands or crossbows, took their position and nocked their arrows.

"Get ready!" Henry called out to his men, who shifted nervously. Several crossed themselves and muttered prayers. More than one fingered an amulet or cross around his neck.

"When do we signal Cerdic?" Ranulf asked, keeping his eye on the opposing force.

"Once Roald's moved his foot soldiers forward," Henry answered. "Down!"

They ducked as the first volley of arrows flew over the castle wall. One man near the gate cried out and fell. His fellows dragged him out of the way, and Henry could hear the man cursing as they did, telling Henry he was merely wounded.

Another volley followed. Henry looked to the men manning the small catapults he'd had built and placed on the wall walk. "Now," he ordered, and in the next moment, rocks went flying over the wall, striking some of the shields, and the men behind them. Other missiles fell short and Henry ordered the men to adjust their distance from the merlons and embrasures.

More of Roald's archers took up positions on the field and soon the air was filled with arrows flying one way, and rocks the other. Men ducked for cover and shouted directions to those working the catapults and loading the rocks. Bits of stone flew off the rocks as they soared overhead and arrows slid and clattered onto the wall walk. Soldiers anxious to fight waited crouched behind the merlons, their arms and shields over their heads, their swords drawn.

Henry commanded the men at the catapults to cease their efforts and remove the catapults to give the soldiers more room on the wall walk, then summoned the archers of Ecclesford to take their places on the battlements.

"We've still got more rocks," Ranulf said, lunging behind a merlon as an arrow shot through the gap beside him.

"I want Roald to think we don't," Henry said. "Then he'll start moving his other men forward."

Although not his archers. They would come no closer; otherwise, their arrows wouldn't be able to get over the wall.

"Shouldn't we signal Cerdic?" Ranulf asked, the merest hint of anxiety in his voice.

"Not yet," Henry replied, glad Cerdic had obeyed his orders to wait.

As he'd once told Mathilde, Cerdic seemed the sort to rush headlong into battle, so Henry had made very sure he understood that to attack too soon could mean that his men might find themselves facing the mercenaries alone. "We'll wait until Roald's men are closer to the walls."

A low rumble of heavy wooden wheels came from the village. "Battering ram," Henry muttered, recognizing that sound at once.

"No penthouse over it to protect the men guiding it," Ranulf noted when a massive tree trunk, supported by four wooden wheels as wide as grindstones and with at least ten men beside it, rolled into view. "He must think that's going to make quick work of the gate."

"A fortnight ago it would have," said Henry. "I had the smith reinforce the gates with iron bands. But that's a fearsome ram."

Henry realized the men around him were muttering anxiously to each other, and exchanging wary looks. "Fear not," he said. "This was expected. While Roald's men are busy trying to break down the gate and scale the walls, Cerdic and his men will be attacking…" He clapped his hand on his backside. "Roald's rear."

That got some grins and chuckles from the men, and more than a few sighs of relief.

Ranulf lifted his head above the merlon, then ducked down quickly as another arrow whizzed by. "I don't see any trebuchets or catapults."

"Thank God for that," Henry said under his breath.

Since Ecclesford had but one outer wall, he'd feared Roald would bring large siege engines capable of hurling huge rocks or boulders. A hole or collapsed portion of that wall would be disastrous, not to mention the damage rocks or balls of flaming pitch thrown into the courtyard could do.

"No doubt he's too impatient to take the time to build them, or the men he's hired lack the knowledge," Ranulf said.

They looked at each other and simultaneously imitated Sir Leonard. "Patience, boy, patience."

Then they grinned, once again youths learning how to wage war from a man who'd been fighting since before they were born.

They came fiercely back to the present when a grappling hook slid over an embrasure close by with a rasp of metal on stone. The men there hacked at the rope until it broke, sending at least one eager mercenary screaming to the ground. Beyond the walls, the ram rolled closer, and more men with grappling hooks and long ladders charged forward.

"Archers!" Henry bellowed, and his own prepared to shoot at the advancing enemy.

Crouching, Henry swiveled to look into the yard below, where ten men held doves in their hands. "Let them go!" he cried. The men threw their hands up, releasing the birds. They flew upward, like a fluttering cloud of smoke. The day was clear, and Cerdic would be watching for just this sight.

"Ready at the wicket?" Henry yelled to those men who would be going out the smaller door cut in the massive gates to attack Roald's men on the ground.

He had chosen the best with swords and axes for this important task.

Every part of him wanted to go with them, swinging his sword, fighting Roald's men. His blood fairly sang with the wish to join the battle, not stay and wait and watch from the safety of the wall walk.

Patience, boy, patience. This was the lot of the commander, to watch and guide and pray your plan succeeds.

"Let me lead the men going out the gate," Ranulf proposed, his hazel eyes gleaming with excitement.

Henry had no choice but to refuse. This was not Ranulf's fight; he was here purely by chance. "Sorry, my friend, I can't." When he saw the scowl begin to darken Ranulf's face, he grinned and said, "If anything happens to you, Merrick would have my hide and little Lady Bea my head."

A ladder hit the wall nearby. Momentarily forgetting Ranulf, Henry grabbed one end and shoved with all his might, pushing it off, grunting with the effort. It tipped back and fell. An arrow barely missed Henry's jaw. Ranulf and two others started slashing at another rope attached to another hook with their swords.

Where the devil was Cerdic? Henry wondered as he hurried to help them and Roald's men continued to press the attack. The signal had flown; Cerdic must have seen it. There was no cloud or mist or smoke to obscure the morning sky.

"Shoot at the men at the ram," he ordered his archers. "Now!" he cried to the soldiers at the gate below.

Henry's men charged out, shouting. An arrow struck the man beside Ranulf. He crumpled to the ground.

Another hook came over the wall and caught on a merlon three down from Henry. Henry stepped over the body of the fallen man and cut the rope, then threw the hook down after it as hard as he could, hitting the upturned face of one of the mercenaries on the ground.

With a shriek the man covered his eye as blood poured from the wound. He staggered back and fell to his knees.

More of Roald's men came running from the village, carrying ropes and ladders.

Even without the catapults and trebuchets, Roald—damn him!—was better prepared than Henry had expected.

His men on the ground surged forward. The ram came to a halt as the men guiding it fell or drew back. Roald's archers kept shooting, sometimes hitting Henry's men on the battlements when they rose to fend off mercenaries trying to scale the walls.

Where the hell was Cerdic and his men?

Another hook sailed over the wall, this time nearly catching Henry with its sharp points. He grabbed hold of the hook before it caught and threw it back.

Another came through the gap between merlons and Henry cut its rope with the help of two of his men.

The garrison soldiers outside the gates put up a good fight, but Roald's men forced them back. More of Roald's men had gone to the ram and were slowly pushing it forward again, despite the battery of arrows from the walls of Ecclesford.

"You command the defense," Henry shouted to Ranulf above the din as he slammed down the visor of his helmet.

He couldn't stand and watch anymore. His blood was up, his whole body anxious and ready to fight, to lead his men by being among them. So with a battle cry on his lips and his sword in his gauntleted hand, he ran down the battlement steps and out through the wicket.

THE HORRIBLE NOISES of battle penetrated even the thick stone walls of the kitchen. The shouts of the soldiers. The commotion of men running. The shrieks and cries of pain.

"Keep to your work!" Mathilde ordered the servants who stopped to raise terrified eyes every time such a noise came to their ears.

As horrible as it was, Mathilde told herself she mustn't show her fear. She must be strong, and brave, so that they would be, too.

All the months of hiding other anguish came to

her aid now. All the pain she'd learned to control, and
the ability to push aside terrible thoughts, helped her
as she briskly cut leeks to go into the great pots of
stew bubbling in the hearth. Other pots of water were
being warmed for washing wounds.

So many injured. So many wounded.

Mathilde silently prayed that Henry and their men
would triumph. She prayed that Henry and her men
would not be hurt, or killed.

She prayed most of all for the battle to be over.

EXCITEMENT SURGING through him, Henry fought his
way through Roald's men, seeking the man who had
hired them and brought them here. Roald's archers
had drawn back, lest they hit their fellows trying to
scale the wall. The ram had been abandoned, left
where it was standing, as Henry and his men moved
closer to Roald's camp.

He fairly rejoiced at the chance to encounter
Roald himself, determined to kill him. One blow,
Henry told himself. One good blow and Roald would
be dead, and justice done for Mathilde. She would
be avenged, and her estate would be safe.

Please, God, bring me to Roald.

First, he had to dispatch the man coming toward
him, a big, stocky fellow wearing well-made mail
and a helmet he'd probably taken from one of his
victims. He was a good swordsman, though, better

than most. Unfortunately for him, Henry was well trained and anxious to fight.

Not taking his eyes from the mercenary, Henry advanced with slow deliberation, gripping his broadsword with both hands, watching and waiting for the man to make a move. Patience had been Sir Leonard's motto. Patience and skill and cunning.

The man raised his sword to strike, and in that instant, Henry swung his blade sideways with the speed of an adder. His opponent reeled back, his mail slashed open by the sharp point of Henry's heavy sword.

Henry finished his opponent off with a lunge through the gap in his mail into the man's belly. He pulled his sword free and moved on to the next man, all the while looking for Roald, and Cerdic and his men, too, who should have joined the battle long ago. Perhaps he was fighting where Henry couldn't see him. Maybe Roald had more men than they supposed.

A Scot, in that skirted garment they wore and with only a shield and a round helmet to protect his body, blocked Henry's way. Although he was little more than a youth, Henry quickly discovered that the young Scot was no mere stripling when he struck Henry's sword with a blow that rattled the Norman's arm and set the metal ringing.

Jumping back and nearly stumbling, Henry swung for the Scot's unprotected right shoulder. The Scot twisted deftly to avoid the hit. By the time Henry had raised his sword again, the Scot was jabbing at him from below.

Henry backed up, silently cursing the unarmored Scot and the weight of his own mail. The Scot, not so encumbered, could move faster than Henry, who was used to being the quickest man in the field. His deftness and ability to turn and twist even in armor accounted for most of his victories, and if he had not that advantage now....

A stone thrown from the walls above struck the Scot's arm. As he gasped and instinctively looked up, Henry moved forward and swung again. But the Scot was well trained, too, for in the next moment he was out of Henry's reach. Another stone fell, barely missing the Scot's head.

And then, at the edge of his vision, Henry saw Roald. The battle must be going in his favor, or he would never have come so close to the walls.

He would be sorry for that arrogant assumption.

"I have more important men to kill today," Henry called to the Scot as he turned away and started toward Roald.

Charles De Mallemaison appeared in front of him, blocking Roald and the rest of the battle from Henry's view.

"Not so fast, my Norman friend," De Mallemaison growled as he swung a bloodied mace back and forth in his right hand. His left side was protected by a tall, conical shield over his arm; his sword was still sheathed at his waist.

"So, here is the brother of the lord of Dunkeathe," De Mallemaison said, his words muffled by the lowered visor of his helmet. "I was hoping I'd meet you in battle today."

Roald would have to wait.

"Say your prayers to whatever demon you worship," Henry returned as he gripped the hilt of his bloodied broadsword, and prepared to fight the most notorious mercenary in England.

De Mallemaison laughed, if that mirthless sound he made could be called that. "You think you can beat me? I've been killing men since I was twelve years old. I only wish I could see the look on your blackguard brother's face when I send him your bloody body."

"While there isn't a soul who'll mourn you when you're dead," Henry retorted, keeping his eye on his opponent, watching, searching, for any weakness.

Nearby, he heard a cry and glanced at the sound. Had Cerdic finally come?

That moment's distraction was a mistake. As he turned his head, De Mallemaison let his mace fly. It struck Henry's visor, jamming the metal into his cheek and forehead. Excruciating pain shot through the right side of his face, so terrible he nearly swooned. Blood clouded his vision and he staggered like a drunken man as he tried to raise his visor and wipe away the blood.

Even in his agony, he heard the sound of a sword being pulled from a scabbard.

Where was *his* sword? Or any weapon at all? As agonizing pain radiated from his cheek, he spotted a broken shield and lunged for it, holding it over his head in time to fend off the blow of De Mallemaison's sword.

Still holding the shield over his head, he scrambled forward, half-blind, searching for his sword. Any sword. A mace. A stick.

He saw his sword, thank God! He reached for the hilt. Before he could get it, De Mallemaison attacked again, aiming for Henry's left shoulder and what was left of the shield. The force of De Mallemaison's blow shattered the shield completely and the blade went through to Henry's shoulder. The remnants of the shield cushioned the blow, and his mail protected the flesh, or Henry would have lost his arm.

Desperately he grabbed his sword and lashed out, but he swung wide, unable to see his opponent.

De Mallemaison's blade caught his, sending Henry's sword flying and leaving Henry weaponless.

Was this the end? Was he going to die here and now, by this man's hand?

No, never. Not now, not this way.

Ignoring his pain, Henry half crouched, summoned his strength, and launched himself at De Mallemaison, tackling him before the man could raise his sword again. Together they fell heavily to the ground.

With a grunt, De Mallemaison shoved Henry off him. Henry rolled and when he came to a stop on his belly, he spotted a foot soldier's plain sword on the ground a little more than an arm's length away. Panting, he hoisted himself onto his hands and knees and crawled toward it.

A booted foot caught him in the ribs and sent him sprawling. "I think not," De Mallemaison snarled.

There was another kick, this time to Henry's wounded shoulder.

Merrick had kicked him, too, like a dog. He wasn't a dog, and he wasn't going to die beaten like one. Inching forward Henry raised his head, looking for that sword. He would find it. He must—

"Oh, for the love of God," De Mallemaison sneered. Henry half rolled onto his back to see De Mallemaison raising his sword for the coup de grace. "Enough."

A fierce cry rent the air. De Mallemaison half turned.

"Cerdic," Henry murmured. And then the pain overwhelmed him, and he slipped to the ground, unconscious.

MATHILDE COULDN'T ignore the frightened faces staring at her. The servants had been terrified by the fighting and were now just as afraid of the silence that had descended upon the castle.

She was not afraid. She must not be afraid. "Our men must be victorious," she assured them, "or Roald's men would have already come—"

The door to the yard banged open, the sound like an explosion.

Mathilde whirled around as the frightened servants gasped. A bareheaded Ranulf, still clad in his mail and bloodied surcoat, stood on the threshold—not some unknown, vicious mercenary.

"Oh, thank God!" Mathilde cried and behind her the servants sighed with relief.

Then dread returned. Why didn't Ranulf look more pleased? Whose blood was on his green surcoat?

Her joyous relief drained away, like the color from her cheeks, and she could scarcely draw breath. Where was Henry? Why had he not come?

He would have too much to do, she told herself even as fear clutched at her heart. He would also have to supervise the capture of the mercenaries, deciding on their fines or ransoms.

"My lady, we've managed to fight off the attack," Ranulf began, walking into the crowded, hot room that smelled of roasting meat and gravy and bread. "But Henry has been wounded."

She stifled the cry of dismay that came to her lips. She must not show fear or despair, because the servants were watching. Her only outward sign of torment was the way she clenched her fingers into fists, as if she would beat the man responsible for hurting Henry if she could.

Which was the truth. She would have thrown herself at him like a scalded cat.

"Where is he?" she asked, managing to keep her voice steady.

"The hall." Ranulf held out his arm to escort her, but she ignored his silent offer of assistance. She would show her people the strength of Lady Mathilde of Ecclesford. She would not weep as she had after Roald had left her. She was a different, better woman now—the woman Henry respected, admired and loved.

Exhausted soldiers, some wiping sweat and blood from their faces, sat or leaned against the walls in the courtyard. Excited villagers milled about, some questioning the soldiers. Many of the people, both soldiers and villagers, saw Mathilde with Ranulf and quickly looked away.

Fear coiled in Mathilde's belly, like a snake ready to strike at her heart. "Is he badly hurt?" she asked, and this time, there was a quaver in her voice.

"I don't know, my lady," Ranulf answered, and she heard truth in his steady voice.

"How did it happen?" She swallowed hard. "An arrow?"

"No. He went out into the fighting beyond the gates."

Mathilde halted, looking at Ranulf with horror. "Beyond the gates?"

"When he saw how the battle was going, he went to join his men and left the defenses to me." He gave her a weary, compassionate smile. "He's a foolhardy, if courageous, fellow, my lady," he said as he hurried ahead of her to open the door to the hall.

"He's the bravest man I know," she replied, stepping into the hall and one of her nightmares—a hellish vision of blood and wounded, moaning men. She reached for Ranulf's arm, clutching it, fighting not to be sick from the smell, let alone the sight.

She must be strong. She would be strong for Henry.

Cerdic appeared at her elbow, and he, at least, looked unhurt. "Where is Henry?" she asked him. "Is he badly hurt?"

"Giselle had him taken to his chamber. She's tending to him herself."

Mathilde told herself that was to be expected. It didn't mean his wound was mortal. "You're not hurt?"

"Nay." He looked as if he would say more, but she didn't linger. At that moment, Henry was all in all. She gathered up her skirts and hurried to the stairs leading upward.

When she had disappeared from sight, Cerdic looked at Ranulf. "Did you tell her?"

"I did not have the heart."

CHAPTER FIFTEEN

MATHILDE CAME to a breathless halt outside the door of Henry's chamber. What if Ranulf and Cerdic had been lying to her, and Henry was dead inside? What if his wounds were serious enough to kill him? What if they had brought him to this chamber so that the servants wouldn't see his body and spread the disheartening word that Sir Henry had been killed?

She told herself they wouldn't do that. Surely they wouldn't do that....

Swallowing hard, she eased open the door to the chamber. From her place by the bed, Giselle rose and turned so that her body blocked the sight of the Henry lying behind her.

A fear greater than any Mathilde had ever known, even in Roald's detestable embrace, threatened to engulf her. Her whole body trembled and her knees went as weak as damp rushes.

"Is he...is he dead?" she managed to whisper, although her throat was so dry with dread, she could scarcely do more than croak the words.

"No," her sister answered.

Mathilde let out her pent-up breath, but fear still clutched her heart and seemingly the rest of her body, too, because Giselle's expression remained grave and she didn't move aside.

"What is it?" Mathilde asked, clasping her hands and trying to still their shaking as she moved closer to the bed. "Why are you hiding him?"

Giselle came forward and took her sister firmly by the shoulders. "He's gravely wounded, but he is alive," she said softly, gently, with infinite tenderness before she moved aside.

Henry lay on his back, his head swathed in bandages, save for his left eye, his nostrils and his half-open mouth. She could see his chest rising and falling as he breathed, but otherwise, there were no signs of life.

A primitive cry of pure anguish rose in her throat; again she forced it back, and after a long, heart-wrenching moment, still struggling between agony that he was so badly wounded and hope because he wasn't dead, she stopped staring at Henry to gaze, searchingly, into her sister's grief-stricken eyes.

She took a deep, trembling breath. "Tell me all, Giselle. How badly is he wounded?"

"He was struck in the face, by a mace I think, and his left shoulder is seriously hurt."

To be hit with a mace, and in the face... But he wore a helmet. "His armor—?"

"If not for that, he would be dead. His visor saved his life, but it was pushed into his cheek and brow by the blow. His right cheekbone is broken, he's lost three upper teeth and his brow was deeply cut. His left shoulder took a severe jarring and now moves too freely. I fear muscles were torn from the bone. I doubt he'll be able to hold a shield again. I cannot tell if his right eye is damaged or not. The flesh around it is too swollen. I stitched the cut and did my best to set the cheekbones." Giselle's eyes filled with pity and sorrow. "I fear he will be disfigured, Mathilde."

Disfigured, his left arm crippled. And his sight...? "Only the right side of his face was hit. The left—"

"Mathilde, I shall be honest with you," Giselle said, taking hold of her sister's cold hands, her expression grim. "Sometimes, even if it seems only one eye has been damaged, the other—"

"No!" Mathilde pulled her hands free and backed away. It couldn't be. He mustn't be... He was afraid of the dark, and to be always in the dark...

Again her sister took hold of her shoulders. "Mathilde, listen to me," she said firmly, sounding more like Mathilde than herself. "It may be that just the one eye is affected. It may be that both are fine. I simply do not know. You must have hope, Mathilde. At least he is alive."

When he awakened and saw the extent of his wounds, or if he was blind, he might wish he were dead.

This was her fault—going to Roald that night, her stupid plan to scare him off, her refusal to listen to Giselle and Cerdic, and most of all, her stubborn and vain pride. If not for her, Henry would be his handsome, merry self, safe and far away from here.

And it wasn't just Henry who was suffering. "How many others were wounded? How many have died?"

"Twenty wounded, six dead," said her sister.

Oh, God. She bowed her head, ashamed, horrified, sick to think that things had gone so wrong. She tried to find some reason not to give in to black despair, and thought of her sister's love. "At least Cerdic wasn't wounded."

Her stomach turned when she saw her sister's expression. "I saw him in the hall," Mathilde protested. "He didn't look hurt."

"*He* isn't, thank the Lord, but of the men who went with him out the postern gate, only he has come back. The others were killed or captured."

"God forgive me," Mathilde groaned, staring at her sister with dumbfounded, numb horror. "What have I done?"

Covering her face with her hands, she bent forward as if being pressed down by a great weight and moaned with despair and sorrow and guilt.

"You did what you thought was right," her sister said softly.

"But I was wrong. So wrong!"

"Would you rather we surrendered Ecclesford without a fight? Do you think there would not have been death and pain and suffering if we had done that? That Roald would be a merciful overlord? No, no, Mathilde," Giselle urged gently, enfolding her in her comforting embrace. "No one blames you for what's happened. They rightly blame Roald."

Mathilde held Giselle tightly as tears slipped out of her closed eyelids. To think she had ever maligned Giselle, in thought or word, bitter about her beauty.

After a long moment, Mathilde drew in a great, shuddering breath and stepped back. "I didn't ask Ranulf about the battle. Have we won? Will Roald go now?"

Giselle regarded her sister with pity and sympathy. Even after Roald had raped her, Mathilde hadn't looked so devastated, so distraught and destroyed. "Not yet, but we will," she said staunchly. "We still have most of the men, and Cerdic and Sir Ranulf."

But not Henry, Mathilde thought with mute misery.

"I should go below and see what more I can do with the hurt and wounded," Giselle said. "Will you sit with Henry, and summon me if he wakes?"

"Of course."

It was the very least she could do for him.

After Giselle had closed the door quietly behind her, Mathilde went to the bed. Kneeling beside it, she took Henry's limp hand in hers and pressed it to her cheek.

No matter whose fault this conflict was, it had to stop. No more men should be killed or hurt. No building, no castle, no estate was worth so much pain.

Yet Giselle was right, too. If Roald controlled Ecclesford, there would indeed be death and maimings as punishments, hunger and suffering as he gleaned every bit he could from the peasants. He must not win this battle.

How could she stop him without more fighting? Was there not some way she could bring about an end to this without giving up Ecclesford?

There must be, and she would find it.

LATER THAT NIGHT, ten men were gathered around the postern gate of Ecclesford Castle. Half of them dozed fitfully, sitting on the ground, their backs against the wall. The other five were anxiously awake. They were on duty, and Sir Henry would have their hides if they slept, or even dozed off.

"Please open the gate," said a woman wearing a cloak, the hood raised but not enough to obscure her face as she stepped into the circle of light thrown by a flickering torch stuck in the ground.

Toft, in charge of this party, regarded Lady Mathilde with understandable surprise and curiosity.

Her face so pale and drawn, she looked like a ghost, except that her snapping, determined eyes were very much alive.

Not quite sure what he ought to do, Toft scratched his head, then his grizzled chin. This didn't seem right at all. Where would she be going? Shouldn't she be doing whatever it was a lady did while her castle was besieged?

"Please open the gate," Lady Mathilde repeated, this time more forcefully.

Toft shifted his feet and glanced at his men, who were now all wide-awake and equally baffled.

"Did you not hear me?" the lady asked with a sharp impatience Toft knew well. "I said, open the gate."

"You can't mean it, my lady," he protested, wishing Cerdic or Sir Henry were here instead of him. "It ain't safe outside the castle."

And Sir Henry or Cerdic would have his head on a platter if she got hurt or killed because he opened the gate and let her go.

Her expression softened, and she stepped closer, speaking to him confidentially and as if he were her equal. "Have no fear. I go with Sir Henry's knowledge and permission. His brother and some men from Dunkeathe are coming up the river from the sea and I go to meet them. I will be safe because Lord Nicholas has sent an escort for me."

That still didn't sound right, Toft thought. Who

was this brother to be trusted with the safety of their lady, anyway? "You should have a guard from Ecclesford, too," he said. "How be some of these lads—"

The lady's eyes flashed a warning that she was losing her patience. "You would have me insult Lord Nicholas by implying that I didn't think he or his men could protect me?"

Toft didn't particularly care what some unknown nobleman thought. He was far more concerned about what Sir Henry or Cerdic would say if he let her walk into danger. "How be I send for Cerdic, eh, my lady?"

"I don't think Cerdic will be pleased to be summoned for nothing. He has quite enough to concern him now. I will be perfectly safe," she assured Toft. "Lord Nicholas's men will meet me not ten feet from the postern gate."

Toft felt powerless beneath her steadfast gaze. She was his lady, and if he disobeyed and Lord Nicholas was indeed waiting…

"Open it up," he ordered the grizzled soldier closest to the lock.

"Thank you," the lady said with a regal nod of her head as Erick eased the gate open. She glided out into the darkness and down the steps leading to the river, the small wharf, and the path along the riverbank.

When the gate closed behind her, Erick looked at Toft, frowning.

"Aye, I don't like it neither," Toft muttered in

response to Erick's silent query, and that of the other men around him.

He nodded at the youngest of the guards. "Herbert, go find Cerdic and tell him what just happened. Wake him up if you have to."

Herbert nodded and did as he was told.

AS HERBERT was seeking Cerdic, Mathilde was running as fast as she could toward the village, and Roald. She was well aware that Toft hadn't believed her explanation, but hadn't felt confident enough to deny her. She suspected he would try to find out if he'd erred by letting her go, perhaps even going to Cerdic himself. If he did that, she didn't have much time. Fortunately, the half-moon was bright enough to light this familiar way. She and Cerdic had gone along the path beside the riverbank many times, sneaking away from the castle by day or at night, full of mischief and unheeding of Giselle's gentle pleas that they stay behind with her. How cruel she'd been to Giselle in those days, how unthinking and selfish.

The stars above twinkled in the darkness, looking as they always did. As they had after that horrid night with Roald, when she marveled that the heavens could look just the same, as if nothing at all had happened.

A bush rustled nearby. She turned—and in the next instant, and with a hand over her mouth, she was dragged into the shadows, kicking and struggling with all her might.

Panic and terror coursed through her like the swash of the sea. Fear and desperation, too—but this time, she'd been tensely expectant, not caught off guard, anticipating only gentle kisses and caresses.

She bit down hard on the hand covering her mouth and when the man let go—for it was a man's rough, calloused hand—she shoved him back and ran.

Her attacker, dressed in a Scot's belted plaid, threw himself at her, catching her around the waist and bringing her down hard onto the soft verge of the path.

She twisted and squirmed, struggled and scratched. But she couldn't get away. The young man was too big, too strong. He grabbed her by her cloak and hauled her to her feet. He had long hair like Henry and was handsome, too, and for one wonderful, wild moment, she hoped her lie was no lie—that this was his brother from Scotland come to help her. "Are you from Dunkeathe?" she gasped.

Still holding her tightly, the man frowned, and she realized he was too young to be Henry's older brother. "No, I'm no' from Dunkeathe," he said sternly. "Where do ye think ye're goin'? Can you no' see the fires o' that camp, woman? Ye're walking right toward men who'll do ye harm." He ran his gaze over her garments as he let her go. "Unless ye're a whore, get out o' here."

"I'm not a whore!"

"Didna think so. Ye'd best go back to yon castle while ye can."

With a terrible sinking feeling, and in spite of his apparent concern for her safety, she realized this could only be one of Roald's mercenaries. She steeled herself and faced him squarely, as she was determined to face Roald. "I am the Lady Mathilde of Ecclesford," she announced, trusting that her rank and relationship with her detested cousin would prevent this man from doing her any harm. "Take me to Roald de Sayres."

The Scot's eyes narrowed. "What for?"

Who on earth did he think he was? "You have no right to question and detain me," she replied, mindful of the possibility that Cerdic and others might be coming after her. "I wish to parlay with my cousin."

His hands on his hips, the Scot frowned. "Parlay?"

"Yes. Speak with, talk to."

His frown became a scowl. "I ken wha' the word means, my lady."

"Then stop repeating everything I say and take me to him," she commanded.

"As you wish, my lady," he said with a shrug. He let out a low hoot, like that of an owl.

There was another slight rustling, and a man appeared, bringing with him the stench of sweat and rotten fish. He was shorter than the Scot and dressed in breeches and a gambeson half-undone to reveal a ragged shirt. A leather hat was pulled over his large ears, and she could see he had about two teeth in his grinning mouth.

"Who's this, then?" he asked with a lisp, looking her up and down as if she were a doxy in a tavern, and a cheap one at that. The Scot's scrutiny seemed the height of politeness compared to the way this man leered at her.

"You ain't gonna get nothin' out of him, deary," the disgusting fellow said. "He's got a woman." He pointed at his concave chest and leered again. "I don't."

She nearly threw up.

"I'm taking this *lady* to Sir Roald," the Scot said with undisguised disdain while she struggled to regain her self-possession. "Take my place here on watch."

"Who died and put you in charge?" the leering lout grumbled.

The Scot reached into the pouch attached to his wide leather belt and tossed a coin at the man. It flashed silver in the moonlight before the lout deftly caught it, his movement swift as a rat darting back into its hole.

"That's for your trouble," the Scot said, starting toward the village. "Now come, my lady."

In spite of this man's seeming kindness, Mathilde knew she was far from safe. Nevertheless, she fell into step beside him, and was glad that she had met him first, and not that other fellow.

"I don't think you belong in the company of evil men like Roald de Sayres or Charles De Mallemaison," she quietly noted—and if he decided he didn't and left before another battle, so much the better. "You seem far too kind a man."

The Scot answered without looking at her. "No, I'm not."

His response was so cold and curt, she felt a chill run down her spine and wrapped her cloak more tightly about her.

When they reached the village, once the happy and prosperous home of their tenants, now half-deserted, the buildings occupied by rough and callous men who would take what they wanted and destroy the rest, she instinctively drew closer to the Scot. If he had not been beside her, she could guess her fate, although this time, death would likely follow.

What these terrible men might not realize was that she'd come armed with two daggers, one in her belt and the other in her boot. If they tried to hurt her, she was more than prepared to hurt, kill or maim them.

The Scot came to a halt and nodded at the large, half-timbered house belonging to the reeve of the village, who was a prosperous wool merchant, too. "He's in there."

Of course Roald would take the finest house for his own.

With a nod, Mathilde started forward.

"Take care, my lady," the Scot called softly after her. "He's not in there alone."

IN THE MAIN ROOM of the relatively fine house, in the glow of the light from the hearth and twenty slender beeswax candles in a nearby iron stand, and under Roald's wary eye, Charles De Mallemaison poured himself some excellent French wine and downed it in a gulp. He poured himself another and finished it, too, before he finally settled his bulk onto a back stool.

The three-legged stool with one leg extended to make a back was made of sturdy oak and had arms, so that it was more like a chair than a stool. Even so, Roald wouldn't have been surprised if it had collapsed under the weight of De Mallemaison's armored body. Although the fighting had been over for some time, the big brute still hadn't taken off his mail. Roald could smell the blood and sweat from where he sat near the hearth, and it was all he could do not to curl his lip and order the man to wash.

"I thought you said they'd be untrained rabble," De Mallemaison complained. "That the garrison'd not put up much of a fight and would run away. The villagers would huddle in their cottages and hovels like scared rabbits. Well, where are they? Where're the women?"

"In the castle, I assume," Roald replied. "The village women weren't part of the bargain."

In truth, he didn't give a damn about the village women, or any woman, for that matter. De Mallemaison and his cronies could do what they wanted with them all and he wouldn't care, as long as he got Ecclesford in the end. But he would remind De Mallemaison who was in charge here.

De Mallemaison sniffed and scratched himself. "They're *always* part of the bargain."

"It was only the first day," Roald said placatingly. Twirling his goblet with his long fingers, he sought to reassure his vicious confederate. "The garrison may have made a brave showing today, but now that that bastard D'Alton's been wounded or better yet, killed, they're surely dispirited. Tomorrow should see the tide turn in our favor once and for all."

De Mallemaison sniffed. "And if it doesn't? I'm not getting paid enough to make a war."

Roald set the goblet down on the table beside him. "You think you deserve more, do you?"

"I know I do. There has to be two hundred men in there."

"I never said anything about the size of the garrison."

"You never told me about men like that yellow-haired demon, either," De Mallemaison retorted.

"Cerdic's only good with the ax. Get that out of his hands and he'll be easy to—"

"The hell he will. He wielded that sword like a Norman born and bred. You can pay me more, or you can lead the assault yourself. But if *I* go, so will most of the others. Without me, they'll doubt your victory and take off for surer profit and greener pastures."

He was probably right, Roald thought, realizing he had little choice. "All right. Another hundred marks."

"Two hundred."

"That's a fortune!"

De Mallemaison shrugged and started to rise.

"All right. Two hundred," Roald grudgingly agreed. There had better be enough in his late uncle's coffers...

"I want the beauty, too. The one who said she'd die before she'd let me touch her."

"I thought you said all women were alike in the dark."

"That was before I saw her—and before she insulted me."

De Mallemaison clearly had more than rape planned for Giselle. A beating would be the least of it, no doubt. Well, so be it. The stubborn ladies of Ecclesford had only themselves to blame for their fates. "Very well."

De Mallemaison's lips curled up into a hideous grin. "You can have her back after."

Roald shuddered to think of the condition she'd be in then. He certainly wouldn't want to touch her.

However, he merely smiled at his companion and nodded.

A loud knock sounded on the plank door.

De Mallemaison jumped to his feet, simultaneously drawing his sword. Roald likewise rose, afraid that this heralded a night attack from Ecclesford, until he realized there would have been more of a commotion outside and certainly cries of alarm. "Sheath your weapon, Charles," he said with a hint of a sneer. "You're as jumpy as a flea." He raised his voice. "What do you want?"

The door opened and a man garbed in a motley collection of mail and leather appeared. "There's a *lady* says she wants to see you," he said with a smirk.

Maybe some clever, ambitious wench in the village had decided to take her chances with the new lord. "Show her in."

That bitch Mathilde marched into the room.

CHAPTER SIXTEEN

IT TOOK EVERY ounce of self-control, every bit of inner strength Mathilde possessed, to face Roald. It sickened her to be this close to the man who'd taken her with vicious cruelty, who'd mocked and vilified her. Before Henry came, she would cringe at the mere mention of his name, but now, for her people and for Henry, she would not even flinch. For their sake, she would try to make Roald leave once and for all.

She saw his shock when she entered and didn't doubt she was the last person he was expecting to see come into this room. She was also acutely aware of Charles De Mallemaison standing a short distance from the hearth, with his sword drawn.

Up close he was even uglier and more monstrous, yet she forced herself to ignore him. "Good evening, Roald."

Having recovered from his shock, her cousin raised a querying brow. She nearly laughed at his attempt to seem master of himself and this situation, to act as Henry would—but Henry would *be* the master of the situation, cool and calm and confident.

"I must say this is an unexpected pleasure," Roald said. "I trust you didn't come alone."

"No," she lied. Let him think there was an armed escort awaiting her outside. "Nor did I come to exchange pleasantries with you." She ran a haughty, derisive gaze over De Mallemaison. "Or your lackeys."

"What of yours?" Roald retorted, returning to the cushioned, thronelike chair she had sat upon many times when she'd visited the reeve. "How fares the handsome Sir Henry? I understand the poor fellow is seriously wounded," he finished with a triumphant glance at De Mallemaison.

"If you've been told that, you've been misinformed," she replied. "He suffered a minor cut. You know how head wounds can bleed—or you would, if you ever actually fought."

She was pleased to see Roald scowl and felt a surge of triumph herself. "No, I assure you, Sir Henry is quite well and, indeed, anxious to fight again. But I said to him, why waste the effort? It is clear Roald cannot win with that rabble he's hired."

She fixed her steadfast gaze on her cousin. "So I have come to spare your worthless life, Roald, which you will surely lose if you attempt to attack Ecclesford again. I have come to accept your surrender and let you leave in peace."

Roald stared at her with stunned disbelief.

"You underestimated us, didn't you?" she continued with every outward sign of confidence. "You expected an easy victory, and now you have discovered it will not be so. Indeed, you *cannot* win against Sir Henry and my men, so unless you are an even greater fool than I think, you will take this chance I offer and end this now. My sister and I will let you leave in peace, as long as you promise to sail back to Provence and never trouble us again."

To her dismay, De Mallemaison laughed, a harsh and terrible sound, as he sheathed his sword. "Surrender? The woman's mad!"

"I am quite sane," she replied, her voice steadier than her knees. "I fear it is you who suffer from delusions if you think you can take the castle. Today's efforts should have shown you that you have no hope of doing so."

"You think so?" Roald spluttered.

"As would any person of any intelligence—which perhaps explains why that truth has eluded you and this—" she curled her lip as she glanced at De Mallemaison "—fellow."

De Mallemaison laughed again and threw himself onto the back stool. "The wench *is* mad." He ran a scornful gaze over Mathilde. "And ugly, too. At least the other one looks good." He stroked himself suggestively. "You know what I'm going to do when I get my hands on her, don't you, my lady? Or are you too stupid to guess?"

His insults couldn't hurt her. Henry's wounds in her cause gave her much greater pain. As for this man's action…

"Are you really going to take counsel from this disgusting pig?" she asked Roald, who gripped the arms of his chair as if for dear life. "Are you truly willing to put your fate in *his* filthy hands? What does he stand to lose if you are defeated? He will simply hire himself out to some other nobleman who requires a murderer. He will not have to face the king's wrath. He will not be excommunicated by the church for defying their judgment."

She ran another contemptuous gaze over Roald's henchman. "He's probably already excommunicated. But you, Roald," she said, looking back at her cousin, "you could lose all, including your life."

Roald shot out of the chair, his face red, breathing hard. "The king agrees that Ecclesford is *mine.*"

The more upset Roald grew, the calmer Mathilde became. As he panicked, she found tranquility. With his fear, she found peace. "Then why have we not received any messages from the king to tell us this? Why has he sent no courtier, no messenger, no document, no word of his decision?"

"Ecclesford is *mine!*" Roald shouted, smacking the back of the chair. "It was always intended to be mine, until you—you whore, you stupid slut—made your father change his will."

"I? I did not make him do that. You did, when you raped his daughter and abused his trust."

"He never wanted me to have it and that was his excuse!" Roald bellowed, his eyes full of bitter rage. "He always hated me and so did your haughty sister, thinking she was too good to even talk to me. But you weren't too good for me, were you, Mathilde? I showed *them* they couldn't treat me like dirt beneath their heels!"

He had raped her because he was angry at her father and Giselle? She was just the object of his vengeance, and barely a person in his eyes? The last of her shame and fear of him disappeared. "You loathsome little toad," she said quietly.

"Bishop Christophus will support my claim!" Roald roared as if he hadn't heard her.

"Because you have offered him a bribe to do so?" she said evenly. "So have *we*."

"Christophus hates Henry. He'll never help you now that you've enlisted that Norman's aid."

"Come, Roald, I thought you were a clever man," she chided. "Do you not see that for a man like Christophus, profit outweighs personal feelings—rather like a mercenary, albeit one in holy robes instead of armor.

"And since you mention Henry—have you forgotten his family? What do you think the lord of Dunkeathe will do when he hears you've attacked a castle commanded by his brother? Or the lord of Tregellas? Even after we win, do you think they will ever forgive or forget?"

The color drained from Roald's face.

"You're not going to let this woman scare you, are you?" De Mallemaison demanded in a low growl, reminding them he was there. "We've got the advantage. That castle has but one wall, one gate. We can take it tomorrow." He got to his feet and came toward Mathilde. "This is a trick."

Mathilde no longer feared Roald, but De Mallemaison was another matter. "Don't touch me!"

"Are you afraid, my lady?" he asked with a derisive leer. "Summon your guards, your escort, these soldiers you think can beat mine." He grinned his cold, malicious grin as he drew his sword. "Go ahead. I'll wait."

"Very well," she said, turning on her heel and starting for the door, the sweat trickling down her back as she tried to remember how many men were outside and think of a way to get past them.

"Not so fast," De Mallemaison said, moving to block the door. He threw it open and looked outside.

Her hand moved toward the dagger in her belt.

"There's only my men outside," he said as he turned back into the room.

"It's dark," she countered.

"Not that dark."

"She *lied?*" Roald cried, hurrying to join him at the door. He swore crudely as he whirled around. "How dare you try to trick me!"

Mathilde backed toward the hearth, her hand on her dagger. "How dare you try to take Ecclesford when you have no right to it!"

"She's a bold fool," De Mallemaison noted with something that might have been a glimmer of admiration, "but a fool nonetheless. Now we have a hostage."

Mathilde had known it was a dangerous gamble to come here alone. She'd remembered what Henry said when he warned her not to leave the castle without a guard because of the possibility of abduction. But it was a risk she'd been prepared to take rather than put any more of her men in danger by asking them to come with her.

So she had her answer ready, like her hand upon her blade. "*You* are a fool if you think Giselle will give up Ecclesford for me, especially to you. She knows what sort of man you are, what kind of overlord you'll be. She knows I'm here, and why, and expects you to take the terms we offer. After all, Ecclesford is well provisioned and our men will die for us, while your paid men will eventually realize your offer is not worth the effort, or their lives."

She managed to walk toward the large chair

without stumbling. Sweeping back her skirts, she lowered herself onto the seat with queenly dignity. "If you kill me, and then try to convince Giselle I am still alive, she won't believe it. She will know that is a lie unless she sees me herself. So you have a choice, Roald. You can either surrender, save your wretched life and go back to Provence, or you can try to ransom me, to no avail, and waste your money paying these men to attempt, uselessly, to take Ecclesford. What is it to be?"

Roald's mouth moved, but no sound came out, until De Mallemaison walked up to him and slapped him hard across the face.

"Don't be an idiot," De Mallemaison snarled in his low, harsh rasp like the voice of the devil himself. "She's lying. And you've got three hundred and fifty men outside. You've captured over forty of theirs and killed how many more? That castle has one puny wall, one useless gate. We can take it.

"As for her threats, who cares what some lord in Scotland and some other in Cornwall thinks or does? You've got the king on your side, don't you?"

"I do," Roald assured him, seemingly as afraid of De Mallemaison as Mathilde was.

"And what does it matter what some churchman says? Get the castle and keep it. You've got the men." He spun on his heel to glare at Mathilde. "And I say D'Alton's *dead*."

She gripped the arms of the chair. "He's not!"

De Mallemaison came toward her like a wolf after an injured lamb. "If he's not yet, he will be. I hit him hard in the face. I saw his crushed helmet."

She half rose, pulling out her dagger, but his beefy hand lashed out and closed around hers, squeezing hard. As he made her drop her weapon, he forced her back into the chair. "He's dead, and they've lost and she knows it."

Still squeezing her hand, the pain excruciating, he hauled her to her feet. "Isn't that right, my lady?"

"No!"

De Mallemaison laughed in her face, his fetid breath making her want to retch before he glanced over his shoulder at Roald. "I tell you what, de Sayres. Give me this one instead of the other." He turned back, his gargoyle face a mask of demonic intent. "I think I'd enjoy taming this one more."

"Roald! You can't listen to this dolt!" she cried, struggling to free herself from De Mallemaison's grasp. "He cares only about his fee, not what might happen to you."

"And you do?" Roald scoffed, coming toward her, an evil gleam in his eyes. "You are still trying to trick me, the way you tricked your father after we made love and you cried rape. The king wants me to have Ecclesford. And De Mallemaison is right. The castle has but one wall, one gate. I have more men than you."

He came around to Mathilde's side and pulled her veil back from her ear. He leaned close and licked her, making her shiver with revulsion, and then he whispered, "Since I've already had you once, De Mallemaison is welcome to you."

"Roald, no!"

He stepped back. "Enjoy her as you will, Charles. I don't care if she lives or dies."

"No!" Mathilde screamed, kicking her captor, striking out at him.

De Mallemaison might have been made of stone for all the results her efforts made.

"Roald!"

Her cousin paused on the threshold, and turned back to look at her as if she were nothing to him but a nuisance he was well rid of. "Farewell, Mathilde. And don't worry. I'll see Giselle gets your body. I'm going to have hers."

"Roald, don't—"

De Mallemaison struck her a backhanded blow that sent her to the ground. On her hands and knees, she looked up through her disheveled hair at the vicious brute standing before her. Roald had abandoned her, but she would fight to the death rather than let De Mallemaison take her.

"What sort of devil's spawn are you?" she sneered. "Does it take rape to make you feel strong? Does it make you feel like a man? You are nothing more than a beast that walks on two legs. If you rape me, God will understand and pity me, and he will surely punish you. I will feel no shame, because none belongs to me.

"*None* belongs to me," she repeated, truly believing that was true, and it had been true before. "But you—you should die of shame. Have you no mother, no sister, that you should treat women thus, as slaves and whores to use as you will?"

"I have no mother, no sisters," De Mallemaison growled as he tore the veil from her head and pulled her up by her hair. "I was left in a gutter. Some of my scars are from the rats that found me first."

He struck her again, sending her hard to the floor on her hands and knees. "Don't try my patience by claiming mercy because you're a woman."

She scrambled forward, grabbed the leg of the back stool and threw it as hard as she could at De Mallemaison.

When he jumped aside to avoid the missile, she reached for her dagger lying on the floor.

"Oh, no, you don't!" he snarled, charging forward and wrenching it from her grasp.

She still had the smaller dagger in her boot. "I'll never let you take me," she breathlessly vowed, inching backward toward the heavy chair. "I'd rather be dead!"

De Mallemaison tossed her dagger across the room

and threw off his coif. The dagger clattered and the coif landed with a metallic thud. "I'm going to make you scream so loud, they'll hear you in the castle."

"You're going to burn in hell!" she cried as she overturned the bigger chair to block him.

With a curse, he leaped back as it fell. Mathilde ran around it for the door.

He tackled her, bringing her down hard. She tried to crawl forward, but he grabbed her foot, the one with the other dagger in her boot.

He laughed, and there was malicious pleasure in the horrible sound. "Go ahead, my lady. Keep fighting. Make me work for it. But I always get what I want in the end."

Not this time, her mind shouted. *Not me. Not again.*

She kicked and flailed, trying to free herself from his grasp without letting him pull off the boot, lest he find that dagger, too. She clawed at the wooden floor, desperately attempting to gain purchase.

He dragged her inexorably closer. "That's right. Don't make it easy for me," he said, his voice now thick with lust.

She stopped kicking her foot and let him pull off the boot. He swore again and went to get the knife that dropped onto the floor, while she got up and lunged for the candlestand. She grabbed hold of its narrow shaft. The weight was nothing, the heat and flame from the candles unimportant, as she swung it at De Mallemaison's head. The candles went flying from their metal holders toward his face.

With a cry, he threw up his arms to protect himself. The candles rolled on the uneven floor at his feet while Mathilde ran at him, holding the stand as if it were a lance, striking him hard in the stomach. De Mallemaison fell backward, onto the wooden floor and some of the candles.

The force of the impact hurt her arms and she dropped the stand to rush to the door. Before she could get there, he kicked the stand toward her, knocking her sideways. She nearly lost her balance and fell, but managed to keep upright. She caught a whiff of fabric burning—and as he got to his feet, she saw what was on fire.

Crouching like a cat about to spring, Mathilde panted, "Fool, your surcoat's on fire."

He glanced at the hem of his garment and then leaped up as if the flames had nipped his flesh. He twisted back to swat out the fire and she saw her chance, dashing for the door, pulling down on the latch and slipping outside.

She paused for the briefest of moments, like a startled deer on the threshold of flight. Some men huddled around a small fire nearby stared at her in stunned disbelief, too shocked by her unexpected appearance to move.

She took off at a run as the startled men jumped

to their feet to give chase and shouts of alarm rang out in the night. Near the edge of the village, she deftly ducked one large lout who came at her with outstretched hands as if he wanted an embrace.

She made for the thicker trees by the riverbank, heading back to the postern gate, alert for any sentries she might encounter, and who would have heard the hue and cry.

She'd failed. Once again she'd failed. But this time, nothing had been lost. She had hoped to gain by her gamble, but as long as she made it safely home, she had not lost anything.

She gasped when a night bird called and rose from a nearby tree—and at that same instant, someone grabbed her and dragged her into the underbrush.

Before she could even begin to struggle, a familiar voice sounded in her ear. "Mathilde, what the devil art thee about?"

She collapsed against Cerdic's broad chest with relief, and only then noticed the shapes of other men around them.

"Take me home, Cerdic," she whispered as the vitality drained from her. "I'll explain everything when we are safely back in Ecclesford."

CHAPTER SEVENTEEN

WHEN MATHILDE returned through the postern gate, Giselle was waiting for her. She gave a rapturous cry of relief and pulled Mathilde into her arms.

Very aware of the curious guards watching, the ones she'd lied to, Mathilde said, "I need to rest" and immediately slipped her arm through Giselle's. She steered her sister toward the hall before Giselle could ask questions that would reveal that she knew nothing about the supposed arrival of Lord Nicholas and his men.

Cerdic followed them as they hurried across the courtyard, making their way around carts and barrels illuminated by the moonlight. For now, the yard was quiet, except for the occasional snuffle or bark of a dog. Up on the wall walk, the men were tense and alert, and one man paced back and forth close to the gate: Sir Ranulf, unless Mathilde was much mistaken.

She hoped she wouldn't have his death or serious injury on her conscience, too. "Has Henry awakened?" she asked Giselle.

"I don't expect him to wake until midday tomorrow," Giselle replied. "If he woke while I was waiting for you at the gate, Faiga was to come and tell me. I left her to watch over him. Oh, Mathilde, I was so worried! Is Sir Henry's brother really coming? Why didn't you tell me before? Where is he?"

"I'm sorry, Giselle," Mathilde quietly replied. "He's not coming. He never was. That was an excuse so the guards would let me go out. I'm sorry to upset you."

"Thou didst upset her, and me, and half the garrison who knows thou wast out there alone," Cerdic growled. "Why didst thou leave the castle?"

"I'll explain in the solar," Mathilde said with quiet resolve as they went up the steps to the hall.

Inside were the wounded, and the smells of dried blood and wet cloth, comfrey, the minty scent of sicklewort and the bitter odor of feverfew that turned Mathilde's stomach.

Fighting her nausea, Mathilde quickened her pace and hurried up the stairs to the solar. She waited until Cerdic had closed the door and gestured for them to sit, while she stood in front of the table. "I went to Roald and told him he should surrender."

They both stared at her, eyes wide, too astounded to speak.

Cerdic recovered first. "Thou sought out *Roald? Alone?* And told him to surrender?"

"I nearly succeeded, too," she replied, "except that Charles De Mallemaison was with him, and he convinced Roald not to give up. Otherwise, I think Roald would have believed me when I said Henry wasn't badly hurt and that his cause was lost."

Cerdic slumped back against his chair. "Of all the strange ideas thou hast ever had…" he murmured before lapsing into silence.

Giselle studied her sister's dirty, torn, disheveled gown. "What happened with Roald?" she asked, her voice thin with dismay and worry. "Did he—?"

Mathilde guessed what she feared. "No."

"Thank God!"

"I look like this because he gave me to De Mallemaison instead, but I set him on fire and got away."

"God in heaven!" Cerdic breathed. "De Mallemaison?"

"You set him on *fire?*" Giselle gasped.

"His surcoat," she clarified. "It caught on fire when he landed on some candles that had fallen on the floor. I hit him with a stand and they fell out. Then I got away and Cerdic found me."

Cerdic jumped out of his chair as if *he* had caught on fire. "And what if I had not found thee? What if Roald had killed thee?"

"Then I would be dead." She clasped her hands

and regarded them beseechingly. "I had to try *something* to stop Roald before any more men could be hurt or killed." She went to Cerdic, putting her hands on his strong forearm. "Before more of your friends died or got captured."

She looked at Giselle. "Before the man *you* love is wounded or dead."

Giselle turned red, while the color drained from Cerdic's face. "Thou knowest?"

"Sir Henry guessed. Was he wrong?"

Giselle rose, and in her usually placid eyes was a determination Mathilde had never seen before. "No, you are not. I love Cerdic, and he loves me, and we are going to be married."

"If thou dost not object," Cerdic said, regarding Mathilde with a combination of anticipation and dread that was so innocent and youthful, it made Mathilde forget, for a moment, that he was a battle-hardened warrior and her sister a woman who could tend the goriest wounds without hesitation—and the danger they all were in. They were young and carefree again, as they had been when they taught Cerdic how to dance in the orchard. "Of course I will not object! I'm very happy for you both, and Cerdic will make a fine lord of Ecclesford."

Giselle gave her future husband a glorious and somewhat smug smile. "I told you she would agree. All your worries were for nothing."

Mathilde wished they could have enjoyed this happy moment longer, but they couldn't. Roald was still outside the gates.

She went to her sister and took Giselle's hands in hers, the hands that could so tenderly care for the sick and wounded. "I think you should leave Ecclesford until the battle is over, Giselle. Should we lose—"

"We will not!" Cerdic and Giselle cried simultaneously.

"Nobody can say how a battle will go," she replied, thinking of her beloved Henry, so battered and hurt. "Please, Giselle, for my sake, leave."

"Who will tend the wounded if I go?"

"Faiga and the other ser—"

"They are not as skilled as I am," Giselle said firmly. "Are *you* planning on fleeing?"

"No. My place is here."

"And so is mine. I am not afraid, Mathilde." Giselle reached out and took Cerdic's hand in hers. "I have faith in our men."

"So do I," Mathilde said, "but Roald told me how many men they have. We are outnumbered. And if he captures you…" She looked to Cerdic. "If he captures her, she will suffer."

Giselle raised her chin. "If he rapes me, I will survive. You have shown me that a woman can go on in spite of the worst a man may do, short of murder. Whatever happens, I will try to be as strong and brave as you, because even if we lose Ecclesford to Roald's army, I will never stop fighting him, as you would not."

Mathilde choked back a sob not of sorrow, but of pride and gratitude that her sister thought her not disgraced and stained, but strong and brave.

Giselle's expression softened. "Cerdic will not leave here, either. How could I abandon the two people I love most in all the world?"

"Giselle, perhaps you *should* listen to her," Cerdic said quietly. He addressed Mathilde with pleading, remorseful eyes. "She is with child—our child. Forgive me, Mathilde."

Henry obviously hadn't guessed this—or hadn't told her if he had.

"There is no need to ask for forgiveness," Giselle said, not a little proudly. "I, too, can make plans, sister. I wanted Cerdic and he wanted me, but he believed he wasn't worthy because he has no title or estate. I thought of a way to overcome those objections. Given that he's such an honorable man, he surely won't refuse to marry me now."

She tilted her head to look up at the face of the strong warrior beside her. "You will marry me, won't you, Cerdic?"

"Thou let me love thee so I would be *forced* to marry thee?" he asked incredulously.

"To overcome your silly notion that you are not

good enough," she replied without a hint of contrition. "But he is, isn't he, Mathilde? He will be a fine husband and a good lord."

Mathilde immediately embraced them both. "Of course he will."

Giselle smiled at Cerdic as Mathilde stepped back. "Am I forgiven?" she asked him.

Instead of speaking, he pulled her close and kissed her.

While Mathilde silently left the chamber and went to sit beside her beloved, holding his hand and praying all would yet be well.

HENRY GASPED, jolted awake by the searing pain. It felt as if his face was being torn from his skull.

The battle. De Mallemaison and the mace crashing…

At least he was alive. At least, he thought he was alive. Surely the pain meant he was alive.

"I'm sorry, Sir Henry. I must change your bandage."

Giselle. That was Giselle. Where was Mathilde?

Oh, God, it hurt! Someone was moaning.

Him.

Finally the last of the linen was removed. He heard Giselle sigh. "There is no sign of infection, thank God," she said. "Can you open your eyes?"

His eye must still be there. That was a relief, even though sweat continued to trickle down his body and the pain swamped him like a drowning man in a storm at sea.

"Can you open your eyes?" Giselle repeated.

Could he? He tried. His left eye opened, and he could make out Giselle anxiously bending over him. Yes, it was Giselle—although there was something not right about the way she looked. It was as if she were a person depicted on a tapestry, flat against a surface.

He couldn't open the other. It was sealed shut with dried blood or pus, or too swollen, perhaps.

"Can you see me?"

He tried to nod, but that hurt too much. He struggled to speak, yet only a croak passed his dry lips.

"Squeeze my hand if you can see me."

He managed that, and Giselle immediately spoke to someone over her shoulder. "He can see!"

"Thank God. Oh, thank God! If you had been blinded!" Mathilde cried. Suddenly she was beside the bed, her head bowed as she took his right hand in hers and pressed a fervent kiss upon it.

Mathilde. Mathilde was there, despite her aversion to wounds and sickness. Of course she would be there, because he was badly hurt. Maybe dying. If so, he had to tell Mathilde or Cerdic what to do….

In the next moment, Mathilde was beside him on the bed, cradling his aching head between her breasts and helping him to drink the most delicious water he'd ever had in his life.

"Slowly, beloved, slowly," she whispered as he spluttered a little.

She laid him back down and he felt the bed rise when she stood up. He managed to turn his head to watch her. If he was going to die, he wanted his last sight to be of her.

"Can you move your left arm?" Giselle asked from the other side of the bed.

Still watching Mathilde as she worked with her back to him, he tried to do as Giselle asked—and sucked in his breath at the sharp, stabbing agony.

"I fear the muscle has been torn from the bone. If you are careful, you may regain some use of it, but it will always be weak."

Some use of it? *Always* weak? That was his shield arm. How could he fight if he couldn't hold a shield? How could he earn money, or hope to win an estate?

What about his right arm?

He attempted to lift it and to his relief, found that he could move it. He was about to feel his face when Giselle grabbed his arm and eased it back down. "You must not touch your cheek. The bones have been broken. I've set it as best I could, but you may cause more damage if you touch it."

His cheekbone was broken? By the blow of the mace. He could guess how the bone would heal; he had seen such wounds before. If he was lucky, his face would be only a little misshapen. If he was unlucky, that side of his face would be like a bowl, permanently indented.

"Your brow was cut. I've sewn it shut."

That would explain all the blood. Such wounds always bled copiously. He would have a scar. A broken cheekbone and a scar and a useless left arm....

But there was more to concern him than his own wounds. "The battle?" he whispered hoarsely.

"Over for now," Mathilde said, returning with a goblet in her hands. "I'm going to give you some of this to drink, Henry. It will ease the pain and help you to sleep."

He didn't want to sleep. He wanted to find out what had happened. "Ranulf...?"

"Sir Ranulf is unharmed," Mathilde said as she put the goblet to his lips. "Please, drink this."

That wasn't what he meant. He wanted to hear about the battle from his friend. But he couldn't avoid drinking the draft.

"Roald...?"

The name came out in a long sigh, and his eyes closed and he didn't hear her answer. He was dimly aware that someone was bandaging his ruined face, and then he knew no more.

THE NEXT TIME Henry awoke, sunlight streamed into the chamber window and Mathilde was seated on a stool beside his bed, her head laid beside him, her eyes closed in slumber.

How long had he been sleeping? How long had Mathilde been there, keeping a vigil at his bedside? What had happened with Roald? Was the battle over? Had they won?

Obviously the castle had not been taken, and it wasn't under attack right now, or Mathilde would not be here and it wouldn't be so quiet.

Either they had won—please God!—or there was a lull in the fighting.

Since there was little he could do in either case, he allowed himself to watch Mathilde sleep. How he loved her. Needed her. But now he had nothing to offer a wife. No land, no wealth, not even a handsome face and decent shield arm. His body was ruined, and his hopes for winning land and wealth dashed. He would have to depend on the charity of others, and he wouldn't ask a wife to live that way.

He must have made a sound, because Mathilde stirred and raised her head. She smiled—and how that broke his heart. "You're awake. Are you in much pain?"

He was in agony, his heartache more painful than the physical blows he'd suffered. "A little," he replied, his swollen cheek making it difficult for him to speak clearly, but at least his throat was not so dry and sore.

She started to rise, until he put his good right hand over hers to make her wait. "Not yet. No more medicine until I speak with Ranulf."

"Then you should eat. I will fetch something—"

"Later." For now, he just wanted to look at her. "Please?"

She returned to the stool and gave him a smile, although there were tears in her eyes. "You weren't supposed to fight," she reminded him. "And after what you said about Cerdic running heedlessly into battle. If you'd been killed—" Her words ended with a strangled sound, as if what she'd been about to say had choked her.

He reached up to stroke her hair. How tired she looked, how weary. She had dark circles beneath her eyes, as if she hadn't slept in days. So much responsibility, so much trouble in her life. He would gladly have died in her service. He wished he had. "Have we defeated Roald?"

Her eyes gave him the answer.

"How long since I was wounded?" he asked before she spoke and confirmed what he already knew.

"Three days."

"Fetch Ranulf. Please."

She nodded and rose, but he kept hold of her hand and pressed a kiss upon it before she gave him a woeful smile and left him alone.

Disfigured as he surely was, he had better get used to being alone. Never more would he be greeted with smiling and speculative glances from the ladies. No longer would they vie for his attention or men linger to hear his stories. He would be stared at, or people would avert their eyes when he came within view.

The door opened. Ranulf, his face streaked with sweat, his hair plastered to his head from the pressure of his helmet, entered the chamber followed by Cerdic, tall and grim behind him. They both looked—and smelled—as if they hadn't been out of their clothes in days.

He wondered why Mathilde had not returned with them. No doubt she had many other things to do.

"Rather an extreme effort to get out of a fight, isn't it?" Ranulf remarked, giving Henry one of his cynical smiles as he stood at the end of the bed.

That was so like Ranulf, Henry felt for a moment as if nothing had changed, and for that, he was grateful. "Roald is still here?"

Ranulf nodded and grew grave. "Unfortunately."

"Has he attacked again?"

"Not yet. It seems he's decided to try to undermine the wall."

That was not unexpected when there was only one wall, and the moat was dry. Roald would set his men to digging at the bottom of a portion of the wall. They'd use wooden props to support the masonry above them, until they had passed more than half its width. Then they'd fill the hole with dry branches and underbrush and set it on fire. When the props burned, the wall would collapse. "Can you stop them?"

Ranulf glanced at Cerdic before he answered. "I'm afraid it's a bit complicated. Cerdic and his men didn't join the battle after the signal that first day because they couldn't."

"Some of Roald's men met us before we could get to the back of their line," Cerdic explained. "My men were either killed or captured, all save me. Roald has set *them* to digging under the wall."

Henry felt for both the captured men, and their comrades. If they tried to stop the men from undermining the wall, they would be killing or injuring their friends.

"On the other hand, captured men generally lack commitment," Ranulf continued. "It will likely take much longer to dig as far as required than if he used his mercenaries."

Henry thought so, too. "No other attacks?"

"A few more forays against the walls," Ranulf replied with a shrug. "Nothing to speak off. I suspect de Sayres promised his mercenaries a quick and easy victory and his men are losing heart. The undermining's a way to avoid casualties until they have a better chance of getting into the castle."

"Your defense?"

"The same as yours would be. I've got men digging from our side, trying to get through before Roald can. If they can get to the other side first, we can fill the hole with rubble before Roald's men can fire the props."

"Good. Losses?"

"Half a dozen men, including those among Cerdic's party."

That wasn't bad, considering.

Henry looked at Cerdic, who'd saved him for such life as he must endure. After all, the man had thought he was doing a good thing. "Thank you."

Cerdic nodded matter-of-factly, one warrior to another.

Henry briefly wondered how Cerdic would feel if their situations were reversed, but defeating Roald and saving Ecclesford, and Mathilde, were more important than his own future. "The provisions?"

"We've got plenty of food. Lady Mathilde made sure of that," Ranulf replied. "I tell you, Henry, that young woman is quite a marvel. She makes Sir Leonard look lazy."

Henry smiled at that—or tried to, but his face hurt too much and he remembered Giselle's admonition about disturbing the bones she'd set.

Ranulf looked at Cerdic. "If you don't mind, my friend, I'd like a few words with Henry alone."

What did this request herald? Was the situation with Roald worse than Ranulf had implied and he didn't want to discourage Cerdic and the rest of the men? Was the defense not going as well as Cerdic seemed to think?

Or were his wounds more severe than Giselle had let on? Had she asked his closest friend to tell him some hard truths?

"Take heart, Norman. We will carry the day yet," Cerdic assured Henry with a grin as he started for the door. "You fight well."

When Cerdic had closed the door, Ranulf looked at Henry and raised a brow. "God's blood, I believe you've managed to impress him." He frowned with mock dismay. "I fear I have some way to go yet."

Henry was definitely in no mood for humor now. "What?"

"You aren't going to like it," Ranulf said as he sat on the stool beside the bed.

As impatient as Henry was, he took heart from Ranulf's expression. What he had to say was serious, to be sure, but Ranulf was not as distressed as he would be if things were truly dire.

"I've sent word to your brother about your wounds and I've asked him to send us some men, if he can spare a few—and before you get angry, it's too late to stop me. The messenger left the day after Cerdic brought you back wounded."

Ranulf must have believed he was on the verge of death to send for Nicholas.

If Nicholas saw him like this, helpless, useless…

His brother had always said he was going to wind up poor and miserable if he didn't mend his ways and act with more wisdom. Now he'd be right.

As difficult as that was, though, Henry wasn't annoyed with his friend because—and the realization hit him with macelike force—he wouldn't have wanted to die without seeing his brother one more time, and thanking him for all the care he'd taken of him, and their sister, too. And if Nicholas could help, that was much more important than his pride. "I looked that bad?"

"Terrible. I confess I didn't quite believe Lady Giselle when she said you'd recover. Thank God you will. That woman's something of a marvel, too. I've never seen anyone tend wounds so successfully. I must ask her about some of her methods and medicines. There's a salve, for instance..." He fell silent and regarded Henry with concern. "Am I tiring you out? Do you want me to go?"

"Not yet. You asked Nicholas to send some men?"

Ranulf flushed, but otherwise betrayed no emotion other than his normal self-confidence. "I knew you weren't going to be pleased, but I thought, since I was writing to Nicholas anyway, and he's going to be involved in this because you are, whether you think so or not, I'd ask. I'm not nearly as proud and stubborn as you, and if there's somebody who's likely to send me aid when I need it, I'm bloody well going to ask for it. Besides, half the men in the garrison already believe your brother's on his way, so why not request a few men to add to our forces? I don't know where Roald found the money, but he's got some expensive men in his company."

"I'm glad you did. I hope he does send men. We need them."

Ranulf looked completely taken aback for one brief moment. That expression was replaced by a relieved smile that was just as brief before his features settled into their usual wry demeanor. "Thank God you've got some sense at last."

There was something else Ranulf had said that puzzled Henry. "Some thought Nicholas was already coming?"

Ranulf hastily got to his feet. "Oh, you know soldiers—always making things up. Always hoping some friendly force will arrive in the nick of time and save them doing any serious fighting."

Henry wasn't fooled. Ranulf's uncharacteristic haste told a different tale. "Who said Nicholas was coming? You?"

It seemed impossible, for Ranulf was not given to reassuring lies, but it *might* be true.

"No!" Ranulf replied, obviously appalled. "I wouldn't do something like that unless I was certain it was true. I wouldn't want to raise false hopes, only to have them dashed and the men disheartened."

"Who then?"

Ranulf shifted his feet, then started sidling toward the door like a merchant trying to back out of a bad bargain. "It doesn't matter now, since his men may indeed be on the way."

Regardless of the pain it caused him, Henry pushed himself up into a sitting position. *"Who?"*

Ranulf struggled inwardly for a moment, but started back toward the bed. "Mathilde."

Stunned, Henry fell back against the pillows, then winced with pain.

"If you promise to sit still and stay calm, I'll tell you why she did it. As I said, she's quite a marvel."

Henry nodded a very little, enough to show that he agreed to sit still, and that Mathilde was a marvel.

Ranulf pulled up the stool and sat down. "The night after you were injured, she told the guards at the postern gate she was going to meet Nicholas and his men. I gather she told them that so they'd let her go out."

She'd lied about Nicholas so she could go out of the castle—*by herself?* And with Roald and his men in the village?

"You said you were going to keep calm," Ranulf noted. "If you get too agitated, I'll have Giselle give you a draught to make you sleep."

"I'll be calm," Henry promised, even though he knew it wouldn't be easy, given what Ranulf was telling him.

"It seems, my friend, that she went to Roald and demanded he surrender."

Henry simply couldn't believe it. She had lied to the guards and gone out of the castle, by herself, to demand Roald surrender?

"Shocking, I know. Outrageous, even, but true. She went to the village all by herself, told him his attempts to take the castle were useless, you were quite unharmed and he might as well give up."

Now that he'd had time to consider, Henry could see her doing it, her gaze resolute, her eyes shining with resolve, her hands clasped in the sleeves of her gown. And yet... "He didn't."

Or Roald's men wouldn't be trying to under-mine the wall.

"Sadly, no."

There was something that, knowing Roald as he did and what he was capable of, didn't make sense. "He let her come back?"

Ranulf didn't meet his gaze. "Not exactly." He raised his eyes and smiled. "She fought her way free. Quite a woman."

There was more to it. "What happened?"

"She got back safe and sound, so there's no need to trouble yourself—"

Henry's good right arm shot out and he grabbed Ranulf's forearm, gripping him tight. "Tell me every-thing."

"You don't need to torture me," Ranulf muttered, pulling his arm free. "I was trying to spare you, since she returned unharmed. Roald didn't touch her."

Relief flooded through Henry, until he realized Ranulf wasn't finished.

"He gave her to Charles De Mallemaison.

De Mallemaison? Sweet Christ!

"But she fought him off and ran." Ranulf's sardonic smile appeared. "Apparently she set the lout on fire."

"Fire?" Henry gasped.

"She attacked him with a candle stand after she lost her daggers." Ranulf stroked his beard. "Like I said, quite a woman."

"Daggers?"

"You don't think she was fool enough to go unarmed, do you? But even when she lost her weapons, she used what was at hand just as Sir Leonard taught us." He coolly raised a brow. "It must be gratifying to have a woman like that care about you."

It was—and humbling, and heartbreaking. "Go now, Ranulf."

"Very well," he agreed, rising. "The ladies will not be pleased if I stay much longer anyway, and there'll be hell to pay if you're exhausted when they return. I would rather not risk their wrath."

He sauntered to the door, then turned back with one of the few genuinely happy and sincere smiles

Henry had ever seen him give anyone. "I'm damned glad you're not dead, Henry."

Henry said nothing as his friend left the room, although in his heart he believed it would have been better to die in battle defending Mathilde than live without her.

CHAPTER EIGHTEEN

DURING THE NEXT few days, as Roald seemed content to pin his hopes on undermining the wall, Mathilde spent as much time as she could with Henry. When he was awake, she helped him to eat and watched as he slowly recovered from the worst of his wounds. As the swelling in his face diminished and he was able to talk with more ease and clarity, they spoke of many things, including their childhoods—Mathilde's that had been so happy, Henry's that had not. She learned that his father had gambled away their wealth and lost the family estates. Nicholas had taken over the father's role and, she gathered, carried out that duty with rather a heavy and unfeeling hand, betrothing their sister against her will, and sending Henry off to be trained by another man. Marianne had thwarted his plans, however, and was happily wed.

Henry sounded as if he'd enjoyed his time with Sir Leonard, although his mentor sounded like a harsh teacher to her. It made her wonder what sort of man his brother must be, if Henry preferred Sir Leonard's martial household. All in all, it must have been a cold, loveless youth; was it any wonder then, if such a handsome young man should seek warmth and comfort in the arms of women? Had she not sought warmth and comfort, too? And she had far less reason.

She helped Giselle tend to his wounds, and although they weren't as severe as she feared, Mathilde was well aware that Henry would never be the same again. Henry never talked about his injuries, though; instead, he asked about the other wounded, and spent some portion of every day with Ranulf and Cerdic, who were now sharing the command of the garrison. Cerdic was in charge of the defenses, while Ranulf guided the efforts of their men digging beneath the wall, trying to break through before Roald's forces. Henry had asked Mathilde to come the moment either Ranulf's men broke through, or if Roald's men attacked the gate again, so that he could watch the confrontation from the window of his chamber.

When Mathilde was not with him, she supervised the distribution of food and mediated the conflicts that arose from too many people in too small an area. Everyone was tense, and even the animals seemed short-tempered.

So it was almost a relief when, finally, Ranulf came to tell her that his men were nearly through the wall. Cerdic's men were gathering on the battlements, ready to attack from above when Roald realized what was afoot. They were keeping their heads low and moving quietly so that Roald and his army wouldn't guess what was about to happen.

Mathilde ran to Henry's chamber, to find him already standing by the bed, clad in a long linen shirt that reached to his knees, his face and shoulder still swathed in bandages.

"They're nearly through, aren't they?" he asked. "Cerdic and his men are massing on the wall."

"You should have waited for my help to get out of bed," she chided, with that pang of guilt she always felt when she saw his bandaged wounds.

"I'm not going to watch the battle from here."

She tried not to look upset, but if he found it too taxing even to stand…. "Let me help you back into bed."

"I'm going to lead the garrison from the battlements," he said with firm resolution. "I want the men to see me. I want Roald to see me and hear my voice as I call out my orders. I want him to know I'm not dead."

He couldn't. He was still too weak—but that was not a word she would use. "You're not yet well enough to be on your feet for any length of time."

"If you can go by yourself to Roald de Sayres and demand his surrender, I can don my mail and command the garrison from the battlements."

She clutched the post of the bed. How had he found out about that failed effort? "Who told you?"

"Are you going to deny it?"

He was so certain, there was no point trying even if she had considered it. But she wouldn't lie to Henry. "No, I'm not. I did go to Roald and tell him he should surrender. I hoped to convince him he couldn't defeat us."

"And you went by yourself."

"Yes, by myself." She wasn't ashamed or sorry for what she'd done, even if her plan hadn't worked. "I didn't want to put anyone else at risk."

"You could have been killed."

"Yes."

"So although you were willing to risk your life for me and everyone in Ecclesford, you would have me stay in here like a child, waiting for the battle to end."

"You're hurt," she pointed out, trying not to reveal too much of her distress. She didn't want him to think he was as helpless as a child, but he would never again be the same powerful warrior he was when he arrived in Ecclesford.

His expression softened. "I know that I'm wounded, and I know you're concerned for me, Mathilde. But can't you see? I can't stay here like an old woman. I *must* do this, or I might as well lie on that bed and never get up again. I want to lead the garrison against the man who hurt you so much.

Who's trying to steal what's rightfully yours and who foolishly thinks he can defeat you and those who love you."

He took her right hand in his. "I would rather die as the garrison commander of Ecclesford defending the woman I love than live another twenty years." He tried to smile in the old, merry way. "And once my brother got over the shock of my chivalrous end, he might be proud of me at last."

Even now, he would try to lighten her sorrow, and her heart broke anew as she looked at him standing so resolutely before her. She studied his bandaged face and saw, deep in his eyes, a plea.

He was a proud warrior, a commander of men. Losing to Charles De Mallemaison must have been as devastating to his pride as the wound to his face. As humiliating for him as Roald's attack had been for her. He, too, had been made to feel weak and helpless, had had his self-worth stripped from him and his pride stolen away. How could she deny him the chance to regain that pride? To be again a warrior, a commander of men? She couldn't. As she loved, honored and respected him, she couldn't. As he had helped her recover her self-worth, she must help him now, no matter how afraid she would be.

Despite her acceptance of what must be, for his sake, it wasn't easy to speak. "Very well, Henry," she said. "I will help you."

334 HERS TO COMMAND

His shoulders relaxed, telling her how tense he'd been.

With his good arm, he pulled her close and held her tight.

"I'm sure the sight of their commander will inspire our men," she whispered, determined not to show him her fear, to be as brave as he as she helped her lover prepare once more for battle.

From the chest holding his clothes, she fetched his breeches, then a shirt and the gambeson, and helped him dress, mindful of his swollen cheek. She gently eased his clothing over his head and carefully maneuvered his left arm into the sleeve. She lowered his mail hauberk over the gambeson, followed by his scarlet surcoat. Henry bit his lip and blanched as he moved, but no sound escaped his lips. Kneeling she tied his leg armor around his shins.

"You'll have to bind my left arm in place."

She mutely nodded and got a wide strip of linen to use as a sling. When she was finished, he said, "My helmet? Or is it too damaged?"

She retrieved it from the chest. "I had the armorer repair it."

Henry took it in his right hand and examined it. "He did a good job."

Mathilde said nothing. She found it difficult to look at that helmet. Whatever Henry thought, it still bore enough evidence of the attack to upset her.

"The visor should hide most of the bandages," he noted with approval. "No need to scare the troops, eh, my beloved? There won't be room for my coif, but I'll manage without it. Shouldn't be as sweaty around my neck, at least."

Oh, heaven preserve him, how she loved him! And feared for him. Yet she couldn't—wouldn't—say anything to dissuade him. She must be brave for him, as he was being brave for her.

He gazed at her with tender sympathy, then reached out to caress her cheek. "I know this isn't easy for you, beloved, but I *must* go."

"I love you more than I can say," she whispered, blinking back the tears that threatened to fall.

"As I love you," he vowed, and then he drew her close, and kissed her.

"SIR HENRY! It's Sir Henry!"

The excited murmur raced first through the hall and then the men waiting anxiously in the courtyard as Henry, with Mathilde by his side, made his way toward the battlements. Ranulf's men digging beneath the wall heard the news and paused in their efforts, until Ranulf reminded them of its importance and urged them to work with a will. They were nearly through and it was imperative that they reach the other side first.

Despite Henry's resolve and Mathilde's support,

the walk to the battlements wasn't easy for him. His whole body ached, and it was difficult to breathe through the helmet and bandages around his face. But when he saw the delight on the men's faces, and their relief, he was more than glad he'd made the effort.

"Well met, Sir Henry," Cerdic said with a grin when they joined him on the wall walk. "I am glad to see thee, as I never thought I would be, and gladder still that we come to battle again at last. Hiding behind walls is not to my taste."

"Nor mine," Henry replied, squeezing Mathilde's hand as he found his balance. His legs were weak from inactivity, but without his coif, he didn't dare lean on the merlon where an archer might see him.

He turned to his beloved and noted her pale face. She was trying to be brave for him, and he loved her all the more for it. "You should go now, Mathilde. It's too dangerous for you here."

He leaned close to kiss her and as he did, he whispered something he hoped would ease her fears. "I promise I won't venture from the battlements."

When she drew back, she gave him a tremulous smile. "God be with you, Henry, and with all of us today," she said.

And then she left him there.

HENRY PAID little heed to the men standing near him as he watched the huge battering ram again being rolled toward the gates. He doubted that, even as re-inforced as they were, the gates could withstand a second onslaught.

Even so, Cerdic had ensured that they were as prepared as possible for another attack on the gate and done everything they could to stop the ram until Ranulf's men broke through beneath the wall.

Sheaves of hay had been brought from the stables and thrown down in front of the gates to block the ram and cushion its blow. Bedding, too, had been tossed over the wall, except for the pallets for the wounded, including the ladies' featherbed.

Several large iron pots full of water had been set on tripods above fires, ready to pour on the men manning the ram or those trying to scale the walls. There was one pot of pitch to throw onto the ram itself. Archers with fire arrows would set it alight once they got the order.

Peering at the oncoming ram, Cerdic cursed softly.

"What is it?" Henry asked, silently distressed he couldn't see very well or far now.

"He's using our men on the ram, too."

"Damn him," Henry muttered.

"We can't throw the pitch on our own men," Cerdic said.

"We may have no choice."

Cerdic looked about to protest, but then he sighed and nodded. It would be difficult to throw heavy stones and boiling water onto the men they knew, and worse to send some to a fiery death from pitch and flames, but it would be worse to have the gate breeched.

"Cerdic, you go to the yard and lead the men there, should the gate fall."

Cerdic nodded and obeyed at once, while Henry stayed where he was.

The ram rumbled closer, picking up speed as it approached the gate. Again Henry cursed his wounds as he tried to scan the army waiting a short distance away, looking for Roald and De Mallemaison. Would they wait for the gates to be broken before they attacked, or would they start an assault on the wall? Or was the ram intended to distract the men of Ecclesford while they finished undermining the wall?

"You there!" Henry called, summoning a short man in ill-fitting mail, a helmet with a noseguard on his head. "Go to Ranulf and see how long before they break through."

The soldier hesitated and Henry didn't hide his annoyance. "Then you go," he said to another, who instantly made haste down the steps. "And you," he said to the man who'd hesitated, curt in his anxiety, "stay out of the way. I won't have a slow-witted man in the first line."

The soldier bowed his head as if rightly ashamed, and stepped back.

Then he was forgotten as the ram struck the gate.

They hadn't done enough to stop its progress. Henry clenched his teeth as the whole wall shook with the force of the impact.

There was no help for it. "Throw the rocks," he ordered as the men guiding the ram started to back it up to strike again. No doubt Roald had arrows trained on them, threatening them with death if they didn't break through the gates. He wouldn't order the pitch thrown until they were desperate.

He saw his men waver, knew they were reluctant. "If Roald gets in the gate, all could be lost."

A rock went over the side. Then another. Nearby, the archers shifted impatiently, anxious to fire on the enemy farther back who were waiting to attack after the gate was breeched or to scale the walls.

"Not yet," Henry cautioned them. "They're too far away. Patience, boys, patience."

Again the ram hit the gate, and this time, Henry had to grab onto the merlon to keep from falling. An arrow whizzed by his head. He peered out from behind the merlon to see that Roald had moved the men with pavises and the archers closer to the walls.

"If you get a shot at any of his archers or their shield men, take it," Henry ordered his bowmen, who eagerly nocked their arrows. "But shoot wisely."

He had trained them well, and they did as they were told. They didn't fire indiscriminately; they held off until they had a chance of hitting one of their enemies.

The ram was coming toward the gate again. Henry moved to the edge of the battlements to look down into the yard. Despite the reinforcing iron bands, the wood of the gate was cracked and the bands themselves were bent. One great iron hinge had come loose from the wall. Another hit, and the gate probably wouldn't hold.

"Throw the pitch!" Henry cried, even though it was an order he hated to give. "Set the ram alight!"

The dark, heavy liquid, heated to boiling, went pouring over the side in a thick, stinking stream. Henry briefly closed his eyes as the screams of the men below filled his ears. The flame arrows whizzed over the wall, and the smell and smoke from burning pitch and wood and flesh rose in the air.

He leaned over and saw, to his even greater dismay, that the pitch had fallen to one side of the ram instead of hitting it directly. Several men lay on the ground, writhing in agony, or not moving at all. More of Roald's men, sensing victory, dashed forward to pull the ram back, ready for another blow.

Henry swore and ordered his men to heave more rocks over the wall. There was one good thing, if such a thing could ever be accounted good: because Roald had thought to use the captured men of Ecclesford to man the ram, he hadn't provided any kind of cover for them. Now his mercenaries were just as vulnerable to anything that came over the walls of the castle.

Roald's archers moved closer, keeping up a barrage that forced Henry and the others to stay behind the merlons. Behind the archers, Henry could see the main bulk of his force lying in wait, Roald or De Mallemaison surely among them even if he couldn't see them.

Despite the efforts of Henry's men, the ram struck the gate again. Once more the wall shook—but this time, he heard the sickening sound of shattering wood. A shout went up from the men in the yard, and at the same time, Roald's men started to run toward the castle.

The gates were breeched. As Roald's mercenaries rushed forward, Henry forgot that he was wounded, forgot that he was weak, forgot he was in command. All he knew was that he must drive back the invaders, by himself if necessary.

The blood rushing through his body, even his pain overwhelmed by the need to protect Ecclesford, he drew his sword with his good right hand and turned to run down to the courtyard.

"No, my lord, you must not!"

He glared at the soldier who blocked his way, the one who'd hesitated. "Coward, out of my way!"

"You promised!"

That was no man. *Mathilde?* What are you—!"

He cried out in horror as she suddenly uttered a little shriek of alarm and pitched forward into his arms, an arrow in her back.

"HOW MUCH LONGER?" Roald demanded as he sat on his horse beside De Mallemaison, glaring at the Scot who'd been summoned from his command of the workers undermining the castle wall.

"Using captured men makes for slow progress," the Scot replied with a shrug.

"It had better be soon. We're nearly through the gate. Go back and tell them if they haven't finished and started the fires by the time I get there, their bodies will be with the kindling when we set the material alight."

The Scot nodded and turned on his heel to return to his command.

"I don't trust that fellow," Roald muttered as he watched the soldiers on the wall walk of Ecclesford toss down more rocks.

"I don't trust any of 'em," De Mallemaison said, his gaze on the castle. "We'd better get in today, or I'm leaving. This is taking too much time."

"What else have you got to do, besides collect the debts of merchants? We're nearly there, and there's plenty of gold inside," Roald countered, Mathilde's warning about De Mallemaison's selfish motives coming to haunt him again. What if the bitch was right and he had made a terrible mistake involving this vicious mercenary in his efforts to claim his rights?

She couldn't be—and her attack on De Mallemaison ought to make the brute more keen to defeat her and the rest of his enemies in Ecclesford. "Don't you want your vengeance on Mathilde?"

De Mallemaison scowled. "Not enough to risk my life."

"Risk your life? Are you mad? Once we get inside the walls, the battle will be over. That garrison is no match for our men."

"They were a match before," De Mallemaison grumbled.

"That was when they had that bastard Henry to lead them, and like you, I'm sure he's dead."

De Mallemaison's answer was a noncommittal grunt, which did nothing to assuage Roald's doubts.

Maybe the man hadn't killed D'Alton. Maybe that Norman was only wounded. Maybe not even that. Perhaps he'd been a fool to believe De Mallemaison when he said he'd killed him.

Maybe he should have accepted Mathilde's offer and gone back to Provence while he could.

De Mallemaison barked a laugh, startling Roald out of his distressed reverie. "They missed. Threw the pitch and missed, the fools." His scarred face twisted with a grin. "I'll stay. Now if only those oafs would finish at the wall."

Roald managed *not* to sigh with relief.

One of the mercenaries working on the wall came running. "They've come through the other way!" he shouted.

De Mallemaison uttered an oath and turned his horse to head toward the wall and the men pouring forth from the hole beneath it.

A pale Roald did not follow.

"OH, SWEET SAVIOR!" Henry cried as, regardless of the agonizing pain in his shoulder, he caught Mathilde and lowered her to the ground, cradling her with his good right arm.

"You there, help me!" he called to the nearest soldier. "Help me lift her. We've got to get her to the hall to Giselle."

Henry couldn't do it himself. He didn't have the strength, his left arm was useless. He called for another soldier to take her other side.

As they lifted her in their arms, one on either side, Henry cursed himself for not, somehow, realizing she was there. He should have wondered who that soldier was, questioned the hesitation, sent her from the wall.

If she died… If she died, he might as well be dead, too.

But first, Roald was going to rue even being born.

As the men carrying Mathilde started down the steps, their enemies began fighting their way into the courtyard through the smashed gate. The men would never get to the hall with Mathilde. They would have to tend her here, as best they could.

"Come back," he ordered. He tore the sling from

his left arm and reached up to try to remove his helmet, but he couldn't do that, either.

"Help me get this off," he commanded one of the archers, who rushed to obey. When the archer got the helmet off, he gasped when he saw Henry's bandaged face.

"Take off my bandages and use them to staunch her wound. Quick, man!"

Breathing hard, the archer did as he was ordered, looking away in dismay when Henry's face was exposed.

Henry didn't care what he looked like or what this fellow thought. He didn't care about his own wounds, or what other damage might be done. All that mattered was Mathilde. "Don't pull out the arrow," he said as the soldiers eased the linen under her gambeson. "Leave it in until Giselle can tend to her."

Unsheathing his sword, he started for the stairs leading to the yard.

"Where're you going, my lord?" the archer who'd taken off his bandages called out.

"To kill Roald de Sayres."

DE MALLEMAISON realized it was hopeless the moment he got to the wall. There were too many soldiers from Ecclesford coming from within; they couldn't stop them, short of pulling down the props, and there was no way to do that now.

Damn de Sayres. They should have used the men he'd hired to undermine the wall, not the captives. They would have been through before this.

Cursing, he pulled his horse hard to the right, away from the castle. To hell with de Sayres and his inheritance—if it *was* his. He wasn't going to die fighting for him. He'd been promised easy pickings, a quick fight and ample reward, and instead found himself besieging a well-defended castle and combating well-trained men.

As for the women, no woman was worth half this much trouble. Beating Lady Mathilde until she pleaded for her life and taking her sister had some appeal, but not enough to induce him to put his life in danger. As for D'Alton, that bitch could say what she liked, but he *knew* he'd killed—

"De Mallemaison!"

With a gasp, he looked back over his shoulder, to see a man charging toward him, his sword upraised, his face—

God damn him, it couldn't be! Some other man must be wearing D'Alton's surcoat. But that long brown hair, the shape of his body—the broad shoulders, narrow hips.

D'Alton was alive and surging toward him to attack. Without a helmet.

Regardless of that shock, and the sight of D'Alton's ruined visage, De Mallemaison reacted with the honed instincts of a trained killer and started twirling his mace, waiting until D'Alton was close enough to hit.

Keeping hold of the grip, he swung the weapon toward his enemy. As he did, D'Alton raised his sword like a beacon. The balls of the mace spun around it and the chains wrapped around the blade. Planting his feet, D'Alton gave a mighty tug, pulling the mace from De Mallemaison's hands and De Mallemaison from his horse.

Stunned, it took De Mallemaison a moment to recover and get to his feet while D'Alton tipped his sword down to make the mace slide free.

It was then, with a rush of triumph, that De Mallemaison realized D'Alton carried no shield on his left arm. That whole side of his body was unprotected, like his head.

Unsheathing and raising his sword, De Mallemaison ran at Henry. Before he struck, Henry dropped his sword and jumped out of the way. As he righted himself, he heard someone call his name.

It was Cerdic, surrounded by three men, one of them a Scot.

"Take my ax!" the Saxon called, tossing his weapon to Henry, who caught it with his good right hand.

As he turned back to De Mallemaison, he saw Cerdic whip a dagger out of his belt and silently begged God to help his friend.

"Look at your pretty face, all spoiled," De Mallemaison jeered as he circled Henry.

"I'm still not as ugly as you," Henry replied as he
tilted the head of the ax toward the ground, letting it
slide through his fingers until he held it near the end
of the handle.

Gripping his sword hilt with both hands, De
Mallemaison raised his sword, preparing to strike. In
that split second when his sword was poised above
his head, Henry brought the ax around sideways,
slicing through the surcoat, mail and gambeson protecting De Mallemaison's chest.

With a gasp, De Mallemaison staggered back,
blood trickling from the wound.

Not deep enough, Henry realized, even as he felt
his strength draining. Not yet, he begged God, not
until I've killed him.

Again raising his sword, although not so high, De
Mallemaison lunged. Henry jumped back, twisting
to avoid the blow, wrenching his wounded shoulder
in the process. He cried out in pain even as he readied
himself to strike again.

"The poor boy is hurt," De Mallemaison sneered,
sidling closer.

Keeping his eye on his enemy, using both hands
and ignoring the excruciating pain in his shoulder,
Henry held the shaft of the ax sideways like a quarter
staff, ready to ward off another blow.

De Mallemaison brought down his sword, and Henry raised the ax. The force of De Mallemaison's blow broke the shaft of the ax in two. Keeping hold of the end with the ax head in his right hand, Henry dropped the other part from his nearly useless left hand.

When De Mallemaison recovered and readied for another blow, Henry swung the portion he still held back, around and up and then threw it at De Mallemaison with all his might.

It sliced off De Mallemaison's right hand. Together it and his sword fell to the ground as De Mallemaison screamed, blood pouring from his arm.

Panting and sickened with the effort of defending himself and the sight of the dismembered hand, Henry stumbled forward and picked up De Mallemaison's sword. Grabbing it, he faced De Mallemaison, who clutched the end of his arm, blood dripping from between his fingers.

The mercenary raised his eyes, and his cold, dead gaze met Henry's.

Winded, sickened and exhausted, Henry lowered his sword.

De Mallemaison fell to his knees, his face pale. His mouth twisted to an angry snarl. "Go ahead, kill me!"

Henry staggered back a step.

"Do it!" De Mallemaison screamed, desperation in his voice. "Kill me!"

If the man could no longer fight, what did he have? Like Henry, he had nothing.

Henry felt no more anger, no more invigorating rage. He held De Mallemaison's sword limply in his right hand, too tired even to pay heed to the other men fighting around him.

De Mallemaison scowled, and then he let go of his wounded arm and let his life's blood flow onto the ground.

"May God forgive you," Henry murmured, turning away—to see Roald de Sayres riding away from Ecclesford.

His grip tightening on the bloody hilt of De Mallemaison's sword, his swollen cheek throbbing, his shoulder agonizing, Henry thought only of killing the man who was responsible for all this. He started toward him at a lumbering jog, staggering and weaving his way through the other men as they fought, determined to get to Roald before he got away. His left shoulder ached as if it had been cut from his body, and his right arm was like lead. He could no longer see out of his right eye. Perhaps the bones had shifted, more damage done.

He didn't care, as long as he had the strength to defeat Roald and punish him for what he'd done to Mathilde.

He was exhausted. He didn't have the strength to catch up to him—and then the Scot who'd been fighting Cerdic appeared as if out of nowhere and grabbed the bridle of Roald's horse.

"Your cause is lost," the Scot declared as Henry, panting heavily, drew near. "Nicholas of Dunkeathe has come, and I willna stay to meet his men."

His brother had come. Thank God Nicholas had come. Now they would win. Now, whatever happened to him, Mathilde would be safe.

Roald lifted his booted foot and kicked the Scot back. "That's a lie!"

The Scot didn't budge an inch as the boot collided with his chest. "Aye, he has, for I know his banner well. And another army has come from Cornwall, carrying Lord Merrick of Tregellas's banner."

Merrick? Merrick had come, too? Henry parted his lips and uttered a heartfelt thanks to God.

"Liar!" Roald screamed, kicking again at the Scot and pulling on his reins to try to turn his horse, until the poor beast's mouth bled.

The Scot lunged, pulling Roald down from his horse and throwing him onto the ground. "I'll kill you for this!" Roald screeched as he scrambled to his feet.

The Scot backed away. "I dinna think so. I'm getting out of this mess and so, I think, are the rest of your men." He glanced at Henry, still coming toward them. "I'm tempted to kill ye mysel' but there's somebody else has a better right."

With that, the Scot strode away, and other mercenaries, seeing him go, took to their heels with less dignity.

"Cowards! Come back!" Roald bellowed, his gaze darting like a trapped rat, his whole body shaking with rage and fear.

"You can't buy loyalty," Henry said, lifting his sword and preparing to fight. "And now that my brother and my friend are here, they'll make short work of any of your men who've lingered. Surrender, Roald. It's over. You've lost."

"No!" Roald screeched, fumbling as he tried to draw his sword, finally succeeding. "I'll kill you!"

He charged forward, his sword upraised to strike.

Henry crouched, feet firm to the earth, as Sir Leonard would say, trying to concentrate and ignore his pain and his fatigue.

But even distraught, Roald was a good fighter. He aimed for Henry's useless shoulder. Henry half turned, his right side forward, his blade raised to block the blow.

Roald was too strong, Henry too weak. Roald knocked the sword from Henry's hands and Henry fell to his knees. He tried to get up, but he couldn't.

Roald's exultant laugh filled the air. "Too bad you didn't stay out of this, Henry. How sorry you must be."

"No, never sorry," Henry gasped, meaning it.

Sir Leonard's voice seemed to thunder in his ears

as his right hand closed around a palm-size stone. *Use whatever comes to hand, boy.*

Whatever comes to hand.

With the last of his strength, he raised his arm and threw the stone at Roald with all his might. It struck Roald in the face, right between his eyes. With a cry, he staggered backward and fell.

Gasping for breath, Henry crawled forward, reaching out for Roald's sword now on the ground beside him.

Roald lay flat on his back, not moving. Grabbing the man's sword, Henry cautiously inched closer, his weight on his right hand, his left arm dragging, to see a dark bruise between Roald's brows. His surprised and lifeless eyes stared up, unseeing, at the sky above him.

God be praised, the man was dead.

As Henry slipped to the ground, pain and fatigue washed over him, and carried him into oblivion.

CHAPTER NINETEEN

"HENRY, ARE YOU AWAKE?" a gentle, loving voice asked.

It sounded like Mathilde. But she had been hurt. Wounded. By an arrow. In the back, on the battlements with him.

Someone was holding his right hand.

"He's still asleep."

Mathilde again? He tried to speak, to say her name, but all that came out was a low moan.

"He really should rest, my lords. He is past the greatest danger, but his wounds are severe and will take some time to heal. We should let him sleep."

That was Giselle.

"I will stay." Wonderful, beautiful, courageous Mathilde, his angel. With an arrow in her back.

And yet… If she was not dead, perhaps not even seriously wounded… Oh, God, could it be? He tried again to speak and to open his heavy eyelids.

"We shall leave, then, until such time—"

Nicholas? God's wounds, that had to be Nicholas. That Scot had not been lying.

"Mathilde?" he finally managed to gasp. He got his eyes open, and the first thing he saw was Mathilde's wonderful, worried face.

She was sitting beside his bed. It was her hand that held his and he squeezed it with all the strength he could muster as she smiled down at him. She didn't look hurt or ill. She looked overjoyed, enraptured. Delightful and delighted. As bold and vivacious as ever. "I thought…"

He started to cough, and she quickly lifted him up and held a goblet of some kind of liquid to his throat. It tasted terrible, but it was soothing for all that.

He lay back, panting, still holding his lover's hand. God help him, he never wanted to let her go.

Two other people came into view behind her: his brother and Merrick. He had only seen his brother look so worried once before, when it was a matter concerning his beloved wife. As usual, Merrick's face betrayed almost nothing, and had Henry not known him well, he would have thought him completely unmoved. But he did know Merrick well, enough to catch the slight downturn of his lips that betrayed anxiety.

Both men glanced across the bed and he realized Giselle was on the other side. "How are you feeling, Henry?" she asked softly.

"Better," he managed to say, again squeezing Mathilde's hand and trying to smile at her despite his aching cheek. "I thought you…the arrow…?"

"If I had not been wearing mail and a gambeson—which I must say is very heavy and I can understand now why the men grumbled so when you made them run in such things—I might not be alive now," she replied. "But I was, so the tip of the arrow did not go deep." She flushed, looking prettier than ever. "I fear, my love, that I fainted, like the weakest woman in the kingdom."

"The bravest woman," he assured her, silently sending another grateful prayer to God for sparing his beloved. "You shouldn't have—"

"I was afraid you would do exactly what you did." She frowned, although her dancing eyes belied any anger. "And after you promised me you would not fight."

"He always was an unthinking, overly courageous fool," Nicholas noted. Henry cut his eyes to his brother, and had one of the great shocks of his life when he realized Nicholas was smiling.

"I always thought it would either be the death of him, or the making of him. Fortunately, it looks as if he's shown me he's a brother I should be very proud of, and I am."

Henry closed his eyes, lest his suddenly tear-filled eyes betray his weakness. Either he was more hurt than he guessed, or perhaps it was the medicine he'd been given....

Damn him, why not admit the truth, at least to

himself? He was thrilled to hear his brother's words. He'd waited all his life to hear Nicholas praise him.

"And he will do what he thinks right, although it costs him dear," Merrick added. "Other men might think twice about interfering in other people's business after the way I beat him when he interfered in mine."

"Thank God he did not think twice about helping us," Mathilde said, as bold and insolent as ever, "and you should be ashamed of what you did to him."

"Mathilde!" Henry croaked.

"Well, it is true, and if you had not interfered, as he puts it, Giselle and I and everyone in Ecclesford would be under Roald's thumb."

"I do believe this lady cares a great deal for my brother," Nicholas said coolly to Merrick. "We should bear that in mind when she upbraids us."

Henry's gaze darted to Mathilde. Had she dared to upbraid Nicholas, who did not take criticism at all well?

Mathilde caught his wary look, but didn't appear the least bit nonplused. "I told your brother he should have ensured that you were in the employ of a lord capable of rewarding you as you deserve, instead of making you travel about like some sort of minstrel."

God's blood, she would, too. Was there a more amazing woman in the world?

Yet he must lose her.

This must be God's idea of punishment for his

vanity and past sins, to have him finally find a woman he truly loved, then disfigure him and make him useless.

"According to her, I've been most remiss in my brotherly duty and ought to be thoroughly ashamed of myself," Nicholas remarked, and to Henry's further shock, it seemed Nicholas wasn't angry but amused. "When you are well, Henry, I shall have to remedy the situation, or I fear this lady's wrath will descend upon me."

In the past Henry would have resented such aid from his brother, but now such help would be pointless. He could be of no use to a lord. "Ranulf? Cerdic?"

"Both are well," Mathilde assured him. "They have the repairs to the wall and gate in hand, and are rounding up any of Roald's mercenaries who might be lingering in the county."

As happy as he was to hear that Ranulf and Cerdic had escaped without injury, this was another reminder that he wasn't needed.

"I gather the tale of the defense of Ecclesford is becoming fodder for minstrels from here to London," Nicholas said, and Henry saw the glimmer of brotherly pride in his eyes. "The brave Sir Henry rises from his deathbed to vanquish the demonic Charles De Mallemaison and the evil Roald de Sayres."

And since Roald was dead, the dispute over Ecclesford was over. Henry could take some comfort from that during the lonely days ahead.

"Gentlemen, you should leave now," Giselle said gently, but insistently. "Henry really must rest. You can speak with him again tomorrow."

Nicholas and Merrick were used to giving orders, not receiving them. Nevertheless, they both nodded with acquiescence, as much as such proud men could, and obeyed Giselle's orders as meekly as the lowliest foot soldier under their command.

Henry continued to hold Mathilde's hand tightly. He hoped she would stay a little longer. One day, and all too soon, he would have to leave her. Until then, he wanted to feast his eyes on her, even though he was already sure he'd never forget her face.

Giselle looked at Mathilde as if she'd like to order her to go, but knew it would be useless, and instead went to the door. "I shall be below if you need anything," she said as she glided gracefully from the chamber.

Once she was gone, Mathilde brushed a lock of hair from Henry's forehead. "Sleep, Henry, my love, as Giselle directs. I will be here when you wake."

In truth, he was still bone weary, but there were questions he wanted answered first. "How long?"

Her brow furrowed. "How long?"

"Since Roald…?"

"It's been five days. After the men brought you

back, Giselle gave you medicine to make sure you would sleep and stay still. You were very lucky, she said, that you didn't kill yourself by going to fight. Why did you join the battle, Henry? And after you gave me your promise you would not?"

"I thought they'd killed you."

"But they had not and if you had died..." Her breath caught in her throat and she looked away.

He hadn't meant to hurt her. He never wanted to hurt her, or see her suffer. That was why she must be free, to choose a better man with better prospects, who could be the sort of husband she deserved.

"I would have wished myself dead if you had been killed!" she whispered.

He let go of her hand to caress her cheek. "Thank God I'm not, then."

She smiled, her eyes bright, and he was both glad and anguished when she leaned down and laid her head against his shoulder. "Thank you for coming here, Henry," she whispered, kissing the lobe of his ear, her breath warm on his face. "Thank you for helping us."

Her heartfelt words nearly unmanned him. "Water?" he rasped. His throat was still sore, but that was not why he asked. He couldn't bear to have her so close, saying such words.

"Of course," she said, hurrying to pour him a cup from the ewer on the table nearby.

As she did so, he reached up and gingerly felt his wounded cheek. It was too covered with bandages to tell much, although he didn't think it was as swollen as before. He moved to his brow bone, and felt the stitches running along its length.

"Here, my love," she said, raising him and putting the cup to his lips. He drank, then sank down again on the pillows. "Rest now."

Closing his eyes, he attempted to feign sleep, but he was so exhausted, he was truly asleep in a very short time.

WHEN NEXT HE WOKE, it was to find Ranulf in Mathilde's place. His red-haired friend smiled, for once without a hint of sardonic world-weariness.

"I sent your nursemaid to eat," he said before Henry tried to speak. "Otherwise, I fear she would starve herself looking after you. She also needs to rest, you know. The tip of that arrow did a little more than prick her skin."

He knew it! She had been sore hurt and was only pretending for his sake—

"Not that it was life-threatening," Ranulf hastened to add, "or would be accounted more than a flesh wound by Sir Leonard, but if she tires herself out, it could slow the healing, and she'll have a scar."

Henry took a deep breath and let it out slowly, while Ranulf leaned back and locked his hands about one upraised knee. "I myself fail to see the fascination in watching a man sleep."

Henry struggled to sit more upright. "Especially one with such a face?" he asked as Ranulf, having adjusted Henry's pillows, returned to the stool.

Ranulf frowned. "To be sure, it's a bad wound, but considering the alternative could have been death, I think you should thank God for sparing your life."

What life was he going to have after this? "I want to see my face."

Ranulf flushed and started to rise, looking for all the world as if he would rather flee.

Whether Ranulf would help him or not, Henry was determined to know the ugly reality. Using only his right hand, he tried to undo the knot holding the linen around his face.

With a sigh of resignation and an expression of annoyance, Ranulf returned to the stool. "Here, let me do it. God knows what damage you'll do if I don't."

Henry didn't care why Ranulf helped him, as long as he did. Sweat started to trickle down his back as Ranulf worked and he watched his friend for any reaction.

Perhaps Ranulf had already seen his wounds, for when Henry could feel the air on his cheek, Ranulf's expression betrayed nothing.

After putting the bandages on the table beside the bed, Ranulf picked up the polished silver ewer that held the fresh water. "Bear in mind that this will distort what you see."

Henry nodded and held his breath as Ranulf lifted the ewer.

It was as if the right side of his face had been made of clay, pressed and permanently indented by the mace's ball. It was still badly bruised, a motley mess of purple, red and yellow. The cut in his brow that had been stitched was scabbed, with dark threads poking through the marred flesh.

He pushed the ewer away. Handsome Sir Henry no more, indeed. It would be a miracle if any woman could look at his face without flinching.

"Mathilde doesn't care, you know," Ranulf said as he returned the ewer to the table.

How could she not? He looked as bad as Charles De Mallemaison.

But it was not of his face that he spoke to Ranulf. "My arm...I can't hold a shield anymore."

"No," Ranulf agreed, sitting on the stool. "I'm afraid your fighting days are over, my friend."

Ranulf hadn't even attempted to make light of his future. This, then, was the hard truth, just as he'd feared.

He regarded his friend with resignation. "Is it difficult?"

"What?" Ranulf asked, confused. "To give up fighting? I have to confess, if someone were to tell me I'd never have to be in a battle again, I'd thank

God. I'd forgotten how terrible they are—the death, the blood, the noise. Losing men. Seeing them hurt. God's blood, Henry, in a way, I envy you."

In a way. That didn't make his fate any easier to bear. Fighting was what he'd trained for, was all he knew. "That isn't what I meant. It is difficult to forget the woman you love?"

Ranulf stared at him with blatantly stunned disbelief, as if Henry had just said something completely, utterly, inconceivably stupid. "You think Mathilde won't want you anymore? God's wounds, I should think that you'd have a better understanding of her by now."

"What have I to offer her?" Henry wretchedly replied. "What lady would want a husband who looks like this? What lord would want a cripple in his household?"

"You've been wounded, and in service to her. If anything, that's only made her love you more."

Oh, God, this was unbearable to hear and worse to believe. "I don't want her to marry me out of pity, or gratitude."

"So you think you should leave her free to find another, better man to marry?"

It was hard to hear the words so bluntly spoken, but that was exactly what had to be. "Yes."

Ranulf's expression hardened into his usual sardonic mask. "And I suppose, being the vain, stubborn and arrogant fellow you are, you won't listen to anyone who disagrees with you."

How could he be vain with this ruined face? How he be arrogant now that he could no longer fight?

Ranulf rose. "I am no expert on women to be offering advice, and the few times I have, I've been rebuffed, so I'm not going to try to tell you what to do, except that I think you're wrong."

"I'm right," Henry replied. "But I'm glad you're not going to argue with me."

Yet there was still something he wanted—needed—to ask, even though it meant treading into a place where his friend preferred not to go. "How long did it take you to forget the woman you loved?"

Ranulf's visage was bleakly grim as he looked down at his friend. "Who says I have?"

The door opened, and Mathilde appeared on the threshold, a tray in her hands.

"Ah, my lady," Ranulf said, once more the coolly genial nobleman. "Come to relieve me, have you? As you see, your patient is once again awake. I trust you managed to get a bite to eat?"

"Yes, thank you," Mathilde replied, her eyes on Henry, and his pale face, his lips pressed so tightly together. She hurriedly set the tray on the table and went to him. "Are you in pain, my love? Would you like something to ease it? Giselle's potion—"

He shook his head, and to her relief, smiled,

HERS TO COMMAND

one side of his mouth rising as it used to, the other not so much.

"I shall leave you two alone, then," Ranulf said, strolling to the door.

On the threshold, he looked back at his friend, formerly the handsomest man at court, and the woman who looked at him as if he still had the face of angel.

LATER THAT DAY, Mathilde gathered up some linen from beside the pallet of a soldier who'd been seriously slashed with a sword. After tending to Henry's wounds she no longer felt ill in the presence of blood and wounds and the smells of the ointments Giselle concocted, so she'd offered to help Giselle with the other men who'd been injured.

Henry's brother had agreed to stay for a few more days, although he was anxious to get home to his wife, whom he very obviously loved. Every time he mentioned Riona, his eyes brightened like Henry's, and his deep voice softened.

Lord Merrick was planning to leave in the morning, because of his wife's condition, or so he said. She was expecting their first child, and he did not want to be away from her for long. However, like the stern Lord Nicholas, Merrick's eyes glowed when he spoke of his wife, and it was clear he loved her deeply, perhaps nearly as deeply as she loved Henry.

Ranulf was going to go back to Tregellas in a fortnight, after the repairs to the wall that he was supervising were completed. Although she had told him
he was welcome to stay longer, he claimed his troops
might fall into disarray and lax ways if he did.
Merrick had replied that they were too terrified of the
mocking Sir Ranulf to do that; however, Ranulf was
clearly anxious to go back to Tregellas, so Mathilde
didn't press him.

Giselle was so quietly pleased about marrying
Cerdic and being with child, Mathilde could only
marvel at how distracted she'd been; otherwise, she
would surely have noticed the relationship between
her sister and their friend earlier. Cerdic, soon to be
the new lord of Ecclesford, never seemed to stop
smiling now, and the tender way he spoke to Giselle
brought happy tears to Mathilde's eyes, even though
she believed it was impossible anybody could be as
joyfully contented as she.

Yet all was not completely blissful. She still had
bad dreams sometimes, where Roald and Charles De
Mallemaison both attacked her. Yet now when she
awakened, panicked and sweating, she could think of
Henry, and the worst of the horror would dwindle.
Occasionally, the troubling memories of the attacks
returned in the day, but now she could vanquish them
with thoughts of Henry, and the happy future they
would share. The laughter. The love. The desire.

Perhaps, if they were blessed, children with his merry smile and handsome features.

"My lady, may I have a word with you?"

She looked up to find Ranulf regarding her gravely.

"Yes?" she replied, leaving the linen to join him in a quiet corner of the hall, away from the wounded.

His expression was grim, and dread crept down her back. "I hope nothing is wrong," she said anxiously. "Do you fear the wall will collapse after all?"

"No, we're filling that hole so firmly, it'll likely be the strongest part of the wall. It's Henry."

"Henry?" she repeated, her chest clenching with fear. She turned to go to him at once, but Ranulf put his hand on her arm to restrain her.

"It's not his wounds," he said, "at least not the ones to his face and shoulder. He's apparently got some foolish notion that if you marry him, you'll be doing so only out of pity, or gratitude, or perhaps remorse. I myself think you have other, very good reasons—"

"Of course I do!" she cried, appalled that anyone, and especially Henry, would think otherwise. "Naturally I am grateful for his help, as is everyone here, but I love him for far more than that!"

Ranulf stroked his beard and gave her a wry smile. "I thought so, but I fear nothing *I* can say will be able to convince him otherwise."

"Then I will find the words," Mathilde vowed,

marching toward the stairs leading to the bedchambers like a general on the way to do battle.

"Yes, I rather believe you will," Ranulf murmured with a chuckle, very pleased with himself.

Until he thought of Beatrice, and sighed.

A SHARP KNOCK on the door interrupted Henry's melancholy ruminations. When Mathilde appeared, he managed to smile, one side of his mouth rising more than the other. He suspected it would always be that way—the best he would ever be able to manage would be a crooked grin.

Mathilde strode briskly into the room and stood at the foot of the bed, as boldly defiant as he'd ever seen her. "Henry, do you no longer love me?"

Caught off guard by her attitude and her brusque, almost angry demand, he shifted beneath his covers. What had brought this... Surely Ranulf would keep a confidence—had he asked Ranulf to keep their conversation private. He—fool!—had not.

What about not offering unwanted advice? Except that Ranulf hadn't, at least not to him and not directly.

"I thought you didn't care about what Roald had done to me before you came."

How could she think that was why—? "I don't!" he protested, pushing himself more upright with his right hand. "That was not your fault."

"Ranulf says you no longer want to marry me. Why not, if that is not what troubles you?"

Damn Ranulf for interfering! "Did he not tell you why?"

"He mentioned some nonsense about your arm and your face, but surely you must know me better than that, Henry—or so I thought. As if I care that you cannot fight anymore! Indeed, it is a great relief to me to know that you cannot, after you broke your promise not to go into battle."

He stared at her, dumbfounded. "But I am a knight! Unless I can fight, I am less than nothing."

She regarded him without a jot of sympathy. "This Sir Leonard of whom you speak so highly—he goes about the countryside engaging in battles?"

"Not often—but we're not talking about Sir Leonard."

"Would you call *him* useless, even though he does not go to battle much himself?"

"No, but—"

"And who was it who planned the defense of this castle? You, was it not? Did you carry a shield when you did that?"

"Mathilde, that's not—"

"Whose presence alone on the battlements inspired this garrison to fight as I never thought they could? Whose leadership gave us the victory?"

"Ranulf and Cerdic and—"

"Who took their orders from *you*. And our men obeyed you without question or hesitation because they knew you are wise in such things—and you are still wise, Henry. Do you think your only worth lies in your face? Or your shield arm? Of course not! It is in that clever mind of yours, and that has not been damaged. Your wounds will not hinder your ability to run an estate, or lead its defense, if need be. Your scars and crippled arm do not make you any the less of a man to me—or if they do, I must believe that what Roald did to me makes me less worthy of your love, in spite of what you say."

He didn't believe Roald had devalued her, and he never would. And yet… "Mathilde, it's not the same."

She put her hands on her hips. "How so? Because you are a *man?*" she demanded, her bold, brilliant eyes flashing. "Do you think me a silly woman after all, Sir Henry? Do you think I am too stupid to know whether or not a man is deserving of my love and respect? Or do you think I am so proud and haughty that I will spurn the man who saved my home, and me and my sister and all that I hold dear, because he was wounded doing so? You must not love me if you can believe that!"

"Mathilde," he pleaded.

She ignored him. "You think because you have no money or estate that you cannot marry me? Would you then tell me Cerdic is not deserving of Giselle's hand?"

Henry felt like he was trapped in a whirlwind—a very passionate, adorable whirlwind that was fast making him believe there could be hope where there had been none before. "Cerdic is marrying Giselle?"

"Yes, and soon, because she bears his child."

In the face of his stunned silence, Mathilde raised an inquiring brow. "Perhaps you are not quite so clever after all, if you didn't see the signs."

"At this point," he confessed, "I could believe you if you said I was Arthur, king of the Britons."

She smiled her beautiful smile. "I admit I was slow to see it myself, she was so sly."

Then her brows lowered and her eyes flashed with determination. "It seems Cerdic has something of the same silly pride as you, for he told her he was not worthy of her, either. But Giselle is not my sister for nothing, and she took matters…well, she took *something*…into her own hands, and now he has agreed, as he should have when they discovered they were in love. So, although he had no estate or any money, and he has gotten my sister with child without marriage, I gladly welcome him as my brother-in-law. Are you so much better that you will refuse the love I offer you?"

Before he could try to explain, her expression softened, and she went down on her knees at his bedside. "For I do love you, Henry, with all my heart and soul, and you will surely break my heart if you leave me." Her eyes shone with unshed tears. "I suppose I could take the bishop's offer and become a nun, but I would be the most miserable nun in all the world. Is that the fate you sought for me when you fought against Roald?"

"Oh, Mathilde, Mathilde," he cried, reaching down for her with his good right arm and drawing her to him. "I'm only thinking of you. You mustn't be tied in marriage to a man like me."

She drew back and regarded him with her flashing eyes. "No, you are *not* thinking of me, my Henry. Otherwise, how could you even consider leaving me and breaking my poor heart? I want to marry you, Henry, and not because I pity you. There is nothing to pity. Nor do I want to be your wife out of gratitude, although I'm grateful for all that you have done, and how you make me feel.

"I admire you more than any man I've ever known, and respect you, too. You are wise, clever, brave—sometimes too much so. You make me laugh. You brought joy back into my life, and hope." She lightly traced his lips with her fingertip. "You gave me back desire. Henry, I love you just as you are now. I will *always* love you, no matter what the future holds."

She smiled tremulously, shyly, bashful as he'd never seen her. "After all, I am no great beauty, either, and too bold for most men's tastes. Yet I believe you want me, in spite of that. I am not wrong to have such hope, am I?"

How could he resist her? How could he not believe her when she spoke with such sincerity, the love shining in her beautiful eyes?

As a happiness such as he had never felt replaced despair, he laughed softly and drew her to him with his strong right arm. "I believe that whatever I think, you will find a way to marry me. So perhaps it would be best to save you making any more astonishing plans. Lady Mathilde of Ecclesford, will you do me the very great honor of becoming my wife?"

Mathilde smiled joyously, with blissful satisfaction. "Yes, Sir Henry, I will."

"Although," he mused as he kissed her lightly on her cheek, "I can only wonder what outrageous scheme you would come up with to win me if I did not ask."

Mathilde laughed softly and cupped his disfigured face in her hands. "I would never give up until I made you mine."

"Thank God I am already yours, forever," he whispered, smiling his crooked smile as he looked into her eyes.

"As you have my heart, forever," she replied, bending down to kiss him.

EPILOGUE

THE WEDDINGS of the ladies of Ecclesford, overseen by Bishop Christophus at the specific request of the stern lord of Dunkeathe and the grim lord of Tregellas, took place at Christmas of that same year. The king and queen gave their consent, even if the notion of a formerly landless soldier ruling an estate went against the grain. It didn't hurt the cause of the young lovers that Sir Henry's brother and the lord of Tregellas had ridden to their aid and were enthusiastic supporters of the marriages. And, the queen said to her husband, better to have such powerful men happy and grateful than enemies.

As the years passed, there were many women who, upon seeing Lady Mathilde's husband for the first time, pitied her greatly. To be sure, she herself was no beauty, but it seemed a hard lot that she should be married to one so disfigured. Others, who had known Sir Henry in his youth, bemoaned the fate that had rendered him such an object of revulsion, and marveled that he could still joke and banter as if nothing had altered his appearance. Noblemen who ran the risk of such wounds themselves were less inclined to be repulsed by the sight of Sir Henry's damaged face and immobile left arm, and were far more impressed by the defense of Ecclesford against an army composed of battle-hardened mercenaries led by Charles De Mallemaison. More than one came to ask if their sons could learn from him. So pleased were they with the results that eventually Sir Henry's fame in that regard came to surpass even that of the renowned Sir Leonard de Brissy.

Those who were better acquainted with Sir Henry and Lady Mathilde, however, knew the couple possessed something few others had: a love that went far beyond outward appearance, and a bond only death could break. And indeed, as the years passed and their family grew, it became apparent to even the most doubtful that instead of pitying the lady or her lord, they should envy them instead.

* * * * *

If you liked HERS TO COMMAND,
be sure to look for Sir Ranulf's story,
HERS TO DESIRE.
Coming in August 2006,
only from HQN Books.

MARGARET MOORE

77003	BRIDE OF LOCHBARR	___ $6.50 U.S.	___ $7.99 CAN.
77040	LORD OF DUNKEATHE	___ $6.50 U.S.	___ $7.99 CAN.
77065	THE UNWILLING BRIDE	___ $5.99 U.S.	___ $6.99 CAN.

(limited quantities available)

TOTAL AMOUNT	$ _____
POSTAGE & HANDLING	$ _____
($1.00 FOR 1 BOOK, 50¢ for each additional)	
APPLICABLE TAXES*	$ _____
TOTAL PAYABLE	$ _____

(check or money order—please do not send cash)

To order, complete this form and send it, along with a check or money order for the total above, payable to HQN Books, to: **In the U.S.:** 3010 Walden Avenue, P.O. Box 9077, Buffalo, NY 14269-9077; **In Canada:** P.O. Box 636, Fort Erie, Ontario, L2A 5X3.

Name: _____
Address: _____ City: _____
State/Prov.: _____ Zip/Postal Code: _____
Account Number (if applicable): _____

075 CSAS

*New York residents remit applicable sales taxes.
*Canadian residents remit applicable GST and provincial taxes.

HQN™

We *are* romance™

www.HQNBooks.com

PHMM0206BL